It was the most 〇 **S0-AYV-236**
Hollywood never made—the truth
about the murder of William Desmond Taylor.

The Cast

King Vidor: Eager to make a movie about the
murder of an old colleague, he began an exhaustive
search for the truth.

William Desmond Taylor: The famed, and
charming, director who made it big in Tinseltown, at
the expense of some conveniently forgotten family
back East.

Mabel Normand: Mack Sennett's blazing young
star, who may have been the last person to see
Taylor. Was she frequenting his bungalow because
he supplied her drug habit?

Mary Miles Minter: The "new Mary Pickford,"
whose career was ended in the Taylor scandal when
silk underwear monogrammed MMM was found at
the scene of the crime.

Charlotte Shelby: The starlet's mother, who was
rumored to be even closer to the director than
her daughter.

In 1922, the police closed the case—with no arrests.
Forty years later, King Vidor solved it—and told no
one of his explosive findings. Now, Sidney
Kirkpatrick gives the full story of Hollywood's hidden
secret in all its riveting, shocking detail.

What the critics are saying about "The best true crime story in ages"

—*Village Voice Literary Supplement*

"This is a mesmerizing chronicle of greed, hypocrisy and misconstrued passion. It reveals much about the macabre world of Hollywood's overnight aristocracy in which powerful personalities play out dramas as sinister as in any Southern Gothic novel."

—**Anne Rice**, The New York Times Book Review

"A Chinese box of a thriller . . . A spellbinder"

—**Time**

"A page turner that is a heartbreaker . . . A jaw-dropping real-life whodunit . . . A mystery so sordidly, endlessly fascinating that, by contrast, Chandler's The Big Sleep *is a big yawn."*

—**Philadelphia Inquirer**

"A Cast of Killers is not mere scholarly speculation on dusty archives involving people long since gone to their graves. In Mr. Kirkpatrick's hands, it is a living case. . . . The reader finds himself hanging on every hairpin turn of the investigator's mind and swerving back and forth with every sharp exchange of dialogue."

—**The New York Times**

"As juicy a tale as you'd expect from movieland"

—**A. Scott Berg**

"This one has everything: an appealing sleuth, a delightful sidekick, a cast and backdrop from the heyday of silent films and a real-life unsolved murder reeking of sex and sensational headlines. . . . So fascinating it should blow the lid off the best seller charts"

—**Kirkus Reviews**

PENGUIN BOOKS

A CAST OF KILLERS

Sidney D. Kirkpatrick has an M. F. A. in film from New York University. A journalist and an award-winning documentary filmmaker, he lives with his wife in Los Angeles.

A CAST OF KILLERS

SIDNEY D. KIRKPATRICK

PENGUIN BOOKS

PENGUIN BOOKS
Viking Penguin Inc., 40 West 23rd Street,
New York, New York 10010, U.S.A.
Penguin Books Ltd, Harmondsworth,
Middlesex, England
Penguin Books Australia Ltd, Ringwood,
Victoria, Australia
Penguin Books Canada Limited, 2801 John Street,
Markham, Ontario, Canada L3R 1B4
Penguin Books (N.Z.) Ltd, 182–190 Wairau Road,
Auckland 10, New Zealand

First published in the United States of America by
E. P. Dutton, a division of New American Library, 1986
Published in Penguin Books 1987

LIBRARY OF CONGRESS CATALOGING IN PUBLICATION DATA
Kirkpatrick, Sidney.
A cast of killers.
1. Taylor, William Desmond, 1877–1922.
2. Vidor, King, 1895–1982. 3. Murder—California—
Los Angeles—Case studies. 4. Murder—California—
Los Angeles—Investigation—Case studies. I. Title.
[HV6534.L7K57 1987]   364.1′523′0979493   86-25605
ISBN 0 14 01.0086 5

Printed in the United States of America by
Offset Paperback Mfrs., Inc., Dallas, Pennsylvania
Set in Baskerville

To Thelma Jeane Vickroy

I returned to the William Desmond Taylor murder case in much the same way as I would return to an old bottle of wine I'd put away. When I searched out the bottle recently and brushed some of the crusted dust off it, I realized it was vintage stuff—the rarest vintage of all: a murder that has never been solved. One opens such a bottle at his own peril. . . .

KING VIDOR, *1967*

PREFACE

King Vidor was a biographer's dream—he saved everything. In assembling information for an authorized biography of the late Hollywood director, I found boxes, file cabinets, entire closets filled with 1925 press clippings, laundry receipts from 1934, valentines dated 1956. Even the smallest detail of his everyday life could be chronicled. But I discovered an intriguing gap in the story these things told. There were no important papers for the year 1967. It was as if the director, or a close personal friend, had picked the estate clean of items for that year.

I asked Vidor's friends and family about this unaccounted-for year. They told me the director had been working on a secret project in 1967, but no one knew what it was. He had traveled extensively, carrying a thick black binder in which he took notes. On one occasion, he called a friend from the Directors Guild and asked him if he wanted to hunt for a bullet lodged in the closet of a downtown mansion. To a second friend, he suggested a trip to Ireland, to do genealogical research.

Nearly a year later, after I had thoroughly cataloged Vidor's estate, 1967 still remained a mystery. The only clues I had to work with were his tax returns and phone bills. He had indeed been working on something and had written off a considerable amount of money for travel and research. He had called police departments as near as Sacramento, California, and as far as Scotland Yard. My curiosity piqued, I put off writing and focused exclusively on finding out what the director had been doing. When all else failed, I instituted a search of Vidor's three homes, prying up floor boards in attics, hunting in basement crawl spaces.

Twenty-three days into my search, I knelt beside the hot-water heater in the garage of Vidor's Beverly Hills guest house and uncovered a locked black strongbox. A tire iron on the wall a few feet away cracked the padlock. A black binder sitting inside, and stacks of loose notes and documents, told me I had found exactly what I was looking for.

I studied the contents of that black strongbox with a deep sense of foreboding, as if this were a prelude to a much longer quest. At first I was intrigued, then shocked. The black strongbox told of the director's briefly turning away from filmmaking to solve the scandalous murder of a friend and fellow film director, William Desmond Taylor.

The results of Vidor's investigation were sensational and explosive. So why had Vidor salted them away?

As I set out to answer that question, I began writing a new book: the story of King Vidor solving the murder of William Desmond Taylor. It wouldn't be the story I had set out to write, but I knew it would be the story Vidor wanted told. To him, a film director was only as important as the story he had to tell. And what a story this was!

The resulting book is as accurate and factual an account as I believe possible. All of the events, episodes, and persons portrayed are real. All living participants were interviewed, and only original documents and source material consulted. Dialogue was reconstructed based on Vidor's notes and the recollections of witnesses.

King Vidor, I had come to learn, had sealed away the contents of the strongbox until such time as the story they told could be made public without injuring the reputations or careers of living participants. The time has now come that the story can be told.

SIDNEY D. KIRKPATRICK
Willow Creek Ranch
Paso Robles, California
January 1986

A CAST
OF KILLERS

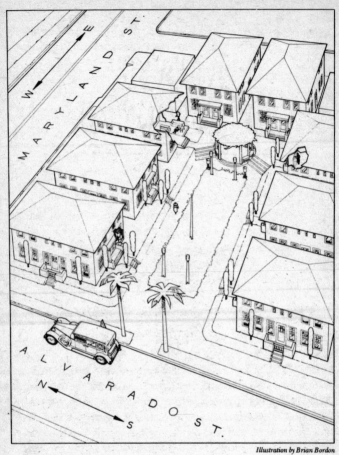

Alvarado Street on the night of February 1, 1922.

Illustration by Brian Bordon

1

King Vidor rose early. While his wife slept, he showered, shaved, ate a small breakfast, and began his working day. As he stepped outside on Monday morning, December 5, 1966, the sun rising over the eucalyptus trees in his yard promised the kind of southern California day that film directors pray for. But Vidor wasn't shooting a picture that day. He had another, more important project at hand: solving a murder.

In dark sunglasses and his favorite brown-checkered cap, he drove his supercharged red Thunderbird down Sunset Boulevard and out of Beverly Hills. Having once dreamed of becoming a race car driver, he loved taking full advantage of the T-Bird's power and maneuverability as he crisscrossed through the side streets of Hollywood and Hancock Park on his way downtown.

When he reached Westlake, the residential slum bordering the business district, he couldn't help remembering the neighborhood's glorious past. Once, not many years earlier, stately homes had sat among palm and citrus trees; now all that remained were seedy boarding houses, unattended billboards, and the abandoned trolley tracks, barely visible through the latest layer of asphalt.

Vidor parked beside a Mexican food stand at the top of Alvarado Street. He bought coffee, then made his way down to number 404, on the east side of the street.

The address was a construction site, a pile of rubble waiting for the dumpster. Workers scurried about on foot and machines, while haggard onlookers watched.

Sidestepping potholes, Vidor took a seat at a bus stop, wondering if any of the others around him had also read the Los Angeles *Times* article about the bungalow court being demolished, or if they were merely passing time, attracted to any activity in the dying neighborhood.

He noticed a deeply tanned man with large, tattooed arms, kicking through the rubble. The man looked up at Vidor, then away. Vidor sipped his coffee and thought back nearly forty-five years, to the time when 404 Alvarado Street, now just another victim of urban decay, had been the setting for one of the greatest scandals in Hollywood history.

On the morning of February 2, 1922, a team of Los Angeles Police Department investigators met at that same Alvarado Street address. The cool morning air still held the acrid odor of the smudge pots that nearby orange

----

growers burned at night to warm their groves. As the investigators entered Bungalow B, to investigate a simple case of natural death, they encountered a flurry of unexpected and quite peculiar activity. Two important executives of Famous Players Lasky, the film production arm of Paramount Pictures, were burning papers in a living room fireplace, while Mabel Normand, the film comedienne in line to inherit—in light of her friend Fatty Arbuckle's recent imprisonment for the alleged rape and murder of a young girl at a wild sex party—the title of Hollywood's biggest comedy star, was rifling through drawers in search of something. In the kitchen, Henry Peavey, black houseman to the bungalow's occupant, was washing dishes, while all around the house individuals not readily identified milled about (one walked out the front door with a case of bootleg liquor and never returned). During all of this commotion, on the floor of the study, William Desmond Taylor, one of the most important film directors in Hollywood, lay dead.

The investigators found Taylor on his back, his arms at his side. His face was composed and his clothes meticulously arranged, as though he had calmly lain down to sleep. An overturned chair had fallen across one of his legs. One investigator found a monogrammed handkerchief on the floor beside the body. He picked it up and placed it on Taylor's cluttered desk.

As the investigators asked everyone in the bungalow to stop whatever they were doing, a middle-aged man made his way through the crowd of reporters and photographers gathering outside. He entered the front door and identified himself as a physician visiting a patient in the neighborhood. He asked if he could be of any assistance and was led to the study, where he quickly examined Taylor's body and said the director had died of a stomach hemorrhage brought on by natural causes.

Mabel Normand and the studio executives told the investigators that Taylor had often suffered terrible stomach cramps, that he had in fact had to travel to Europe a few months before to visit specialists about his condition. Henry Peavey, long a trusted employee of Taylor's, concurred, saying that only the night before, Taylor had asked him to get him some medication on the way to work the next morning. He showed them the bottle of milk of magnesia, still wrapped in the brown paper from the druggist down the street.

The investigators pieced together what had obviously happened: Taylor had hemorrhaged, fallen from the chair he had been sitting in, and died. They asked everyone in the bungalow just what he or she was doing there. Mabel Normand said she had come to retrieve letters and telegrams she had written to Taylor. They had nothing to do with his death, she said; she just wanted to keep them private. She said Taylor kept them in the middle drawer of his bedroom dresser. But when investigators looked in the drawer, it was completely empty.

Others in the bungalow claimed to be after similar personal items, but like Mabel Normand's letters, none of those items was ever found.

Investigators were puzzled by this air of mystery surrounding an otherwise routine case. But then, as people had long liked to suspect, and as the Fatty Arbuckle scandal confirmed for them, a lot more went on within the motion picture community than was ever made public.

Then, less than an hour after the official investigation into the death of William Desmond Taylor was closed, it was reopened, with a completely new emphasis. After questioning everyone in Taylor's bungalow and sending them on their way, the investigators watched as Taylor's body was placed on a stretcher to be removed to the funeral home. On the floor where the body had been was a small, dark pool of blood. Investigators turned the body over and found a neat bullet hole in his back.

Anyone could see that Taylor had been murdered.

Why then had the man claiming to be a physician declared death by natural causes? The investigators would never know for the man was never seen again, nor was he ever identified. The monogrammed handkerchief that had been found by the body also disappeared forever.

Taylor's neighbors were immediately questioned. Douglas MacLean, a noted actor who lived across the courtyard, said he had heard what might have been a muffled shot the night before, sometime between 8:00 and 8:15. His wife, Faith Cole MacLean, had looked out the window and seen a man wearing a cap and muffler leaving Taylor's front door. She described the man as about five feet, ten inches tall, of medium build, and roughly but not shabbily dressed. Upon later questioning, Mrs. MacLean said she couldn't be certain it had been a man she had seen; it might have been a woman dressed as a man. Hazel Gillon, another neighbor, was even less sure. All she said she had seen was a dark figure.

Two Hartley Service Station attendants remembered seeing someone shortly before 6:00 P.M. the night of the murder who fit Mrs. MacLean's description. They said it had definitely been a man, and that he had asked them directions to Taylor's house.

The Third Street Red Car line conductor said a man fitting the description had boarded his train that night at Maryland Street, near Taylor's bungalow, at either 7:45 or 8:27 P.M.; he couldn't remember which.

Taylor's body was delivered to the coroner. Seventy-eight dollars had been found in his pocket, a diamond ring on his finger, and a two-thousand-dollar platinum watch on his wrist. Apparently, robbery hadn't been the motive.

The coroner's report stated that Taylor had been shot at close range with a .38-caliber snub-nosed revolver. The bullet was of an obsolete design, not commonly used at the time. The bullet hole in his coat was considerably lower than the one in his vest. Only by lifting Taylor's left elbow could the holes be aligned. Taylor had had his arms raised when he was shot.

Cigarette butts found behind Taylor's bungalow suggested that someone had lurked in the darkness, entered through the den, then shot Taylor in the back and left by the front door.

But who was the mysterious "police physician"? And what was the significance of the missing handkerchief? And why were Taylor's friends and associates so concerned about their "personal items" at the scene of the crime?

The press had a field day with the case. People were eager to read about scandal in the sordid world of Hollywood. And the film community, already becoming the most influential force in Los Angeles, was eager to avoid any investigations that might give the press further ammunition against it. The L.A.P.D., caught in the middle, wanted to solve the murder as quickly and undramatically as possible.

A thorough search of Taylor's bungalow turned up just the sort of ammunition the press hungered for. Pornographic pictures were reportedly found of the director with a number of easily recognizable actresses. Police also claimed to have discovered a secret, locked closet containing a large collection of women's lingerie, each item tagged with initials and a date, presumably souvenirs of encounters the director wished to remember, or, as police began to suspect, evidence for possible blackmail. Most interesting was a pale silk nightgown embroidered with the letters M.M.M., the initials of Paramount's blonde bomb-shell, Mary Miles Minter. Love letters were also reported, suggesting that Minter had been having an affair with Taylor.

In the study, police found an open checkbook and a partially completed tax return for the previous year, 1921. Further investigation would reveal that Taylor had visited his accountant, Marjorie Berger, the morning before his murder, and that Berger also handled Mary Miles Minter's finances. Though Taylor drew a considerable salary, only a small fraction of the money he was supposed to possess could be found. His bank reported that, a few days before he was killed, Taylor had withdrawn a substantial sum from his account, and then redeposited this same amount the day of the murder. Perhaps, the press quickly suggested, Taylor was not a blackmailer, but was in fact being black-mailed himself.

Police also found an assortment of keys, but no locks that they fit.

In time-honored tradition, the police compiled a list of suspects. Henry Peavey was an obvious candidate. He had been the first to discover Taylor's body. When the inves-tigators arrived at the bungalow, he had been calmly wash-ing dishes—or was he destroying evidence? Less than a week before the murder, Peavey, a homosexual, had been arrested in a public park on a morals charge. On the very morning that Taylor's body was found at the bungalow, Taylor had been scheduled to appear in court at Peavey's hearing—an appointment Peavey's employer never kept.

Mabel Normand also made the list. She had been at the bungalow when the investigators arrived, and the let-ters she claimed to be searching for, in light of the other letters subsequently found, suggested that she, like Mary Miles Minter, had been having an affair with the director.

As for Minter, though she was still underage, stories abounded of alleged affairs with directors she had worked with, including Taylor. These affairs were ended by Minter's mother, Charlotte Shelby, who was said to have gone as far as threatening directors with her own .38-caliber pistol, which, of course, made Shelby herself a possible suspect.

The list continued to grow every day. A federal narcotics officer claimed Taylor had been helping a famous-actress friend kick her drug addiction. He said Taylor had had a fight with the actress's supplier, a studio employee suspected of supplying many important stars. Another man reportedly had asked Paramount Studios where Taylor lived two days before the murder. Another had asked at a downtown movie theater, and yet another at the Los Angeles Athletic Club, where Taylor was a member. At least a dozen studio associates came forward with strange stories that the director had been plagued by unidentified telephone callers and burglars.

The police amassed so many suspects that even questioning them all would take weeks, maybe months. And with each addition to the list, the case grew more and more mysterious.

On the first day of the police investigation, police discovered that Taylor had been sending monthly checks to a southern California woman who claimed to be the abandoned wife of Taylor's brother. Taylor had never mentioned to anyone in Los Angeles that he had a brother, though the description his alleged sister-in-law gave of her missing husband did fit uncannily that of Edward Sands, the personal secretary Taylor had fired a few months before for stealing jewelry and forging checks.

Apparently there was a lot about Taylor that he had wanted no one to find out. Investigators in New York, running down leads provided by Taylor's alleged sister-in-law, made the astounding discovery that William Desmond Taylor's name had not even been William Desmond Taylor. It had been William Deane Tanner, the name of a man who had vanished from Manhattan in 1908, leaving behind a thriving business and, like Taylor's alleged brother, a wife and child. The police in Los Angeles were absolutely baffled, as they realized, days into their investigation, that they didn't even know the true identity of the victim of the murder they were investigating.

Vidor finished his coffee and poked through the rubble. The tattooed man, also still kicking through the debris, attempted small talk. He and Vidor both claimed innocent curiosity at what was going to be built in place of the old bungalow court. Vidor wondered if the man, like himself, was lying, if perhaps he too had secret reasons for wanting to dig back into a forty-five-year-old mystery that the greatest investigative minds in Los Angeles had never been able to solve. The man didn't look like a detective, but then Vidor knew he himself didn't either. At seventy-one, he looked more like a grandfather than a sleuth. But he knew he possessed something no one ever involved in the Taylor case had possessed: insight into the victim's private world. Vidor had been a contemporary of Taylor's, and had had a long, distinguished career, making fifty-four feature films —all successful—including such classics as *Our Daily Bread, Northwest Passage, Stella Dallas, Ruby Gentry, The Fountainhead, Duel in the Sun,* and *War and Peace.* He had directed such stars as Charlie Chaplin, Lillian Gish, Marion Davies, Douglas Fairbanks, Spencer Tracy, Bette Davis, Clark Gable, Audrey Hepburn, and Henry Fonda. Who better to probe the life of one central figure in early Hollywood than another? And now, with the motion picture industry in the hands of young executives who had less need each year for the creative contributions from members of his generation, Vidor had the time and money to do just that. He didn't plan on retiring: he would turn the story of William Desmond Taylor into the most spectacular screenplay and film of his career. No one before him had ever attempted such a task, because no one before him had ever been qualified to find the one crucial element missing from the story: Taylor's killer.

Vidor found a doorknob in the rubble. He picked it up, dusted it off. He looked at it and turned to see the tattooed man watching him. He stuffed the doorknob into his pocket for a souvenir paperweight, and waved good-bye to the man. Then he walked back to his car.

2

At his Beverly Hills office several days later, Vidor studied his face in the bathroom mirror, manually supporting the tired muscles under his crystal-blue eyes and pinching his cheeks to give them color. Through his wire-rimmed glasses he saw the brown spots around his temples. His wife, Betty, called it cancer, but he didn't believe her.

The director turned quickly from the mirror when he heard his secretary, Thelma Carr, fumbling with her keys at the front door. He didn't want her to see him at the mirror again. She thought he was vain enough as it was, and had told him so after one of the Christian Science therapy sessions they attended once a week.

Vidor dashed to his desk and greeted Carr as she walked in with an armful of papers she had typed over the weekend. She was a pretty brunette in her late thirties, with an electric smile Vidor always wanted to take a closer look at. Her smile soured as she looked for a place to set the stack of papers. Vidor hadn't spent the weekend straightening up the office as he had promised, but running around town in his T-Bird.

Vidor didn't fault himself for the office's condition. It hadn't been designed as an office, but as a three-room guest house, a hundred yards from his own home. He had built it in the late fifties with strong clean lines, spacious rooms, and the large sliding glass windows that he wanted. Like his home up the driveway, it was quiet and functional, a far cry from the opulence of the homes of his neighbors, two of the wealthiest, most important families in Beverly Hills. But since he'd lost his office on the MGM lot, he'd filled the guest house with film cans, clippings, awards, file cabinets, a pair of Spanish guitars, and film gear. His golden retriever, Nippy, sat beneath the ten-foot-high poster of *The Fountainhead* that was precariously balanced over a baby grand piano.

As Carr settled into her cubicle in the far corner of the room, Vidor swept aside the mass of correspondence neatly stacked in front of him and told her to pull the Taylor papers. He didn't remember exactly where they were, but he remembered a black binder. He suggested she look in his files under directors. If not there, under murder, or whodunits. When he asked a second time, she reluctantly put down the morning mail and headed toward the broom closet where the file cabinets were kept. Vidor picked up the telephone, swiveled his armchair away from her, and put in a person-to-person call to Chicago, to Colleen Moore, financial analyst, silent-film star, and half owner of Vid-Mor Productions.

"Madame Zaza," Vidor said, smiling and playfully rolling his antique doorknob across his desk blotter.

"Professor La Tour," Moore answered immediately, pleased with his call. "What have you got in your hands this time?"

Vidor enjoyed the Madame Zaza gambit. It was part of a mind-reading act they had played at cocktail parties years before, often to the applause of mutual friends like Scott Fitzgerald. Vidor was Professor La Tour, Moore was Madame Zaza. While she was blindfolded, Vidor passed among party guests, picking up various objects such as coins, jewelry, and silverware. Madame Zaza then identified each object without seeing it. Vidor would say, "Madame Zaza, what is it that I am holding in my hand?" She would reply, "A fountain pen," or "A wedding ring," whatever their prerehearsed code called for. When an object came up for which there was no code, she would hold her hand to her head and say, "The object is not clear. Dark vibrations are swirling through my mind."

This morning, Vidor told her exactly what he had in his hand, the doorknob from the Taylor bungalow that he had swiped last weekend, before wrecking crews could shovel it into a dumpster. He was off and running, he said, on the Taylor screenplay. But, he added, he still needed a killer.

Several years earlier, in a Paris hotel, Vidor and Moore had sat down and talked about the Taylor murder for two hours. Turning it into a film had been her suggestion—Vidor desperately needed another film property. The last four Vid-Mor development projects had been shelved. Their latest, with coproducer Sam Goldwyn, Jr., was on hold until a suitable script could be drafted.

Moore was the ideal producer for the Taylor project. She not only knew, like Vidor, the Hollywood of the twenties, but could put financing together faster than any of the young incompetents at the studio. She hadn't become a partner in Merrill Lynch by her good looks. She worked at breakneck speeds, taking only an occasional day or two each month for a Hong Kong shopping spree with friends like Clare Boothe Luce, or a retreat to a Scottish castle, where British royalty kept a suite of rooms reserved for her visits.

Moore was restless. It was a nasty day in Chicago, and she was sitting with her secretary in front of her Smith-Corona churning out pages of her autobiography and waiting for a snowstorm to clear the air. On the phone she told Vidor that if he were with her, they could bundle up and run across the street for champagne and pancakes, or to the Chicago Museum of Science and Industry to view the permanent exhibit of her million-dollar doll house.

Silent Star, the autobiography on which she was putting the finishing touches, would be complete within the month. She assured Vidor that he was included, but that he wouldn't have to worry about what she said. Greta Garbo, Erich Von Stroheim, and Louis B. Mayer were the ones who had to worry. Also, a letter had just arrived from her publishers suggesting she follow the book with a second, *How Women Can Make Money in the Stock Market.* Vidor wasn't surprised. Moore's investments for him over the last two years had made it possible to add a wing to his ranch in Paso Robles, a few hours outside of San Francisco. The Taylor film, she suggested, was the perfect interim project between books.

Moore continued, talking cross-collateraliz&ation, end money, joint ventures, and negative pickups. Vidor understood the language, but when he spoke, he used terms like dolly shots, crossfades, and character motivation. Both kinds of talk were part of filmmaking. Colleen Moore was as important to getting the Taylor project launched as Vidor was.

They both realized a key problem: they had a "rug show" on their hands, the kind of film with too many interiors. It would be up to Vidor to develop a script that didn't all take place inside the Taylor bungalow and smoke-filled police interrogation rooms. They needed action. Moore suggested a car chase: Mabel Normand drove her lavender limousine like a maniac, and Mary Miles Minter knew how to fly. They could show Henry Peavey casing Westlake Park for young boys, or Taylor might be seen taking a cable car up Echo Mountain to his favorite speakeasy, or perhaps buying drugs in Chinatown.

Casting would come naturally, once they had a killer, Moore said. Michael Caine looked just like Taylor, and he had the right kind of English accent and debonair appeal. Sandy Dennis would make a good Mabel Normand, and she had been great in the recent *Who's Afraid of Virginia Woolf?* Kim Novak might be good for Mary Miles Minter, if she could still pass for a teenager. Bette Davis might be good for Minter's mother, Charlotte Shelby. If Moore asked her, Gloria Swanson might even come in as a dialogue coach, and she had been closer to Taylor than either Vidor or Moore herself.

Flashbacks would be a must. Vidor might even have to bring in Taylor's bizarre past in New York. Undoubtedly, there were still those around who knew what Taylor had been up to. His daughter, Daisy Deane Tanner, might still be alive. Moore said she knew a woman from the Midwest whose father had known both Taylor and his brother. She would write her immediately. Other friends she had might be able to get hold of Taylor's diaries, a hot property that had circulated in Hollywood during the thirties and been auctioned off with the Clara Bow sex letters and Valentino candid photo library.

Locations would also be important. Vidor suggested San Francisco. It still had a lot of buildings from the twenties that could be used for exteriors. And in San Pedro, the deep-water seaport of Los Angeles, there was a police station that hadn't changed at all. The bungalow complex could be built on the MGM backlot. Vidor had the door-knob, didn't he?

They were going to have to be careful. It would be easy to step on the wrong toes. They wanted to make a film, not put anyone in jail. Both Moore and Vidor were close friends with Claire Windsor, an actress who had dated Taylor on the Saturday night before the murder. One of Moore's favorite directors was Marshall Neilan, a man who had hinted to both of them that he knew a great deal more about the murder than had ever been leaked to the press. If possible, his reputation had to be protected. Vidor had done a film with Minter in the early teens; Moore had gone on double dates with her. Everywhere, they would have to tread carefully.

Moore gave Vidor the green light. They were talking millions. The director would be in on the cut. The producer would carry development when Vidor had the story nailed down. The first title card would read "Colleen Moore Presents," followed by "A King Vidor Production." But no announcements would be made until they had the screenplay. Arrangements would be kept top secret until Vidor had time to circulate and collect what information he could from Taylor's friends and associates. The killer might still be at large—and all they wanted was a screenplay, not another murder.

"It's going to be a pleasure working together again, King-zzy," Moore said, signing off.

Vidor swiveled his chair back around to face Thelma Carr. She had been listening in, and though she pretended not to, she suspected that Vidor was getting romantically involved again, only this time it wasn't with the script girl, production secretary, or star of the picture. That was for younger directors. He was becoming involved with his producer. As for Vidor, he was so flushed with excitement at that prospect that if Carr's desk were any nearer his own, he might have tried for a closer look at that smile of hers. He hadn't looked forward to a project with this much enthusiasm since he had locked horns with Cecil B. deMille back in the fifties. And Colleen Moore was much better looking than C.B.

As she handed him the morning mail, Carr told him she couldn't find the Taylor files, and she didn't want to look a second time. They were obviously lost in his filing system, not her own. She suggested he try the basement, and take Nippy, his dog, with him.

Vidor didn't like that idea. The basement was the repository for everything that didn't fit upstairs: a set of golf clubs he hadn't touched for ten years, the stationary bicycle his doctor had made him buy, columns of books that literary agents sent him, clothes, photographs, toys, car parts, and more file cabinets. And on top of that, Vidor hadn't called Western Exterminators as Carr had suggested nearly two weeks before. Even Nippy wouldn't step inside that rodent-infested storage room.

3

Nippy sniffed curiously at the stack of old papers on the bedroom floor. Betty, in the bedroom across the hall, still had her light on, but the hallway door was closed. Vidor sat in his own bed, wrapped in the comforter his daughter had given him, poring over the details of the Taylor story, and taking notes on a yellow legal pad. He had found the black binder containing the Taylor file under his baseball mitt and binoculars after a two-hour search through the contents of the basement. Now he reviewed the story he had put together so far.

Taylor's story began at the turn of the century, in New York. The future Hollywood director had been an actor named William Cunningham Deane Tanner, about whom very little was known. He had told some acquaintances that he had come from a very wealthy Irish family and had graduated from Oxford. He had told others that his father, an officer in the British Army, had sent him and his younger brother, Denis, to receive a practical education at Runnymeade, a ranch near Harper, Kansas, a claim substantiated by residents of Harper.

In 1901, Tanner married actress Ethel May Harrison. Soon afterward, both gave up the stage, Tanner becoming vice-president of the English Antique Shop on Fifth Avenue, at the impressive salary of $29,000 a year. The Tanners moved to Larchmont, where Tanner was remembered as a highly respected citizen and member of the prestigious Larchmont Country Club.

Then, apparently, Tanner began drinking heavily and seeing other women. On October 23, 1908, he left the antique shop to attend the Vanderbilt Cup Race, an annual automobile rally held on Long Island. He was not seen for several days, though later reports placed him drinking at the Continental Hotel during that period. Then, from a public phone at Broadway and Nineteenth Street, he called his office, asking for five hundred dollars in cash. The money was delivered, and Tanner disappeared for good.

Four years later, Tanner's younger brother also disappeared, leaving behind a wife and two children and another successful antique business. Denis's wife, Ada, depleted the family savings looking for him, then moved to California to live with relatives.

Meanwhile, according to various articles Vidor had collected, William Tanner was working as a hotel manager in Telluride, Colorado; as a timekeeper for a Yukon mining operation; even as a prospector in the Klondike. One report placed Tanner in San Francisco, back on the stage, where fellow actors described him as a "shell of a man."

Whatever happened during the five-year interim between the disappearance of William Deane Tanner from New York and the arrival of William Desmond Taylor in California, Taylor's meteoric rise to the top of Hollywood's royalty was well documented. He worked first as a film actor, then as a director, reaching his stride with Paramount's production of *Huckleberry Finn*. He also directed Mary Pickford in *Johanna Enlists* and *Captain Kidd Jr.*, and after a short stint in World War I directed Mary Miles Minter in such pictures as *Judy of Rogues Harbor* and *Jenny Be Good*, all popular, highly regarded films of their time.

As Taylor became increasingly successful in the industry, he began enjoying more and more the lifestyle it afforded him, joining the exclusive Los Angeles Athletic Club, taking expensive vacations, acquiring a staff. He hired as his personal secretary a man named Edward F. Sands, who later, in 1921, disappeared with Taylor's money, jewelry, and an expensive automobile while Taylor was in Europe. This was a man, reports would later claim, who might have in fact been Denis Deane Tanner. Vidor made a note to investigate this possibility further.

Around this time, Denis Tanner's wife, Ada, having seen Taylor on the screen, burst into Taylor's office, demanding that he tell her what had happened to Denis. She said she needed him to help pay for her daughter's education. Taylor claimed absolute ignorance of everything she was talking about, though he began secretly sending her fifty dollars every month.

Coincidentally, three thousand miles away, in the fall of 1919, Taylor's own wife, Ethel May Harrison, had been watching a reissue of one of the season's biggest hits, *Captain Alvarez*, when a familiar face appeared on the screen. She watched Taylor with disbelief. She'd obtained a divorce after his sudden disappearance, claiming he had carried on an affair in the Catskills and that she had not seen or heard of him since. Ethel May had no idea what had become of Tanner, but she never dreamed he would be a Hollywood celebrity. As Taylor walked across the screen, she gripped the hand of her daughter, Daisy, and said, "That's your father."

Little Daisy wrote Taylor a letter, expressing a desire to see him, and Taylor, in another rare and perhaps imprudent admission of his former identity, wrote back, promising to meet with her whenever he could get away from his busy work schedule.

They finally got together, on July 21, 1921. Though no details were made public, friends of Daisy's family said the reunion had been a happy one, that by the end of their meeting Daisy had been calling Taylor "Father." In the months that followed, Daisy and Taylor exchanged many letters, promising they would see each other again soon. It never happened.

By this time, 1921, Vidor had met Taylor on any number of occasions. The meeting he remembered most clearly took place when his own studio, Vidor Village, was having a hard time making ends meet. He had made the rounds of all the other studios in hopes of taking on a free-lance project, when he happened to be walking through Echo Park, a beautiful tree-shaded lake area that was often filled with the Keystone Kops and other slapstick comedians from the nearby Mack Sennett Studio. Though a light rain was falling, Vidor saw a group of Boy Scouts standing on a grassy clearing listening to a man on a raised platform. As his black servant held an umbrella over his head, the man addressed them on the importance of making clean films, doing one's duty, and living upstanding,

Christian lives. The man was William Desmond Taylor; the servant, Henry Peavey.

On the evening of February 1, 1922, at 6:45 P.M., Taylor had a visitor. Mabel Normand, the actress, stopped by to pick up a book Taylor had bought for her. As she approached the bungalow, Taylor either answered his ringing telephone or was already engaged in a conversation—Vidor's clippings presented both possibilities. Either way, Normand waited until Taylor finished his conversation, then enjoyed a forty-five-minute visit. Afterward, Taylor walked her to her chauffeured limousine and said he would call her at nine to see how she was enjoying the book.

Vidor found no explanation in Normand's recollections for why Taylor was going to call her an hour later about a book he had just given her.

Only a little later that evening, Taylor's neighbor Faith Cole MacLean saw someone else casually leaving Taylor's bungalow, someone who appeared to be a man, but had "an effeminate walk" and seemed to be wearing what looked like heavy movie makeup. Hazel Gillon, the second neighbor, could neither confirm nor deny Mac-Lean's account.

The next morning, at 7:30, Henry Peavey arrived for work. He saw a light burning in the living-room window and decided to enter through the front door. The door was unlocked. Peavey pushed it open and saw his employer lying on the floor beside the desk. Peavey panicked, ran through the bungalow court screaming for help. It was an hour before the police arrived, an hour in which any number of individuals hurriedly tampered with what would be discovered to have been the scene of a cold-blooded murder. Mabel Normand, studio head Charles Eyton, actress Edna Purviance, the MacLeans, E. C. Jessurum, wealthy oilman Verne Dumas, and others—they all had reasons for beating the police into Taylor's bungalow.

Vidor's list of unanswered questions covered his legal pad as he reached up and turned the bedroom light off. By this time Nippy had lost all interest in the dusty documents at the foot of the bed, and Betty's room was dark. Vidor had to find out what the police had eventually learned about such puzzles as the identities of Denis Deane Tanner and Edward Sands; what became of the mysterious "doctor" who first examined the body; and the missing monogrammed handkerchief. He wanted to know why Faith MacLean gave different descriptions of the person she saw leaving the bungalow, why the police had been so long in arriving in the morning, and many other details that would help him map out the events and the motives that had led to Taylor's murder. But he wasn't simply looking for a dramatic *theory* of what happened that night; that was not the way King Vidor approached a film story. He wanted to make the definitive statement on the life and death of William Desmond Taylor. It would not only be dramatic, moving, and revelatory—it would be true.

4

0n Monday, December 19, 1966, Vidor cruised Fifth and Flower streets looking for free parking. After twenty minutes, he pulled into a pay lot, twenty-five cents an hour. He hadn't always been so tight with a dollar. Three marriages and two settlements had that effect on some men.

Thelma Carr met him at the south entrance of the Los Angeles Public Library, and together they walked through the wide tile hallway to the Newspaper Annex. The librarian expected him. She knew him by reputation, and she had a note from upstairs in front of her on the desk saying

Vidor was to be given special access to anything the library had.

A long oak table had been set aside, stacked with canvas-bound volumes of the New York and Los Angeles newspapers, maps, and a rare 1920s telephone directory. Vidor brought the number-two pencils, a pair of sharpeners, antacid tablets, and tissues. Carr brought the lunch, ham on rye.

Vidor had read about the seventy-eight dollars found on Taylor's body, his two-carat diamond ring, and the platinum wristwatch. What surprised him were all the variations on the rest. This was shoddy reporting at an all-time low.

Some published reports failed to mention the set of mysterious keys that fit no locks; others presented this as fact, speculating that Taylor led a double life, his keys fitting the ignition of a sports car no one knew about, an apartment where a second wife lived, or a hidden trunk where the answers to all the Taylor mysteries sat like the contents of Pandora's box.

Such was also the case of the handkerchief said to have been found beside the body. Many accounts failed to mention it at all, while others claimed it was monogrammed with the letter S and removed by the "doctor." Still others claimed that Taylor owned a matching set of them, offering no explanation of why the director's own initial wasn't on them.

Reporters agreed on Taylor's financial profile. Taylor's partially completed tax return showed $37,000 income in 1921. Taylor's accounts at the First National Bank of Los Angeles revealed that he had saved only six thousand dollars in his lifetime. A second account, in New York, contained only $18.96, after initial deposits totaling

$7,811.52. Though reports varied on the exact amount, Taylor had withdrawn around $2,500 in cash from his Los Angeles account on January 31, the day before the murder, and redeposited the same sum, or a figure very close to it, back into the account the day of his murder.

The police—and in turn, reporters—claimed blackmail and pointed to Edward Sands as the most viable candidate, as evidenced by the fact that Sands had cashed some of the checks found on Taylor's desk, and others that he had forged. The generally accepted theory was that Sands knew about Taylor's secret past and used this information to bleed his employer until Taylor turned on him.

Reporters also agreed Taylor was a drinker. Police found a cocktail shaker and two large goblets with traces of orange pulp and gin in the dining room. A full liquor cabinet was well stocked with whiskey, bourbon, gin, and vodka. Prohibition aside, this evidence was important because police were said to have known that Taylor had recently been fighting with his bootlegger. No details were released to the press, but it was generally assumed by all the major papers that the bootlegger may have been angry enough to pull the trigger. Though reports indicated police knew who the bootlegger was, no arrest was made.

In the same room as the liquor cabinet, police were said to have found an ashtray with cigarette butts. Outside, behind the back door leading to the pantry, more cigarette butts had been found, along with footprints. Again, no details were released to the press, firing more speculation: Taylor smoked, but so did Edward Sands, Mabel Normand, Henry Peavey, and Mary Miles Minter's mother, Charlotte Shelby.

Much was also made of the letters written by Normand and Minter. On February 7, 1922, a reporter from the Los Angeles *Times* stated that he believed a man of high position in the film industry had taken Normand's letters and others in an effort to protect Normand's reputation and those of others in whom he had a vested interest. For legal reasons his name was not mentioned, though Charles Eyton, studio manager of Paramount, was considered the number-one suspect. Inexplicably, Normand's letters, not found when Taylor's house was first searched, showed up in a locked upstairs closet days later. If Eyton had replaced them, the press had not been told. Like the others at the bungalow on the morning of the murder, Eyton was under police orders not to speak with reporters.

District Attorney Thomas Woolwine, head of the investigation from 1922 to 1923, announced that he had read the letters and that they contained nothing helpful to their investigation; he had returned them to Normand. Their contents were never made public, and Normand was officially exonerated when her chauffeur and maid provided alibis.

Normand, however, remained a suspect in the eyes of the press. Though she clung to her account that she had visited the director the night of the murder, had spoken and shared peanuts with him, she denied any involvement in his slaying and denied being at the bungalow looking for her letters when police discovered the murder. She told reporters that she returned to the bungalow days after the murder, at the investigator's request, to identify the exact location of furniture possibly shifted by the killer. Retrieving her correspondence, she claimed, was an afterthought. Investigators neither supported nor denied her claims.

It was obvious that Normand and Taylor probably chatted about more than books. Less than a year later, both Normand and Edna Purviance were linked to a second shooting, again involving drugs and liquor, which suggested that these ingredients, not literature and peanuts, might have led to the Taylor murder.

At about the same time that Normand's letters appeared, so did Minter's, and these did find their way to the press. The first one found was a scented note on purple butterfly stationery that reportedly dropped from between the pages of one of Taylor's books, *White Stains,* a scandalous book by black-magic proponent Aleister Crowley:

> Dearest –
>   I love you – I
> love you – I
> love you – – –
>
>   Yours always!
>   Mary

Between the last "I love you" and the bottom were ten Xes.

Other letters from Minter were reported to have been written in a simple schoolgirl code of straight lines and dots. One, deciphered, read:

> What shall I call you, you wonderful man. You are standing on the lot, the idol of an adoring company. You have just come over and put your coat on my chair. . . . I want to go away with you, up in the hills or anywhere. I'd go to my room and put on something soft and flowery, then I'd lie on the couch and wait for you. I might fall asleep, for a fire always makes me drowsy—then I'd wake to find two strong arms around me and two dear lips pressed on mine in a long sweet kiss.

Press accounts differed concerning Minter's silk nightgown. Some stated quite bluntly that it was an expensive frilly pink one, embroidered with the initials M.M.M., and found in the top drawer of Taylor's bureau. Other accounts claimed the nightgown was just one of many, all belonging to Minter. The *Herald-American* even claimed that the nightgown had been found along with hundreds of pairs of frilly pink panties, each labeled with the owner's initials and a date.

Minter denied ownership of the nightgown, as she denied any involvement in the murder. When interviewed, she said she had been at her forty-room mansion, Casa de Margarita, on the night of the murder, reading a book aloud to her sister, grandmother, and mother.

How well she had known Taylor was never a question; the frilly pink nightgown and her love letters attested to that. It was the rest that reporters wanted to know: were the rumors true that her mother owned a .38-caliber pistol, that she was jealous of her daughter's attentions to older men, and had been seen threatening them?

As with Normand, Minter's denials didn't satisfy the press. Rumors persisted even years later after Mary, in a long court battle filled with mutual recriminations, successfully sued her mother for money her mother had managed for her. In the late 1930s, Minter and her mother, fed up with insinuations about them, demanded that the police reveal any evidence connecting them with the Taylor murder. Police said they didn't have anything to reveal, and granted the entire family complete exoneration from any wrongdoing. Still the rumors continued. If police had never had the Minter family pistol, or the Minter nightgown, why hadn't the public been told back in 1922, before Minter's career was killed, along with her favorite director?

The pornographic photographs were as difficult to trace through the newspaper accounts as Minter's nightgown. One account stated that Edward Sands was the photographer who captured his employer on film with famous actresses; other reports claimed that the only photographs found were tasteful, signed portraits of actresses Taylor had directed. Official police spokesmen neither confirmed nor denied any of these accounts, merely claiming it was in the best interests of their investigation that the truth not be made public until arrests were made.

As Vidor read more, he began to notice that, though no drugs had been reported found in Taylor's bungalow, they were mentioned in nearly every article. One report said Taylor was a pusher, another just an innocent bystander. Both stories were based on statements by Assistant U.S. District Attorney Tom Green, who claimed that Taylor came to his office in 1920 with stories of a dope ring operating out of one of the studios. Green went on to claim that the director told him a certain prominent actress was buying upwards of two thousand dollars' worth of narcotics from them every week. Taylor urged Green to ask federal authorities to undertake a war on dope in Hollywood. Other story sources were based on supposed eyewitness accounts of Taylor's haggling with a known pusher. All the reports stated that police had begun a war on dope traffic in the studios, but none claimed any arrests had ever been made.

By the end of 1923, over a year after the murder, the District Attorney's Office had over three hundred suspects and confessions in the Taylor case, and they were still coming in, sometimes as many as ten a week. But still no convictions.

One of the most promising leads came from a rancher living near Santa Ana, some forty-five miles south of Los

Angeles. The rancher claimed that shortly before the murder, he had picked up two tough-looking hitchhikers who said that they had served in the Canadian Army under a captain they called "Bill," a man they said had been responsible for their being "sent up." The rancher thought nothing of the story until one of the hitchhikers dropped a .38-caliber revolver onto the floor of his Ford pickup.

Another story, recounted in a letter to police from a former British Army officer, described a meeting the officer had had with Taylor in a London hotel in 1918. Taylor and the officer were seated in a hotel dining room when an unidentified individual in a Canadian Army uniform crossed the room. Taylor told the officer, "There goes a man who is going to get me if it takes a thousand years to do it." The man appeared to resemble one of several descriptions given by Faith MacLean, and the rancher's gun-toting hitchhiker as well.

Shortly after the police took the rancher's testimony, a man fitting his description was arrested in Mexicali. The rancher identified him as one of the hitchhikers. The suspect, Walter Kirby, was reported to have worked as a chauffeur in Los Angeles, possibly for Taylor.

The facts about Kirby looked suspicious. Along with fitting the suspect's description, he was reported to have been wearing a brown cap at the time of his arrest, the same kind MacLean's stranger wore. A search of his room uncovered a pair of Army breeches and several .38-caliber bullets. By his own admission he had served in the Canadian Army under Bill Taylor. Then, within twenty-four hours of his arrest, Kirby produced an airtight alibi, and the Santa Ana rancher who had positively identified him suddenly changed his mind.

Kirby was released from custody, but not from the news. A friend of his told police that Kirby was a notorious drug addict, and that someone was after him and would "end him quick." In May 1922, Kirby was found dead in the swamps of New River, west of Calexico, in the Imperial Valley. Journalists posed a question that police were not able to answer: had Kirby actually died of exposure, as some accounts claimed, or had he died of a forced lethal overdose of drugs?

That same month, another man named Walter Kirby, along with five others, was arrested for the Taylor murder. The men were being held principally on the strength of information given by a woman who claimed that she overheard the men threaten Taylor with his life the night before his murder. She said the men operated a bootlegging outfit that had sold liquor to Taylor and many of his friends. Their threat had terminated an argument with Taylor. During the arrest, detectives seized what they called a "quantity of evidence" but provided no specifics. The only other information given the press was that two of the suspects had recently arrived in Los Angeles from Chicago, where they had reputations as hired gunmen.

Another potential suspect turned himself in, claiming to be a friend of a certain motion picture actress he did not wish to name. He said he had passed by the Taylor bungalow on the night of the murder and seen the director and the actress in a heated argument. Entering the apartment, he saw that Taylor had a pistol, and in a struggle to pull the weapon away, had shot Taylor in the back.

Another confession came from a Folsom Prison convict, Otis Heffner, who claimed he had tried to rob the Taylor bungalow on the night of the murder. Taylor's unexpected arrival forced the burglar to hide behind the piano, where he reportedly witnessed a fight between Taylor and a woman who was dressed like a man. The fight ended in murder.

In Cleveland, police were said to be closing in on other murder suspects, based on "hot tips." In Flagstaff, Arizona, deputies located a man who looked identical to Sands, who had arrived in that area only two days after the murder. In Carlin, Nevada, police had a man barricaded in a hotel room. Police in St. Louis, New York, London, and Paris had suspects as well. But none of them had a killer.

As Vidor was quickly discovering, he had quite a task before him. The latest reports covering developments in the Taylor murder stated that Faith Cole MacLean, the closest the police department had to an eyewitness, had died in the 1950s. D.A. Thomas Woolwine had also died, as had his successor, Asa Keyes; Marjorie Berger; Mabel Normand; Henry Peavey; Charles Eyton; and Charlotte Shelby. Mary Miles Minter had just dropped from sight.

Peavey, lying on his deathbed in a ghetto in the Napa State Hospital for the insane, had screamed "the master's killer" was after him.

Mabel Normand, dying of tuberculosis, had asked, "I wonder who killed poor Bill Taylor?"

Vidor had read all he wanted to read. He snapped the bound volume shut and dismissed Carr. The Los Angeles *Times* hadn't wanted this murder solved. Nor had the New York *Times*, the *Herald-American*, or the *Times-Courier*. The longer the investigation ran, and the more sordid the details, the more papers they would sell: "Hollywood Babylon" at three cents a pop.

Outside, he pulled the T-Bird out of the lot, asking for a receipt for the dollar and a quarter. He knew he needed a lot more than the old newspapers had given him. He needed flesh and blood, living people, who remembered what had really happened.

5

0

n Saturday, January 21, 1967, Vidor took American Airlines Flight Six to New York. He hated the expense of flying first class, but he didn't want to risk anyone from Hollywood, especially one of the young studio executives, seeing him in economy. Straight bourbon helped mollify his lifelong fear of heights, and he made a point of directing his gaze away from the window, to his desk diary in front of him. Doing so, he thought of Colleen Moore, the woman who had helped him overcome his fear of flying and the woman he planned to meet when he arrived.

Few knew the story of his relationship with Moore. To

all but the most trusted friends, they were simply business partners. But in fact, as Vidor had been lately writing in his diaries at night, they were much more than two motion picture veterans teaming up to keep their creative spirits alive. Theirs was a romance born nearly half a century earlier, when Hollywood itself had only just come into being.

When Vidor and Moore first met, the Hollywood community was trying to rise above its reputation. Largely founded by fugitive filmmakers from New York trying to escape paying the patent rights on motion picture equipment, the town was still popularly thought of as a haven for the wanton and the wicked, filled with back-alley dealings, narcotics, prostitution, and general amorality (a view nurtured by such early fan rags as *Moving Picture World* and *Motion Picture Magazine*). To an extent, these stories were true. The towering sums of money that movies brought their creators and players—most of whom, coming from vaudeville, carnival, burlesque, and circus backgrounds, were unaccustomed to wealth of any kind—created a climate wherein excess and extravagance could flourish.

But there were also talented workers whose primary concern was their new art form, the motion picture, and who believed that their dedication and tenacity could raise the world's opinion of Hollywood, show that it could outgrow its problems, which were really no different from those common to any boomtown. Among these dedicated people were King Vidor and his first wife, Florence.

Vidor had come from Galveston, Texas, in 1915, with ambitions to direct. Florence had dreams of becoming an actress. By 1921, Vidor had his own studio, Vidor Village, next door to the brand-new Mary Pickford Studio on Santa Monica Boulevard. The family-run studio—his parents, sister, and wife all worked there—quietly produced movies while scandal raged around them, the most virulent being Fatty Arbuckle's. Involving rape and murder at a show-folk orgy, the scandal inspired over a hundred legislative bills calling for film censorship, a ban on all movies by one town in Massachusetts, and a foundation for the anti-Hollywood sentiment around the country. But Vidor, though his fortune and future were hardly secure, had found something to keep his mind off the doomsayers' predictions that Hollywood was heading for a rightful fall: Colleen Moore.

Colleen Moore was the most beautiful and charming girl he had ever met. Her short black hair was a refreshing change from the blonde Mary Pickford curls popular among actresses, and her eyes—one blue, one brown—were unlike any he had ever seen. She was seventeen years old, King was twenty-six.

Vidor planned his most ambitious production for her, *The Sky Pilot,* about a young girl in a small Canadian town coming to grips with life and religion. During shooting on location, while Vidor's wife, Florence, was off at Paramount acting under the direction of William Desmond Taylor, Vidor and Moore fell in love. Keeping their flirtation secret from everyone around them, they concocted symbols of their affection: a circle on a dressing-room door signified eternal love; three vertical lines meant "I love you"; the initials LND stood for Love Never Dies. They gave each other nicknames: Madame Zaza and Professor La Tour. The picture was behind schedule and going over budget—with the producers demanding a new ending, and creditors threatening to close Vidor Village—but Vidor and Moore were living a true-life fairytale romance.

On February 1, 1922, the new ending finally completed, a blizzard hit their northern California mountain location, completely burying the steep roads back to Hollywood. As the cast and crew all settled into a nearby mountain lodge to wait out the storm, Vidor and Moore found their first real time alone together, each completely in love but neither knowing what would happen when they got back to Hollywood, and reality.

When the blizzard finally let up, the company left their cars and some of their equipment behind and made the eight-mile trek down the mountain to Truckee on foot. When they arrived, they all went into a speakeasy behind the hotel to thaw out with hot coffee and brandy. Vidor's father was waiting for them. While everyone told spirited tales of their ordeal, Charles Vidor didn't seem to be listening. Finally, he slid onto the barstool next to King's and announced that William Desmond Taylor had been murdered the night before. A hush fell over the room.

In the days and weeks that followed, Taylor's story was retold many times, for it seemed, together with the Arbuckle scandal, to mark the imminent end of Hollywood. The Vidor company returned to Los Angeles, not knowing when they might have to pack up and leave, returning to the carnivals and theaters they had come from. Colleen Moore, a good Catholic girl, knew that her dating a married man would not sit well with a public bent on censorship and enforced morality. So, days after the New York release of their film, they bid each other farewell on a Manhattan street corner, vowing never to see each other again.

For forty years Vidor and Moore kept that vow. And yet, for forty years, each continued sending the other messages in their lovers' code, always hidden in an innocent motion picture scene. Moore would tell each leading man that "love never dies," and Vidor would decorate his sets with violets, which he had always given Moore during their short time together.

Then in 1964, Vidor was in Paris, walking along the Champs-Élysées and contemplating his stalled career, when he recognized a woman in front of him. He tapped her on the shoulder and said, "Madame Zaza, what is it I am holding in my hand?"

Without turning around, Colleen Moore replied, "A dime, Professor La Tour."

They walked back to Vidor's hotel, and the years that had elapsed disappeared. They talked of the early days in Hollywood, and the opportunities they had in the new, youth-oriented film industry of the 1960s. Vidor had some scripts, and ideas for others he felt would make good, personal motion pictures. And Moore had the abilities to oversee the business side of filmmaking. Vid-Mor Productions was born.

And now, three years later, Vidor was on his way to New York to see Moore and to work on the script that would for the first time present those early, explosive days of Hollywood as they actually were. He'd arranged meetings with a dozen old friends, and others who might have knowledge of William Desmond Taylor that would answer some of the questions surrounding his life and death. Moore had done her work as well, contacting friends she had in the Midwest who had known Taylor and helping make appointments. It should be a fruitful trip—and not all of it would be business.

6

Taylor certainly wasn't an Oxford man," Robert Giroux, the New York book publisher and Hollywood historian, told Vidor. "That's what he may have told his friends, but the official record doesn't bear him out. . . ."

As Giroux spoke, he spread his private collection of original Taylor documents out on the table in front of Vidor like a museum exhibit. The sight was nothing out of the ordinary at the Players Club, where they met on January 27, 1967. Publishers like Giroux often conducted business upstairs in the formal dining room. Downstairs, by the pool table and bar where Vidor and Giroux sat, those deals were sealed with a cigar and brandy.

"It's the disappearing acts that bother me," Vidor confided as he nursed a glass of French wine. "A lot of people arrived in Hollywood pretending to be people they weren't. Taylor just did it exceptionally well. What I'd like to know is what he was running from."

Giroux had no easy answer, nor did Vidor expect one. If he had, Giroux would have published the monumental amount of research he had accumulated on the life of Taylor. The fact was, he had only half the story, just enough to keep Vidor on the edge of his chair.

Irish genealogical records Giroux had collected showed the Tanner family living in Carlow, Weatherford County, not Mallow, Cork County, as the official studio biography publicized—the same biography that failed to mention his first marriage, or the fact that he had ever worked as an antiques dealer. This was a small but important distinction, Giroux pointed out, for Carlow was a great deal more rustic and provincial than Mallow, and Taylor's origins far more humble than he led one to believe.

The birth certificate of William Cunningham Deane Tanner read April 26, 1872, not 1877, as reported in dozens of newspapers. And the family wasn't from a long and important line of Irish families, as Taylor had told many of his Hollywood friends, but from a simple, hard-working, and upright Catholic family that placed a high premium on firm discipline, good education, and Irish nationalism.

The information Giroux had collected presented William Tanner as a handsome, friendly, and hard-working young boy. He enjoyed traveling, even if it was only to the next town where he attended school. He had two sisters and two brothers, including Denis Deane Tanner. He didn't get along very well with his father, known as a hot-tempered major in the British Army who had severely punished his son on occasion. Nothing was known about William's mother.

Giroux, like Vidor, was particularly interested in the details of an early, unsuccessful marriage arrangement between William and a young neighbor and companion. That friend, Eva Shannon, like William, was only fifteen. From what Giroux had been able to cull from published records, William's interests didn't lie in her charms as a lady, but in her abilities to catch salmon in a nearby river, where William often went to be alone. Giroux had little more to go on. All he could say for sure was that wedding plans had suddenly soured, and William had left, destination unknown.

Giroux's guess was that Tanner had left with an actor, Charles Hawtrey, then managing a repertory company touring that part of Ireland. He based his guess upon the fact that two years later, William was playing major roles in Hawtrey's company. The young boy might have begun building sets or running errands, Vidor suggested. Whatever happened, in May 1884, at age seventeen, William was waiting for his cue to go on stage in London when a family friend spotted him and wrote his father.

Within days, Major William Tanner had snatched his son from the stage and sent him to Clifton College, then to Heidelberg, Germany, to study engineering, and prepare to follow his father's footsteps to the military academy at Sandhurst. The exact details of what followed were unimportant, but it was clear that William spent very little time at school, resulting in bitter arguments with his father over the acting profession—considered by the head of the family to be the lowest form of gypsy existence.

Disgraced, Tanner's father turned to friends he had in the military and, at their suggestion, sent him to Runnymeade, a ranching settlement in Kansas run by Ned Turnley. In the American West, where Turnley promised a disciplined environment and strenuous physical activity, William's father believed his son would develop more in his own image.

Vidor helped fill in the rest of that story. Turnley's daughter was still alive. While Vidor and Carr had been doing research at the Los Angeles Public Library, Colleen Moore had made contact with the daughter. In a letter from Kansas to Moore she recounted what she remembered.

Runnymeade, so the story unfolded, had been set up as a retreat for young Englishmen who had failed to live up to the standards set by their families. Though William got along well with the other residents, he didn't fit the mold. While the others went into the next town and raised havoc in the saloon, William kept to himself, reading heavily, drawing, writing, and spending time in the company of one or two carefully chosen friends. He left Runnymeade after a year and a half, when money from home dried up.

According to Giroux's notes, William's father demanded nothing short of a ten-year term defending his country when his son returned to Ireland. Perhaps there was some kind of showdown, perhaps not; neither Vidor nor Giroux knew. Official records only showed that he took the physical but failed for poor eyesight. And yet Taylor never found the need for glasses, nor did his eyesight prevent him from joining the Canadian Army years later.

Vidor and Giroux could only read between the lines. William may have found the idea of following in his father's footsteps distasteful, and decided it was easier to fake an eye exam than to face his father's wrath. But whatever happened, William soon disappeared from home a second time, and this time he never returned.

Back in America he roamed the railroad yards in Kansas City, wrote for a magazine in Leavenworth, sold crude sketches in Milwaukee, shot craps in Chicago, and finally, through connections he had made in London years before, landed a job in the theatre in New York.

There was little doubt that women on and off the stage were attracted to him. He was tall and good-looking, with a finely proportioned body and gentle eyes—the perfect accompaniment for a popular feminine star—and Fanny Davenport, the famous Broadway star, signed him as her leading man.

Neither Vidor nor Giroux had found any detailed information about the relationship between Tanner and Davenport. All they knew was that they had gone their separate ways after three years, when they had reached the height of their respective stage-acting careers. As Vidor well knew, three years with an actress was a substantial emotional investment, and Tanner and Davenport were both receiving high salaries and good reviews when Tanner inexplicably left for an uncertain future on the road in stock companies in Boston, Seattle, and Chicago. Perhaps there had been artistic differences, or perhaps, as Vidor began to believe, their relationship had become too intimate for Tanner's tastes; Giroux didn't know.

On the road, money became tight. Then Tanner heard of a gold strike in Alaska. A retired miner from the Klondike told reporters in 1922 of spending several days in a small mountain cabin with Bill Tanner, days during which Tanner had told him of a great love that had ended in a bitter affair and lasting sorrow. Could he have been talking about Fanny Davenport?

In another account Tanner had said that he had gone to prison in England for three years to protect a woman's honor. Neither Vidor nor Giroux had found any official records to substantiate either of these claims. As with the later accounts concerning his murder, there were literally dozens of conflicting stories, all of which agreed only on Tanner's return to the New York stage in 1901, when he met Ethel May Harrison, a member of the famous Floradora Sextette.

Ethel was a vivacious beauty who acted, sang, and played the piano. There was no question that she appreciated the handsome, cultured, well-spoken Irishman. But Tanner, who had entrée to theatrical circles all over the city, could have chosen any of dozens of stage beauties. "Why Ethel May Harrison?" Vidor asked.

Giroux had some ideas. Tanner was now thirty-four years old, and virtually penniless. He knew firsthand that on the stage he couldn't make the kind of money he wanted. And while the Floradora Sextette was famous, its individual members, and their families, were not—except Ethel. Ethel's father, a wealthy stockbroker, was in a position to help get Tanner set up in business, and at the same time eager to see his daughter off the stage. So Tanner married Ethel May Harrison in 1901 at the Little Church Around the Corner, and became the new vice-president and part owner of the English Antique Shop at 246 Fifth Avenue, at a salary of nearly thirty thousand dollars a year. Ethel gave up the stage.

As Vidor knew, Tanner and Ethel May settled in Larchmont. Tanner grew a mustache, bought and sold lovely furniture, and was generous to everyone he knew. In 1903 a daughter was born to the couple, whom they named Ethel Daisy Deane Tanner. For seven years Tanner played the dutiful husband; then abnormalities in his behavior began to bother Ethel. William had begun to drink. He acted restless at night, and took an intense interest in psychology and neurosis, often shutting himself up for hours to read.

At about noon on October 23, 1908, Tanner told associates in the antiques shop that he was going to the races and would not return that day. Friends saw Tanner at the track. He was drinking quite heavily, as he had during the previous week, and was accompanied by a notorious spendthrift, "Fudge" Alexander. Tanner didn't return home that night.

The following day he telephoned the cashier at his shop and had cash taken to his hotel room, which was the last his associates ever saw of him. Tanner had pulled another disappearing act, only this time the reasons were a great deal more difficult to pin down.

As both Vidor and Giroux knew, Tanner's next four years were spent on the road as a timekeeper for the Yukon Gold Company in Alaska; a night clerk at the Inter Ocean Hotel in Cheyenne, Wyoming; a prospector in Colorado and Alaska. He arrived in San Francisco penniless, wracked by flu. Back on the stage, he drew rave reviews from Geraldine Farrar, the great opera singer, and Thomas Ince, the powerful studio producer. Hollywood was the next natural step. The new film frontier, like the Alaskan Klondike, offered a challenge. He could not only put his acting skills to work, but rake in the kind of dollars others made panning for gold.

A great many journalists and writers said that this very challenge had made him leave his wife and family. Giroux wasn't convinced. Nor was Vidor.

The least credible theory held Tanner to be in a state of frenzy and temporary memory loss brought on by excessive drinking and intense business pressure. But, as Giroux pointed out, he had left his finances in perfect order. His savings, which were turned over to his wife, were substantial. And though he drank, he had no record of alcoholic tendencies, drunken binges, or mental disorders. Quite likely, this theory was generated by his wife—her way of saying her husband must have been crazy to leave a lovely woman like herself and young child.

Another theory promulgated by the press assumed that Tanner had left his wife for another woman. This theory was based upon an eyewitness account claiming that Tanner was often seen in the homes of beautiful women and, years later, recognized by a hotel clerk in an Adirondack honeymoon lodge where he was said to have spent a weekend in the arms of a blonde.

The fact that Tanner was seen with various women in New York was easily explained, Giroux pointed out. The majority of his customers at the antiques shop were either interior decorators or the wives of wealthy men making purchases for their new homes and apartments. Part of Tanner's duties as a salesman had been to see to all their needs, even if it meant sitting in a quiet restaurant discussing trends in decorating, or making house calls in the homes of prospective clients.

The claim that Tanner was seen in the arms of another woman was not as easily dismissed. Giroux, however, pointed out the coincidence of this "eyewitness" account occurring at the same time that his wife was seeking a divorce. Adultery was the only ground for divorce in New York State, and as Vidor knew from his own experiences in divorce court, a few dollars paid to the right hotel clerk could provide the kind of testimony that Ethel Tanner needed. The man she intended to marry, L. C. Robbins, the owner of Delmonico's, had the money. According to this theory, Tanner's partner went "unnamed" because she didn't exist, except to furnish grounds for a divorce. Tanner wasn't about to come forward and say otherwise.

A third theory became prevalent at the time of Tanner's murder—that a mysterious killer, revenging some wrong committed by Tanner in Ireland (perhaps the "bitter love" suggested by the Klondike miner), had followed Tanner to New York. Tanner had become aware of the killer's presence and left town immediately, changing his name to Taylor to try to cover his tracks. The killer had continued his search, discovered him in Hollywood, and completed his mission.

As interesting as Vidor and Giroux found the latter theory, it still would not explain why Tanner chose such a high-profile career as an actor, director, and eventually president of the Motion Picture Directors Association. If Tanner were really a hunted man, he could have virtually disappeared into any of a hundred professions.

"I think he was just disillusioned with his marriage, his job, and the life he had cut out for himself in Larchmont," Giroux said. "Tanner struck off on his own to seek adventure and freedom, as he had done years before in Alaska. He hadn't acted on the spur of the moment, but had coolly planned his escape in advance."

As enticing as this theory sounded, Vidor said he thought there was more to it. He cited the example of Ethel Tanner's discovery in a Broadway theater that Tanner had become a Hollywood actor. She gasped, not because she suddenly realized that Tanner was alive but because he had become a celebrity. Her reaction was not one of bitterness or vindictiveness but rather of curiosity. Later, she permitted her daughter to strike up a correspondence with her former husband and expressed happiness at the thought that someday Daisy would visit Tanner in California. Ethel was a wealthy and important woman by that time from her second marriage and had no apparent desire for Taylor's money or status as a celebrity. Vidor wanted to know what kind of man could inspire such enduring affection and loyalty in a woman he had deserted.

As Vidor's and Giroux's evening was drawing to an end, the director decided to leave Giroux with a theory he figured Giroux wouldn't agree with. Vidor had heard rumors, he said, back in the twenties, stories that a New York publisher wouldn't have heard.

"Tanner was obviously a man torn by inner conflicts," Vidor said as he finished off the bottle of wine in front of them. "It looks to me like Ethel May knew what it was, and sympathized. Losing Tanner might very well have been a relief. If I didn't know better—considering the nightgown and loose women—I'd say the problem was his job or his family. Could Taylor's problem have been a growing awareness of his homosexuality?"

Giroux's expression suddenly changed as Vidor spoke these words, and Vidor knew he had mentioned the one possibility that Giroux had never considered.

7

I gave Taylor his big break," Allan Dwan, the film director, said proudly as he munched an apple tart in a small office in a midtown brownstone, a day after Vidor's meeting with Giroux. "I couldn't say whether he was a homosexual or not. Didn't knock up any of the girls on the lot, but then he didn't molest the electrician, either. Tell you the truth, I wouldn't have cared either way. He kept the action going, his films on budget, and his hands to himself, which is a lot more than I can say for most of the crowd I had to work with."

Dwan conveyed these sentiments to Vidor with the eager bravado of a caged animal. Retirement hadn't softened him one bit. Nor had the cold shoulder that he, like Vidor, had been getting from the studio executives. He was still as self-assured and boisterous as when he himself had held studio reins, and had no doubt that, were he and Vidor reinstated into rightful positions of authority in Hollywood, the young hot-shots now in charge would be out clipping lawns.

He sat in the office off the living room and recalled all the gossip published after William Desmond Taylor's murder.

"It was patently false," he said. "Taylor was a gentleman and an artist. He was fair, friendly, and extremely talented—not at all the libertine and dope fiend the papers suggested."

Dwan also dismissed with a wave of his tart any mystery surrounding Taylor's name change.

"Everyone did it. I was christened Aloysius Dwan. Mary Pickford was Gladys Smith. It was a matter of setting the right image. And Taylor's name choice was brilliant. It sounded like someone from an English novel, the kind Hollywood liked making into films. It set him apart from all the aspiring actors arriving by the trainloads from places like Kansas and Nebraska. Taylor was sharp."

No sooner had Taylor arrived in Hollywood, Dwan said, than he set up headquarters at the Alexandria Hotel, on the corner of Fifth and Spring streets in downtown Los Angeles. The Alexandria was the place to see and be seen by everyone who was anyone in the motion picture industry. It was at the Alexandria bar that, over its celebrated free roast beef sandwiches, Taylor first met Mary Pickford's director, Marshall Neilan; Mary Miles Minter's director, James Kirkwood; and Dwan himself—all men in positions to help Taylor's career.

It was on Neilan's advice that Taylor took every acting

job offered him. Most were very small parts in Civil War dramas and Westerns shot at Thomas Ince's studio, but gradually he earned more substantial roles.

In *The Iconoclast,* Taylor was a heavily mustachioed villain; in *A True Believer,* a clean-shaven soldier; and in *Millions for Defence,* a buffoon—all bread-and-butter roles in pictures Dwan and Vidor remembered only by name.

But they both remembered Taylor's first starring role in a feature production: as Robert Wainwright, the pistol-carrying hero of a rebel brigade in *Captain Alvarez.* The film brought Taylor fame, and helped turn the West Coast branch of Vitagraph Studios, then a three-man operation with rented tents, into a major outfit with its own barns and darkroom.

The role of the rebel leader required a quiet but powerful actor, and director Rollin Sturgeon decided on Taylor immediately. Sturgeon, a Harvard graduate, saw in Taylor an element of class, something not easily found at a studio where problems were still solved with fists and six-shooters.

"Sturgeon," Dwan said, "introduced Taylor to Mabel Normand. I think both men were a refreshing break for her from all the rough-and-tumble cowboys always turning the Vitagraph set into free-for-alls. I don't know if Taylor ever slept with her. He wasn't the kiss-and-tell type. He didn't even stand in line to peep through the secret holes in the walls of the actresses' dressing rooms."

Dwan laughed and finished his breakfast. Vidor asked if Taylor and Normand ever worked together.

"I don't think so. Normand was always the comedienne, Taylor the dignified hero. If she was tied to a track with a locomotive barreling toward her, Taylor'd be more likely to be sipping a goblet of wine and striking a handsome pose than racing off to save her."

Soon, tired of constantly traipsing from the Alexandria to the studio casting offices, Taylor turned to directing. His first opportunities were at the financially unstable Balboa Studios, where he directed his future fiancée, Neva Gerber. Though newspapers at the time made much of the romance, Dwan told Vidor it was more studio publicity than anything else. Besides, just weeks after the romance hit the press, Taylor moved to Santa Barbara to work for Flying A Studios, where Dwan was head director.

"And I never once saw them together," Dwan said.

At Flying A, Dwan hired and fired as he saw fit, hating the nepotism that existed at all the other studios. He gave jobs to people who might never have gotten breaks otherwise, including Victor Fleming, who would later direct *Gone With the Wind,* and an eager, young, all-around gofer from Texas with the highfalutin name of King Vidor.

Taylor completely enchanted Dwan as he did everyone else on the lot. He displayed such confidence that no one doubted he was destined for greatness both on and off the screen.

And yet he made no truly close, lasting friendships at Flying A. Where most of the directors shared their private lives with one another—everyone knew of Victor Fleming's rendezvous with a certain studio head's wife—Taylor remained secretive about himself. He passed on the popular trips to the local brothel, and was not known to have approached any of the Flying A actresses, even, Dwan recalled with another laugh, Mary Miles Minter, whose mother made a nearly full-time job of saving her from the clutches of amorous directors like James Kirkwood, or actors like Monte Blue.

"Maybe he *was* homosexual, I don't know," Dwan said. "But I do know about the dope, and Taylor was against it. He actively tried to stop the drifters who used to come up from Los Angeles with cocaine and opium."

"Were there a lot of those drifters?" Vidor asked.

"There were as many dope dealers as there were prostitutes—and there was never a shortage of prostitutes, believe me. But I don't recall Taylor actually fighting any of them, though he was known to throw a mean lecture on the evils of drugs, which makes all those later reports about his Paramount years highly questionable."

Taylor's crowning achievement at Flying A was directing twenty episodes of the serial *The Diamond from the Sky*. The serial's star, Lottie Pickford, Mary's younger sister, was highly temperamental, pregnant, and saddled with a serious drinking problem. But Taylor handled her expertly and the serial was a smashing success, gaining Taylor industry-wide recognition as an important young director. The two-carat diamond ring found on Taylor's finger on the day of his death was Flying A's way of saying thank you for *The Diamond from the Sky*.

"You make him sound like the boy wonder of the movies," Vidor said. "He must have changed dramatically when he moved to Paramount."

"Maybe so," Dwan replied, "or maybe the newspapers just didn't give the whole story. They're not known for emphasizing one's finer points, you know."

Vidor wondered if he were getting the whole story from Dwan.

"Is there anything else you remember about Taylor?"

Dwan rubbed his hand over his bald head, then, sitting back, rested it on his belly.

"There is one thing. In *Captain Alvarez*, there was a blacksmith, and the man who played him, when he had his makeup off, looked strikingly like Taylor. I never met the man myself, but everyone I knew on the lot said there was no doubt they were brothers. I don't know why this wasn't mentioned in the papers, and I don't know what might have happened to him, whether, like some people seemed to think, he might have become . . . what's his name? . . . Taylor's secretary that some people thought killed him and disappeared . . . ?"

"Sands," Vidor said.

"Right, Sands. I don't know about that, but whatever later became of him, for a while at least, Denis Deane Tanner was definitely in Hollywood with Taylor."

8

Vidor sat alone in the Russian Tea Room on Sunday, January 29, 1967. Around him the lunch-hour crowd bustled noisily in and out, the air filled with the patois of show business. Names and faces that Vidor recognized surrounded him, but he paid them no more mind than they paid him. He ordered the lunch special and made screenplay notes into his pocket notebook. His talk with Allan Dwan had further convinced him that the Edward Sands / Denis Deane Tanner connection was something worth looking into. If, as Dwan suggested, so many people were convinced that the bit actor in *Captain Alvarez* had been Taylor's brother, then it was likely that when Denis Tanner's wife, Ada, stormed into Taylor's office demanding her husband's whereabouts, she wasn't simply assuming that Taylor would know, but had seen *Captain Alvarez* herself and knew perfectly well Tanner was somewhere in Hollywood. And if that was the case, why hadn't she—or anyone else for that matter, including Dwan—said so to the press? Why had Denis Tanner's very existence been shrouded in so much mystery?

Vidor finished his chicken cutlet and checked his watch. He had an hour before his appointment with Gloria Swanson. She probably hadn't known Dennis Tanner, having met Taylor only after his return to Hollywood from Santa Barbara and Flying A Studios. But she was an integral part of Taylor's social crowd once he made entry into Hollywood royalty at Paramount. She knew who Taylor's friends—and enemies?—were in the years prior to his death. Perhaps she had met Sands.

Vidor had encountered Swanson nearly fifty years earlier at a Hollywood party where she and William Desmond Taylor had had a great laugh at Vidor's expense. Vidor had worn to the party a special shirt he had bought at his favorite discount basement, Knock-'Em-Dead Murphy's, for $3.50. The exposed cuffs and collar were silk, but the rest of the shirt, designed to be hidden under a jacket, was made of matching but decidedly cheap cotton. Vidor had enjoyed the party, drinking his share of bootleg punch, until the men all started removing their jackets. It was a summer afternoon, and everyone implored Vidor to make himself comfortable. Vidor begged off, claiming his Texas blood was unaccustomed to the California chill. Finally, after a spirited round of joking, Swanson and Taylor egged Vidor into a mock wrestling match that exposed Vidor's deceptive shirt to the entire party.

The incident had embarrassed Vidor but had made

----

him known to everyone at the party. Afterward, several who had attended, including Taylor, offered jobs to both Vidor and his wife, Florence.

Vidor reached Swanson's Fifth Avenue penthouse precisely on time. She met him at the door. It had been nearly twenty years since Swanson had appeared as the tragic Hollywood has-been, Norma Desmond, in *Sunset Boulevard*, a film in which many had cruelly said Swanson had merely played herself, yet Vidor detected nothing of her most celebrated character in her. She was still, at a very health-conscious sixty-seven, as vibrant and attractive as Vidor remembered her.

"So, what is this project you're working on?" she asked after friendly reminiscing.

"It's about the old days," he told her. "Up to around the time Bill Taylor was killed."

Swanson looked at Vidor in silence, as though her clear blue eyes were boring right through him. Finally, slowly, her famous toothy smile appeared.

"Well," she said, "it's about time someone told that story. Or at least as much of the story as anyone knows to tell. How can I help you?"

"When did you meet Taylor?"

Swanson seemed amused by the subject matter, as though she suspected Vidor's specific interest in Taylor were not as casual as he was trying to make it seem. But to Vidor's relief, she didn't push the matter. She settled comfortably onto her love seat and answered.

"It was just after he'd been working up in Santa Barbara. He came to work for Oliver Morosco at the old Bosworth-Morosco Studios. Then Paramount bought them out. Adolph Zukor took Charlie Eyton as his right-hand

----

man, and Taylor went with the package. Eyton and Taylor were friends right up to the end."

Under Zukor, at Paramount, Taylor directed no fewer than twenty films in three short years, including such hits as *Davy Crockett, House of Lies,* and *Tom Sawyer.*

"Taylor fit right in in Hollywood," Swanson said. "He always arrived at places in style, always spoke with that impeccable English accent. I think Zukor liked him because he wasn't always after all the actresses in his films the way most directors were. That and the fact that he knew how to keep his mouth shut."

"What do you mean?" Vidor asked.

"You know what I mean. Secrets have always been harder to keep in Hollywood than youth and marriage partners. And Taylor wasn't a talker. Take Wallace Reid, or Mary Pickford's brother, Jack. They both had horrendous drug problems. Morphine. At least with Reid, the studio supplied the drugs, and Taylor knew it but didn't say anything.

Vidor wondered if Taylor had kept any sort of diary or had any other evidence that might hurt the reputations of the people he'd worked with at Paramount. That might explain what Charles Eyton was looking for in Taylor's bungalow the morning after the murder.

"I wouldn't know about that," Swanson told him. "But I doubt it. Taylor didn't seem the type even to risk hurting someone, should his diary ever be stolen or anything."

By the time Swanson met Taylor, he was living at the Los Angeles Athletic Club, an exclusive residence where his neighbors included Charles Chaplin and friends Marshall Neilan and James Kirkwood. He was in demand socially as well as professionally, always seated beside the guest of honor at formal affairs, and welcomed heartily at such less formal gatherings as the boxing matches at the

Vernon Club, dinner and dancing at Nat Goodwin's on the Santa Monica Pier, and the regular Saturday night parties at the Sunset Inn on Ocean Avenue, where Fatty Arbuckle, Buster Keaton, and other comedians entertained everyone well into the morning hours.

"But what Taylor liked more than anything else," Swanson recalled, "was going up in the mountains and sitting around the Mount Lowe Lodge with his drinking buddies."

"Who were?"

"Oh, let's see. James Kirkwood, Marshall Neilan, Tony Moreno, Doug MacLean, that bunch. They're the ones you should be talking to, any of them still alive. It's too bad Marshall's gone. He could have told you all kinds of things. Including who killed Taylor. I'm certain of it."

"He told you?"

"He never told me anything about it. But the night Taylor was killed," she said, then paused, as though deciding whether to complete the sentence. Then she went on, "The night Taylor was killed, Marshall Neilan and I were . . . together. Early the next morning, an emergency meeting was called at the studio. All the studio heads were there. The meeting lasted all day and into the night. When it was over, I met Marshall at the studio commissary. He was in a hurry, said he had to talk with Mary Miles Minter. So we picked her up at her house and took her back to Marshall's. She seemed to be in a good mood. She cooked up some scrambled eggs, and we had a lot of champagne.

"Then all of a sudden, Marshall told me to go home. He said he had some 'heavy talking' to do with Mary and would come over later that night. He showed up the next morning, just in time to shower, shave, and get to the set. He never did tell me what it was all about, and when every thing started coming out in the papers, I knew better than to ask. Are you listening, King?"

The question jarred King back to attention. The mention of the emergency meeting at Paramount had reminded him of something MGM head Louis B. Mayer had said after Taylor's death. Mentioning the same secret meeting, Mayer had talked of "all the things we have to do now, in light of the Taylor murder." At the time, Vidor had assumed Mayer was referring to general efforts to improve the movie industry's public image. Now he wondered.

"I'm listening," he said. "Neilan never told you anything at all about the meeting?"

"Not a word. But it was obviously not because he didn't have a lot to tell. Same with Jimmy Kirkwood. He once told me he knew more than the police did about Taylor's murder, but he wouldn't go into any specifics. Except that the Saturday night before the murder, he was at a party with Taylor and Claire Windsor, the actress. I don't know if that's important, or even if Kirkwood's still alive, but Claire Windsor is, if you want to talk with her. I got a letter from her just a few weeks ago."

"I may do that." Vidor wrote the names Kirkwood and Windsor in his notebook. "And you mentioned Tony Moreno and Doug MacLean?"

"Yes, they were part of the Mount Lowe bunch. MacLean wasn't just a neighbor, but a good friend—he was in a number of Taylor films. Moreno knew Taylor for years. He lived at the Athletic Club. Apparently, Moreno had a meeting scheduled for the morning Taylor was murdered—with Taylor and District Attorney Woolwine."

"How do you know that?"

"That's what Mickey—I mean Marshall—told me. He never said what the meeting was supposed to be about, but the fact that Woolwine was put in charge of investigating

Taylor's murder makes the whole thing sound pretty suspicious."

"Is Moreno still alive?"

"The last of the Latin lovers? Yes."

Vidor returned his notebook to his pocket.

"You've been a great help. You seem to have given this Taylor thing a lot of thought."

Swanson laughed her famous laugh.

"Not for years. But at the time, how could I help it? Being that close to Marshall Neilan, I felt like an accessory or something."

"Any theories?" Vidor asked.

"Dozens."

Vidor joined her laughter.

"I mean, aside from all the obvious ones that have been tossed around now for . . . what? . . . forty years? . . . you shouldn't overlook Taylor's professional colleagues who just happened to make it big only after he was killed. Like his writer, Julia Crawford Ivers. Whoever heard of her before the murder? But after, it was as if she had a golden pen. Or how about some of his close friends that the same thing happened to? Like George Hopkins, or Douglas MacLean?"

While Swanson was completely enjoying herself, facetiously adding to the already laughably long list of suspects, Vidor grew tense. He knew George Hopkins. Hopkins had been the art director on a film Vidor had made for Warner Brothers.

"George Hopkins knew Taylor?"

"Oh, yeah. Taylor gave him his first big-time job in pictures. They were very close friends."

"Interesting." Vidor took out his notebook, added Hopkins's name to it. He thought Hopkins might be able to answer an important question about Taylor. When Vidor had worked with Hopkins, Hopkins was having an affair with a friend of Vidor's—an important Hollywood director, a man.

Douglas MacLean, Taylor's neighbor, had become a big-time Hollywood producer—a producer of a King Vidor film. Paramount had always been good to MacLean.

Swanson walked Vidor to the door.

"You really think you're going to solve this mystery?"

Vidor was ready for the question.

"I'm not a detective, Gloria," he said. "I'm just a moviemaker."

Swanson accepted a kiss on the cheek and returned it.

"Yes, you are, King, and a very good one. But you haven't answered my question."

9

William Desmond Taylor was a hero in the First World War.

He was an infantryman wounded at Belleau Wood.

He was an ace pilot decorated by the Royal Flying Corps for shooting down German biplanes.

He was a buck private whose selfless bravery earned him officers' commissions.

The roles he played in the war were as varied as the sources that reported them. Vidor read newspaper accounts, interviews, studio publicity releases, even Taylor's own war journal, which Vidor had acquired from a Hollywood souvenir dealer. All that the various reports had in common were that Taylor had served for Great Britain and that he had served heroically—two facts Vidor had believed from the beginning, having witnessed, along with six thousand other spectators, a full honor guard composed of officers of every army of the British Commonwealth firing a hero's salute over Taylor's Union Jack–adorned casket. Some of the reports smacked of pure Hollywood PR. Others, such as those from friends like Mary Miles Minter, might have resulted from self-promotion on Taylor's part. And still others—who knew? But whatever the truth of Taylor's wartime experiences might be, Vidor felt it might play a part in Taylor's postwar life, and death.

There had been stories about Taylor's testifying in a wartime court-martial, and speculation that the soldier he testified against might have tracked him to Hollywood and taken his revenge. But like every aspect of his life, Taylor's war years were clouded with contradictions, and Vidor needed to understand what really happened. So he asked his friend Laurence Stallings if he might be able to help. Having directed such a wide variety of movies—pictures set from Coney Island to the Russia of *War and Peace,* and taking place in every era from that of biblical Sheba to the present day—Vidor had had occasion to work with experts in many geographical, historical, and cultural fields. Stallings's area of expertise was World War I. He had met Vidor, in fact, during the twenties, while writing a script about the war. They were on the same Pullman, heading away from Los Angeles, Stallings's berth directly above Vidor's. For several hours they talked, Stallings telling Vidor about the horrors he had seen at Château-Thierry and the Metz. As he spoke, the train bounced over a rough length of track, causing Stallings's wooden leg, hanging on a wall hook, to swing into Vidor's berth, offering visual proof of just how real the horrors had been. In the forty years since, Stallings had become Vidor's chief screen-writer as well as confidant, drinking buddy, and yachting partner.

He arrived at Vidor's room at the Lombardy Hotel armed with street-vendor hot dogs and an oversized brief-case. Vidor had just come back from seeing Swanson.

"Hope you know what you're getting into, King," his deep gravel voice said as he made his way inside to a large overstuffed chair by the window, the only chair big enough for him. "Isn't every day I'm asked to dump on a guy's reputation. Even if the reputation isn't deserved."

He sat his hot dogs on an ottoman, offering to share them with Vidor but letting Vidor know with a laugh that if he weren't hungry not to worry—nothing would go to waste. He opened his briefcase. It was filled with papers from the British Recruiting Commissioner, and Taylor's war journal, which Vidor had given him to study.

"Taylor's reputation wasn't deserved?" Vidor asked.

"Well, not his soldier's reputation at least. Taylor did serve, there's no question about that. But he was no hero."

Stallings told Vidor all he had been able to find out.

On July 3, 1918, thirteen months after the United States had declared war, William Desmond Taylor, agé forty-one, enlisted as a private in the British Army, not the Canadian Army. He signed up in Los Angeles, which delayed the processing of his papers so long that by the time he actually arrived on the other side of the Atlantic, the Armistice had already been signed. He was stationed in Hounslow, south of London, then reassigned to Nova Scotia, where he was appointed temporary lieutenant shortly before being discharged. In all, he served approxi-mately nine months in uniform, during which he saw no wartime activity at all.

Vidor wasn't surprised. It was typical of Hollywood to

canonize its celebrities, to take a known fact—such as Taylor's having worn His Majesty's uniform—and exaggerate it in the name of glamour. But he still wondered why, especially that late in the war, Taylor had enlisted at all. If the studio had pressured him to participate in the war effort as they had others in the public eye, he could have done so by selling war bonds, as had Chaplin and Douglas Fairbanks. Or he could have enlisted in the U.S. Army as an officer—a letter from Zukor or Eyton could have arranged it with no problem. But he had enlisted as a buck private for the British.

"Well, look at his background with the military," Stallings suggested, shifting, Vidor could tell, into his screenwriter's mode. He laid out a plausible story line.

"Taylor's father was a British officer who apparently governed his family the way he governed his troops. When Taylor ran away from the military life, he lost his father's respect. Maybe he tried to get it back when he was in Kansas. Who knows? But we do know his father was later killed defending Taylor's homeland, so maybe Taylor enlisted as a private to prove his worth to his family and his country. And to himself."

"But what could he have proved?" Vidor asked. "He didn't see any action. In fact, from what I got out of his journal, he didn't see much of anything, except Friday night variety shows."

Stallings finished off a hot dog and licked mustard from his fingers. "That's true." He picked up Taylor's journal, randomly flipped through it. "Private Gale, magician; Corley, pianist and singer; Hendry, bagpipes. Not like most war journals I've read." He sat the book back down, readied another hot dog.

"Maybe his commanding officers knew who he was and gave him the assignment he was most suited for, directing their shows. I mean, how many men were there named William Desmond Taylor?"

"Yeah," Vidor said, "and he certainly wouldn't have enlisted as Tanner and risked that whole ball of wax being found out."

Vidor picked up the journal, turned to a small entry Taylor had made about the court-martial at which he had testified. The note said he had hidden his evidence behind a barracks window for safekeeping until the trial.

"What about this court-martial?"

"You know as much about it as I do," Stallings said. "It would be next to impossible to find out any more now. We don't even know the name of the soldier on trial, or what he was being tried for. And the name of one witness doesn't give us much to go on."

"Maybe it was one of the men Taylor mentioned in the journal, one of the ones he directed."

"I checked those names with the records. No courts-martial," Stallings replied.

"Oh."

Vidor stood, looked out the window. Across the street, construction workers walked on girders and platforms, raising another high-rise office building, oblivious to the height and the weather.

"I appreciate the help, Larry," he said. "This Taylor story gets more interesting the deeper I get into it."

"Well, as I said, I hope you know what you're getting into. This sounds like the kind of story that, no matter how you end up writing it, you're always going to know another way that'd be just as good."

Stallings wadded his lunch wrappings into a ball and stuffed it into his briefcase with the recruiting papers.

"I almost forgot," he said. "I found this stuck between a couple of pages in Taylor's journal." He handed Vidor a small, wrinkled photograph. "Looks like our man with a couple of his buddies."

Vidor inspected the photograph in the light from the window. It showed Taylor in his uniform, standing with three other officers. Two of the officers Vidor didn't recognize. But the one on the far right looked exactly like Taylor's brother, Denis Deane Tanner.

10

Herb Dalmas fancied himself another Raymond Chandler. The celebrated hard-boiled author was his idol, and, like him, Dalmas had abandoned an early career choice—he had been an associate professor at Rutgers; Chandler, an oil company executive —to try his hand at mystery writing. Like Chandler, who had called the industry "poison to writers" but had been forever attracted to the money it offered, he had moved to Hollywood, hoping to find work in motion pictures. His first novel, *Exit Screaming,* released the year before, seemed to be providing the break he needed. Upon the novel's publication, Vidor had expressed interest in developing the book as a movie project and, especially impressed with the mystery's structure, had asked Dalmas for any insight he might have into the Taylor case. Dalmas had jumped at the opportunity to work, if only in a minor advisory capacity, on his first real Hollywood mystery, researching the case throughout the promotional tour for *Exit Screaming*. Now, the tour ended, he stood in the lobby of the Lombardy Hotel, an inscribed copy of the novel under his arm, waiting to share his ideas with Vidor.

Vidor exited an elevator and was taken by Dalmas's appearance. More than his literary idol, he looked like one of Chandler's characters, worn and haggard, as if the book tour had been marked by constant travel and no sleep. Vidor shook Dalmas's hand and was about to suggest they postpone their meeting until after Dalmas had had a good night's rest, when suddenly Dalmas seemed to come alive.

"I think I've come up with something very interesting," he said as he led Vidor outside into the snow. He flagged down a Checker cab and instructed the driver to take them to the public library.

On the way, Vidor gave Dalmas a vague progress report, referring to his pocket notebook and listing the areas requiring further investigation.

Dalmas listened carefully and agreed that Vidor could never be too thorough in his research.

"The more I read, the more I understand why Chandler once said the only reason the Taylor mystery was a mystery was because no one had ever taken the time to do an adequate investigation. All anyone seemed interested in were the scandals surrounding the murder. The crime itself was almost secondary."

At the library, Vidor found a pair of empty seats at a long wooden reading table populated mostly by transients driven inside by the snow. He waited nearly twenty minutes, memorizing the graffiti carved into the tabletop, until Dalmas emerged from the next room carrying a stack of bound magazines and a dust-covered blue book. He set them in front of Vidor and opened one of the thick volumes to the cracked cover page of a 1919 fan magazine.

"I think I threw them for a loop in the stacks. No one's checked these out in years."

"It's no wonder," Vidor said, carefully turning the brittle pages. "You can't believe a word of this stuff. It's all just publicity blather."

"Exactly." Dalmas commandeered the volume, quickly flipping for specific pages. "The studios used these rags to print whatever they wanted printed. They put these stories in here for reasons, and if you read between the lines, you can pretty well guess what the reasons were."

He found a six-page photo spread announcing the birth of Realart, a motion picture corporation formed after the First World War by Paramount Studios to feature the combined talents of their top director and newest star, the "priceless" and "profound" William Desmond Taylor and the "dainty, delicious, and delectable" Mary Miles Minter.

"Did you ever wonder," Dalmas asked, "why this Taylor thing ended the careers of Mary Miles Minter and Mabel Normand, but didn't affect other people who were close to Taylor at all? I mean, we read a lot about monogrammed panties in Taylor's bedroom, but M.M.M.'s the only monogram anyone ever singles out. I think there's a reason for that.

"After the war, Paramount's biggest star, Mary Pickford, quit, eventually forming United Artists with her husband, Doug Fairbanks; Chaplin; and Griffith. Paramount desperately needed a replacement, and who could have been better than Minter? I mean, she looked just like Pickford, and she was younger. So they started the old publicity ball rolling, giving her her own company and everything, trying to make her seem like the greatest thing that ever happened to movies. But what happened?"

Dalmas flipped through more pages, illustrating with articles and reviews what had happened.

Realart's first production under Taylor was *Anne of Green Gables.* It was a hit, with Taylor receiving praise as the director, but Minter was being compared unfavorably with Mary Pickford. The movie was followed by *Judy of Rogues Harbor, Nurse Marjorie,* and *Jenny Be Good.* With each picture, Taylor was praised and Minter panned.

Then, with no public explanation for her sudden disappearance, Taylor made ten films without Minter, including *Huckleberry Finn, The Soul of Youth, The Furnace, The Top of New York,* and *The Green Temptation.*

"You see," Dalmas said, "by the time Taylor was murdered, he was on top of the world, but Minter was just an embarrassment to the studio. They still had her under contract, even used her in minor pictures, but basically they just considered her dead weight. The Taylor scandal gave them a perfect excuse to get rid of her once and for all. The same with Mabel Normand at her studio."

Vidor absentmindedly rubbed the brown spots around his temples. "That's an interesting theory," he said, "but what does it have to do with Taylor's being killed? You're certainly not suggesting the studio killed him to set up an excuse for firing a couple of bad actresses?"

"Of course not," Dalmas said, pushing the magazines aside. "But the way they used the murder for their own benefit, they might as well have. I know this doesn't help us find out who the killer was, but I think it says something about the world that Taylor, and probably the killer, lived in. I mean, to the studio, ruining someone's career was a small price to pay to get rid of a bad investment. Hell, you know—things went on inside those movie studios that would have made the Taylor scandals seem like Mack Sennett comedies if they ever got out."

"That's what the publicity departments were for," Vidor said. "To see that they never got out."

Dalmas picked up the blue book he'd brought out with the magazines. "That's my point. The studios looked out for their own interests at all times, making sure we all believed what they wanted us to believe. And they didn't care one bit what side effects their efforts might have, like who they might hurt, or what truths they might be helping to obscure. Even if some of those truths were—"

"The truths about a murder." Vidor finished the sentence.

Dalmas nodded. He handed Vidor the blue book. "In making sure that everyone knew about those M.M.M. panties, and about Mabel Normand's affair with Taylor, the studio could very well have inadvertently steered reporters' attentions away from what should have been their primary concern: a man had been killed. I mean, like I said, all anyone ever seemed to write about were the scandals."

"Not bad," Vidor said. "Maybe this script will say more about Hollywood than I'd even planned."

Dalmas said, "It's something to think about."

Vidor looked at the book in his hand. It was entitled *Round the Room*, and was the autobiography of Edward Knoblock. Knoblock was a playwright who had written *Kismet* and worked on motion pictures, including the classic Douglas Fairbanks production of *The Three Musketeers*. Knoblock had been staying in Taylor's house at the time that Taylor's secretary Edward Sands robbed Taylor.

Vidor opened the book to a photograph of Knoblock

with fellow writers Somerset Maugham and Hugh Walpole.

"He just calls himself a 'bachelor' in the book," Dalmas said with a smirk, "but hanging around with those two, I'd have to make the same guess about his sexual preferences that you're wanting to make about Taylor's. They were great writers, but they were both queer as three-dollar bills. They were all friends of Taylor's, too."

Dalmas found for Vidor a twenty-five-page section recounting Knoblock's days in Hollywood, his friendship with Taylor, and the trouble with Edward Sands. Combined with what little Vidor had already learned about Knoblock, this presented quite an intriguing addition to Taylor's life story.

In the summer of 1920, at the suggestion of actor Douglas MacLean, Taylor moved from an apartment on Orange Street to a vacant bungalow across from MacLean's own, at 404 Alvarado Street. He hired Sands as his personal secretary and a man named Earl Tiffany as his chauffeur—both recommended by friends at the studio.

When Taylor, suffering from stomach problems, decided to take a vacation in Europe, Knoblock gave him the use of his London townhouse while Knoblock himself, writing scenarios for Paramount, stayed at the Alvarado address.

Knoblock liked the bungalow, but didn't like Edward Sands at all, feeling that Sands always seemed to be nosing around in his personal affairs.

About a month after Knoblock moved in, Sands asked if he might have the final week of Taylor's trip off, so he could get married and honeymoon on Catalina Island. Knoblock didn't hesitate to grant the request.

The next day, a trunk arrived at the bungalow, in

which Sands said he was going to pack his belongings for his new home.

Sands left while Knoblock was at the studio—and never returned. The day before Taylor was due to return to Los Angeles, Knoblock telephoned the Catalina Hotel, where Sands said he would be staying, and was told that Sands had never been there. And no one at the studio or in the bungalow court who knew Sands had been told anything about a wedding.

When Taylor returned home, he discovered that his checkbook and his entire wardrobe, as well as many smaller, personal things, were gone. In a bedroom wastebasket were sheets of paper on which Sands had practiced forging Taylor's signature.

Taylor called his bank and was told that Sands had cashed at least one check for five thousand dollars and several smaller ones.

Sands had also stolen Taylor's roadster (which was later found, wrecked, in a Los Angeles suburb).

In the following weeks, Taylor fired Tiffany, and hired Henry Peavey as his cook and Howard Fellows as his chauffeur. He apparently never saw Sands again, though an envelope did arrive one day containing pawn tickets and a note saying that he could find some of his stolen possessions at a pawnshop outside San Francisco. The envelope was delivered to Taylor's address, though the name on it was not William Desmond Taylor—it was William Deane Tanner.

Vidor closed the book, set it on the table. Nearby a librarian was trying again to roust some of the vagrants hogging space from legitimate patrons of the library.

"Do you think Sands was Taylor's brother?" he asked Dalmas.

"Well," Dalmas replied slowly, thinking it over. "He certainly seems to have known Taylor's real name, which was more than anyone else knew at the time. I hate to think of someone killing his own brother, but from everything you told me, and from everything I've read, Sands looks as good as anybody to be the killer. I mean, the chauffeur himself, Tiffany, said Sands always carried around a little pistol, like the one that did Taylor in. Doesn't anyone have any pictures of Sands?"

"Not that I've been able to come up with."

"What about the police files? They must have pictures of everybody involved in this thing."

"I hope so."

They stood up to leave. Outside, the snow was blowing harder than before, slowing even more the snail's-pace midtown traffic. As they waited for a cab to approach, Vidor thanked Dalmas for his help.

"My pleasure," the writer replied. "Besides, I figure the more sensational this mystery is, the more Hollywood will be clamoring for your next one."

"Exit Screaming?" Vidor asked.

"Of course," Dalmas said with a grin. He spotted an unoccupied taxi and stepped into a curbside snowbank to attract the driver's attention. "You think I do this detective work because I like it?"

11

The spots at his temples aggravated him. They were in no way uncomfortable, so he could discard Betty's worrisome diagnosis of skin cancer; they were just damned unattractive—shapeless splotches of discoloration that reminded King of the spots on his grandfather's hands when Vidor was a child in Galveston —spots that, even more than his own wrinkled forehead and sagging eyes, betrayed the ineluctable fact of old age.

He adjusted the angle of his new hat from Bloomingdale's, imagining himself in the bathroom mirror as others must see him. Tilted just so, the hat hid most of the discoloration. But seeing in his reflection a vanity that his grandfather—a musician whom Vidor fondly recalled running his bent and spotted fingers magically along the neck of his violin—never once displayed, Vidor settled the hat more naturally, comfortably, on his head. He wanted to look his best for Colleen Moore, whom he planned to meet that morning, and for everyone at the party that Gloria Swanson was throwing that night, but he knew that trying to one-up nature was a lost cause. For the first time in his life, Vidor had lately begun to feel his age, seventy-one. He fastened one of the monogrammed silver buttons of his blue blazer, slipped his new Brooks Brothers trenchcoat over it. It was not such a bad figure he cut, all things considered.

One week and three days had passed since he had arrived in New York. Outside, the snow had let up, but the sky was still overcast, concrete gray. According to the morning *Times*, it shouldn't be too cold for the walk through Central Park that Colleen Moore had planned to kick off her and Vidor's reunion.

Vidor anxiously checked the bedroom clock. The telephone rang.

"King Vidor?"

The voice was faint, obviously calling long distance, and sounded old and, Vidor thought, somehow familiar.

"Tony Moreno," the voice said. "I hear you're working on a new picture, the Taylor murder."

Vidor sat on the bed. Antonio Moreno—William Desmond Taylor's best friend.

"How did you find me?" Vidor asked.

"We'll talk about that later," Moreno replied. "Right now let's talk about this picture of yours."

Vidor was silent. He hadn't even known if Moreno was still alive.

Finally, Moreno continued. "A lot of people were hurt

by Bill Taylor's murder. Lost their jobs, their careers, some lost much more. Do you really think it's a good idea to dredge it all back up again?"

"Who said I was dredging up the Taylor murder?"

Vidor heard Moreno's long-distance distorted laugh.

"I'll play it any way you want to, King," Moreno said. "I'm just wondering if you know what you might be getting into, if you *should* try to tell the Taylor story. That is, assuming you even know the real story."

"Do you?" Vidor asked.

Moreno laughed again. "Hell, I don't think anyone knows the whole story. But I think I know enough not to run around New York and Hollywood sounding out new theories to everybody. Somebody might not want to hear some of those theories."

Vidor took off his coat, leaned back against the headboard of the bed, careful not to wrinkle his blazer.

"Why not? Taylor was killed over forty years ago," Vidor said.

"Well," Moreno's voice droned monotonously beneath the static of the connection, "you and I are still around. Maybe we're not the only ones left from the—" he seemed to chuckle again, "the good old days."

A wave of excitement came over Vidor, as it dawned on him that Moreno had a specific reason for calling, that Moreno had some specific knowledge that would aid his search for Taylor's killer. And Moreno seemed frightened.

"You sound afraid of something. What is it?" Vidor decided to hazard a guess. "Is it Edward Sands?"

Now Moreno's laughter drowned the static almost eerily, mocking Vidor with an air of superiority that confirmed Vidor's feeling: Moreno knew something.

"Sands was a horse's ass. Bill snapped his fingers, and Sands drooled."

"Was he Taylor's brother?"

"No more than you or I."

"How about Taylor's lover?"

"Sands?" Moreno said in a near falsetto. "Sands jumped on anything in a skirt. Faith MacLean wouldn't let the man near her. Edna Purviance either. He considered himself a royal cocksman, even though he was ugly as a boot."

"Then why are you calling me?" Vidor said. "Why are you so worried that I might be dredging it all back up again?"

"King," Moreno said, then paused so long that Vidor thought he might have hung up.

"Are you there?"

After another short silence, Moreno said, "I'm here."

"Then what is it?" Vidor implored. "Is it something someone found in the bungalow that morning?"

"King," Moreno began again. "I don't know what anyone found. I didn't find anything myself."

"You were in there that morning?"

"You know there were a lot of us in there that morning."

"What were you looking for?"

"Hell, King, you knew Taylor. He was a major director. Paramount didn't want anything getting out that might be scandalous. Especially after the Arbuckle fiasco."

Now it was Vidor's turn to laugh. "Well, they sure did a good job saving his image," he said sarcastically. "Twenty years of front-page stories about assumed identities, extortion, and women's underwear."

Moreno waited until Vidor was silent, then said, "Maybe they did a better job than you think."

Then there was another, more ominous silence. This time, Moreno really had hung up.

12

The concierge in the Lombardy Hotel directed Vidor to a florist's shop just blocks down Lexington Avenue. While his cab waited, Vidor purchased violets. The florist wrapped them in green foil, affixing a card on which Vidor had quickly jotted the three initials that conveyed his and Colleen Moore's shared eternal slogan, Love Never Dies.

At Columbus Circle, he pocketed his Checker cab receipt and walked on a frozen sidewalk to the statue where many years before he and Colleen had said good-bye, vowing never to see each other again. Moore had chosen the meeting place, though she was also staying at the Lombardy. And though Vidor, anxious for their reunion, had arrived early, she was waiting for him, looking as beautiful as he had ever imagined her.

"Don't you look like quite the detective," she said as he approached in his trenchcoat and tilted hat. "What happened to the young director with the breeches and riding crop?"

Vidor handed her the violets. "He ran off with the young flapper in the sequined dress." He kissed her gently on the cheek.

Moore brushed her short black hair away from her face and read the card with the flowers. She smiled, tucked the card into her purse, and, taking King by the hand, led him across the street into Central Park.

"How was your trip?" King asked.

The air was crisp and cool, freezing their breath in front of them as they walked.

"Bermuda was glorious," she said. "And the yacht was unbelievable. Three stewards, and I had my own maid."

Vidor smiled, fighting the urge to ask Moore about her traveling companion: a well-known film producer, a millionaire owner of supermarkets. Jealousy had been outlawed early on in their relationship, and Vidor struggled determinedly not to succumb to it today. He and Moore were together now, and he told himself that that was all that mattered.

"How's my handsome detective's investigation coming along?" Moore asked.

King warmed to the new subject, as he felt her grip on his hand restoring his self-confidence, like a double shot of adrenaline.

"It's more involved than I'd anticipated," he replied. "I just talked with Tony Moreno."

"Tony Moreno? I didn't even know he was still alive. How'd you find him?"

"I didn't. He found me. I don't know how, but he did."

"What did he have to say?"

"Not a lot, but he gave me the impression that he thinks Paramount was involved in Taylor's murder."

"Really?"

"Or at least that the studio knew more than they ever let on."

"Well, we already knew that," Moore said. "Why else would everybody have been rooting around the bungalow that morning?"

Vidor shook his head. "No, he seems to think it's more than that. I don't know. The whole thing is odd, his calling me and everything. I think he's scared of something. I'll have to call him as soon as I get back to L.A. If he's in L.A."

"Well, in the meantime," Moore said, a twinkling hint of suggestion in her eyes, "we have some time before the party at Sardi's, and I have a bottle of champagne chilling at the hotel."

For the next several hours there was no mention of business, Taylor, or the supermarket millionaire. Everything was champagne and violets. Then, as they were preparing to leave for Gloria Swanson's soirée at Sardi's, Moore asked, "When are you going back to Los Angeles?"

"I'm not sure," Vidor said. "Soon. I've talked with everyone I need to here, and I do want to find Moreno. I think he may be able to answer a few key questions. Doug MacLean as well."

Vidor caught himself checking his reflection in a mirror, something he'd been doing altogether too much lately. He turned self-consciously away; Moore hadn't mentioned the signs of ever-advancing age that so bothered him, and he didn't want to draw her attention to them now.

"Why don't you come back to Beverly Hills with me?" he asked. "You can stay in the guest house. Give us a good chance to work on the script with Dalmas."

Moore's eyes answered Vidor before she spoke. Then she said, "I can't, King-zzy."

"Why not?" Vidor could think of several reasons why not. "Is it Betty?"

She shook her head. "I'm afraid Betty's your problem, not mine."

Vidor feared another intrusion by his rich rival.

"Then what is it?"

"The Chicago *Tribune* has asked me to write three columns about Kenya. I'm leaving on safari the day after tomorrow."

"Safari?" Vidor asked incredulously.

"Only with cameras instead of guns."

"How big a safari?" Vidor said, sidestepping his true question.

Moore picked up on the question anyway, and touched his arm with reassurance.

"Well, I'm not exactly sure, but there's certainly room for one more. Want to come along? We can put the project on hold for a while, get back to it when we return."

Vidor considered the offer, then thought of Betty and the simple note he'd left, telling her he was going to New York for a few days. That was easily explained behavior. But disappearing to the Dark Continent without telling her? He didn't think he could do it.

"I don't know. I probably shouldn't interrupt this investigation," he said. "I should get back and see about finding Moreno while he's in a mood to talk."

"Don't look so disappointed," Moore told him. "I won't be gone all that long. Besides . . ." She handed Vidor his trenchcoat and, smoothing with one hand her new Yves Saint-Laurent suit, picked up her mink from the bed. "We've still got the next two days."

13

Vidor's arrival turned heads at Sardi's. With Colleen Moore and Gloria Swanson on either arm, he strutted proudly to their reserved table. At the table, Bob Giroux, NBC founder General David Sarnoff, and musician Artie Shaw stood to greet them. Other guests had been invited—Jennifer Jones, David Selznick, Lee Remick, Groucho Marx, all friends of Vidor —but would not be able to make it.

Vidor helped Moore and Swanson into their seats and took the place saved for him at the head of the table. He ordered appetizers and bottles of California champagne— and a cup of herbal tea for the health-conscious Swanson.

As the conversation turned to the reasons for Vidor's trip east, everyone ventured an opinion on the Taylor murder case.

"It's obvious," said Artie Shaw, who of all those at the table was the least familiar with the case (and consequently the least aware of the ironic plausibility of his remark). "The butler did it."

Everyone laughed.

Giroux suggested that Taylor might have been killed by a narcotics kingpin in retaliation for his war on dope.

"I always figured it was a love triangle," General Sarnoff offered. "That one of Mabel Normand's other lovers did it."

Vidor grinned and said, "If Groucho were here, he'd say that theory wouldn't substantially narrow the field of suspects."

Everyone laughed again and Vidor, sharing a warm glance with Moore, refilled their champagne glasses.

"Who do you think it was, King?" Gloria Swanson asked.

"What?" he said. "You want me to spoil the whole movie for you?"

The bottle empty, he pulled another from a silver ice bucket.

"King's been working on some interesting angles into the mystery," Moore said. "It's just fascinating."

"Like what?" Giroux inquired.

"King's been studying Taylor's last day," Moore replied, looking toward Vidor, waiting for him to take the lead.

Vidor returned the bottle to the ice. He took a sip from the glass.

"Nothing Taylor said or did that day could lead a detective to believe that it would end in violence. Why had the murderer selected that day? Was it motivated by some series of events, a sudden decision, or a bit of information that has somehow been overlooked?"

He had everyone's complete attention. He paused as a waiter removed the empty bottle from the table, then continued.

"On February first, nineteen twenty-two, Taylor was not engaged in the actual process of shooting a film. That morning he could lie in bed until he heard Henry Peavey, busy in the kitchen below his bedroom, or could doze until Peavey came up with an eye-opening cup of coffee.

"Peavey arrived as usual at seven-thirty, stepping off the Maryland Street trolley, then walking up the gravel path through the building courtyard, then to the back door of the small bungalow, where he picked up the morning's milk delivery. Interviewed the next day, he did not remember seeing any strange footprints or cigarette butts by the back steps—as the police would later find.

"Taylor took his gold cuff links from his middle dresser drawer. What else was in there with them? Obviously, something soft and pink. Was it a handkerchief? A woman's nightgown?"

Vidor made eye contact with everyone at the table, drawing them into his story as his film would draw its audience.

"At breakfast, Taylor read the front-page newspaper story about the raging Fatty Arbuckle scandal. As Peavey cleared the dishes, he noticed his employer's gold cigarette case beside his coffee cup. Peavey specifically remembered seeing this because the cigarette case had been missing for many months—since Edward Sands had stolen it, along with a package of Taylor's specially made black cigarettes with gold tips.

"At eight-thirty, Taylor's chauffeur, Howard Fellows,

dropped Taylor off at the Los Angeles Athletic Club where during his morning swim and workout he encountered Chaplin, Jimmy Kirkwood, and Mickey Neilan. No one seems to know what was said between Taylor and these men, but all, to one degree or another, figured in the later mystery. Were these encounters merely casual, or were they planned?

"Next, Taylor arrived at the studio where Charlie Eyton and Julia Crawford Ivers were waiting for him. From reports I've gathered, they had an argument over the next picture Taylor wanted to direct, *The Rocks of Valpre*. Ivers said that there wasn't enough action, Charlie Eyton said the picture would be too expensive. Taylor pleaded his case, and very well might have offered Mary Miles Minter as the lead—which would not have gone over well with any-one besides the director. Minter, from what I've learned, was all washed up, a hasbeen."

Vidor paused only to sip champagne. "So Taylor left, disappointed, of course, but with too much work to do to brood about it. After lunch at the studio commissary, he left for Projection Room C, where he did some editing on his latest picture, *The Green Temptation*, with coworkers he treated with utmost respect. His editor, Edy Lawrence, reported that Taylor kissed her hand at the end of that editing session—a remarkable gesture, when one considers the way most directors treated their editors. Significantly, many of Taylor's coworkers who attended this session were thought to have been the same people at Taylor's bungalow the next morning, picking through his possessions.

"After work, with Fellows driving, he stopped briefly at Robinson's Department Store, but returned to the car without having made a purchase. Next, at the First National Bank, he deposited twenty-three hundred dollars in cash. His last stop before going home was Fowler's Book-store, where he bought two copies of *Inhibition, Symptom, and Desire,* by Sigmund Freud."

"He actually did this?" Artie Shaw asked.

"Of course," Vidor said, hoping he didn't sound short with Shaw. "Back at home, Taylor changed his clothes and called Mabel Normand on the phone, Her maid took the message, and told Taylor that Normand was out shopping, and would be returning at suppertime.

"Taylor walked to his regular dance class on Orange Street. He was learning to dance the tango. His regular instructor was away for the afternoon, and Taylor prac-ticed with his instructor's assistant, a young man named Duncan.

"Taylor returned to his bungalow at six-fifteen, where Marjorie Berger, his tax accountant, was waiting for him. During their meeting, Taylor expressed his frustration at not being able to distinguish his own signature on checks from those forged by Edward Sands. Berger told Taylor that she was glad that Taylor was finally rid of Sands, whom she obviously disliked. Taylor did not comment on this point but was reported to have looked at Berger with an expression that seemed to say: 'I'm not so sure of that.'

"Before Berger left, Taylor wrote a check for her ser-vices, then another to Ada Tanner—which was how police were able to locate his sister-in-law."

Vidor finished his second glass of champagne and, allowing Moore to assume the honor of pouring another, went on.

"It was nearly dark, dusk, when a limousine pulled up in front of the bungalow court. A beautiful woman got out carrying a bag of peanuts. Mabel Normand. As she ap-proached Taylor's open front door, she saw the director inside talking on the phone. She waited outside until he hung up, then went inside. Taylor greeted her with a kiss, and the offer of a drink.

"Then, a short while later, at seven-forty-five, Taylor walked her back to her car. She was carrying one of the Freud books. On the back seat, along with peanut shells, was an issue of *The Police Gazette*. Taylor affectionately chided her on her choice of reading material, then kissed her good-bye. As the limo pulled off, Taylor walked back into his bungalow and shut the door behind him. The next morning, he was dead."

When he finished, Vidor looked at each of his friends, their nods and thoughtful expressions telling him that they had indeed been captivated by the story. A good sign, he thought, and smiled at his producer. Moore returned the smile and raised her champagne glass in toast.

"I think it's a real mystery," Artie Shaw said, clicking his glasses with the others.

"Especially when we see what the police discover in the morning," Sarnoff added, puffing on a large Cuban cigar.

14

In the cab from Los Angeles International Airport, Vidor imagined the confrontation that awaited him at home. It was February 4, 1967, two weeks since he'd left his wife Betty the curt note informing her he was going to New York, and he wondered what her first words would be when he walked in the door.

She was sitting on the front porch when he arrived. Vidor paid the driver, forgetting even his customary receipt, and made his way inside. He deposited his bag, as well as his trenchcoat and hat, in the living room, then stepped out a side door to where Betty was waiting.

"Toby's dead," she said in a weak voice. She set aside her *Better Homes and Gardens* and turned toward her husband, a single tear, thick with mascara, slowly marking one side of her pale face. Toby was Betty's German shepherd, a vicious animal Vidor had never liked. The dog had once bitten Vidor's grandson and was the reason that Vidor's own dog, Nippy, was forced to live in the guest house. Still, Betty's crying, not an unfamiliar sight the past few years, filled Vidor with sympathy. He felt even worse than he had imagined on the ride from the airport. He knelt beside Betty, took her hand.

"When I came back from the country club this morning, I thought she was just sleeping."

Vidor handed her his handkerchief.

"Maybe it's for the best," he said. "She was old, could hardly get around any more."

"She was a good protector," Betty said, the sudden defensiveness in her voice betraying, along with her sorrow, an anger that Vidor knew was directed toward him.

"Did you call the vet?" he asked.

She shook her head no.

"I'll take care of it."

Betty nodded and, saying nothing more, turned back to her magazine.

Vidor walked into the house. He unpacked, showered, and put on a pair of corduroys. He dreaded the inevitable confrontation that had only been postponed.

Walking down to the guest house, he could hear Nippy barking inside. Thelma Carr opened the door to let him out, and showed mild surprise at her employer's unannounced return.

"So," she said, "just dropping by for a visit?" Her electric-green sweater, she remembered, was one of

Vidor's favorites. She quickly turned back into the office. "Or do you think you might want to do a little work today?"

Vidor followed her inside.

"What kind of work do you have in mind?"

Obviously in no mood for a round of suggestive cat-and-mouse, Carr handed him the last two weeks' mail and started reading from a numbered list on her stenographer's pad.

"You have a speech at the Toastmasters Club on Monday, which by the way is your wife's birthday; UCLA coming to pick up whatever papers and scripts you're donating to them on Tuesday; a Directors Guild symposium to moderate on Thursday, which is your sister's birthday; and a poker game at Dick Marchman's on Friday night."

"Nothing on Wednesday?" Vidor said with a smile.

Carr was not amused. "It's not easy running this office when I have no idea where you are or how long you're going to be gone."

"You do a great job. Any calls?"

She handed him another list.

Vidor sat at his desk and sorted his mail. Tax forms, *Christian Science Monitor*, Directors Guild Retirement Fund, Dodgers Season Ticket Office. He opened first a large manila envelope whose contents he already knew. It was his biographical screenplay, *Cervantes*, returned by Spanish producers who said the failure of their last movie had inspired them to abandon cinematic pursuits and rechannel their capital into a retail chain.

Not good news.

Next, a letter from his lawyer, John Chapman, informed him that under the homicide division of the California Public Records Act #6254, all police records concerning the Taylor case—because it involved a capital offense that had never been solved—were closed to public inspection. What Vidor had planned to use as a primary source of information, including, he hoped, photographs of Denis Tanner and Edward Sands, was unavailable to him.

More bad news.

Vidor checked his phone messages. Nothing from Sam Goldwyn, Jr., concerning Vid-Mor's development project with him. Hoping that no news was, for at least his current endeavors, good news, he set the rest of his mail and his phone calls aside and dug an old address book from the bottom drawer of his desk. He dialed a fifteen-year-old number. A woman answered.

"Hello, this is King Vidor. I'm looking for Tony Moreno."

There was a short pause, then the woman said, "Tony's dead, Mr. Vidor."

Vidor felt himself holding his breath. "What?" His hand, gripping the telephone receiver as tightly as it could, began to perspire.

"He died a couple of days ago."

"I just talked to him."

"He had a heart attack."

After a pause as the news sank in, Vidor said, "I'm sorry, my sympathies."

He hung up. Another potential source of information was gone now. He opened his pocket notebook to his notes on Moreno's call, wondering if the questions he had planned to ask him would ever be answered. Especially the first two on the list: "Who told him I was working on the Taylor case?" and "How did he find me in New York?"

He closed the notebook and looked around the office, noticing for the first time that Thelma Carr had cleaned and straightened it in his absence. The stacks of loose papers were gone from the top of the piano. His film and news magazines, mostly unread, were neatly arranged on top of his obviously dusted file cabinets. His guitar leaned in a corner outside its case, its blond surface polished shinier than he had ever seen it. Even the top of his desk, except for the clutter he had already made of his unopened mail, had been organized.

"The place looks great," he called to Carr. "I've never seen it this straight."

"I had to do something in the last two weeks besides fielding your telephone calls," she said. "You want to sign some checks now?"

"Okay."

She brought him a dozen prewritten checks. Signing them, he thought of Taylor and Edward Sands, wondering how easily his own signature could be copied.

As Carr returned to her desk, Vidor decided to make one more phone call before catching up on the work he had set aside to go to New York. On the same page of his address book where he had found Antonio Moreno's was another number he hadn't called in years, that of Douglas MacLean, William Desmond Taylor's neighbor on Alvarado Street.

Again, a woman answered, and again, Vidor sat silent as he was told about the man he was calling. MacLean, too, had had a heart attack, and though he was alive, he was paralyzed and unable to talk. Vidor offered his apology and sympathy and hung up, stunned. This was not his day. And he still had to face Betty about New York. He arranged his mail into a neat pile, more fitting with the office's new look, then searched his desk for something. Finally, he called out, "Where's my doorknob?"

"In the gray file cabinet," Carr responded without having to ponder. "With your catcher's mitt."

Vidor didn't know whether she was being sarcastic or just systematic. But he had too much to do to worry about it. He told Carr he'd be back in an hour and left.

Betty was still on the porch as Vidor and Nippy walked up the driveway. She looked thin, not at all the vibrant, buxom script girl he had fallen in love with all those years ago in Hawaii. He wished he had talked with her about New York before the trip, but the fact that he would be meeting Colleen Moore had made him too uncomfortable. He knew he would have to do it soon. Tonight. But first, he had to take care of Toby.

15

Vidor hated pajamas. He never slept in them, only wore them in the morning when he made his breakfast. Every year on Christmas and his birthday he received new pajamas as presents and, after graciously thanking the well-meaning friends and relatives who had given them to him, added them to the plastic-wrapped collection in his bedroom closet. With the use Vidor got out of them, one pair could, and did, last for years.

Vidor was wearing his current pair, very slowly pouring Cream of Wheat into boiling water, when he heard Betty step into the kitchen behind him.

"Good morning," he said without diverting his attention from the water. Cream of Wheat was his favorite breakfast, and making it correctly (lumpless) required constant stirring and concentration.

"Good morning." Betty poured a cup of coffee from the pot Vidor had brewed. She held it in front of her, steaming, and looked out the window at the backyard. Nippy was barking at something, already happily at home in Toby's old kennel.

Betty had yet even to mention the New York trip, and Vidor wondered if she ever would.

"Are you playing poker at Dick's tonight?" she asked, turning from the window.

"I thought I would." Vidor turned off the stove, still stirring his cereal. "Do you have plans?"

"Evelyn's having a bridge party."

"Sounds like fun." Vidor hated bridge but had learned to play and often joined Betty and her friends for mixed doubles.

Betty looked down into her coffee, then padded off to her bedroom. Vidor ate his Cream of Wheat with honey, washed his breakfast dishes, then dressed for the day.

At ten, he taught his film class at the University of Southern California. Afterward, he met with a few of his favorite students and assigned special extracurricular research projects. Then he drove to Paramount Studios, choosing a circular route that took him again to the site that had once been William Desmond Taylor's bungalow court. The lot had already been cleared for construction, leaving no indication at all that anything had ever stood there.

At Paramount, Vidor pulled up to the DeMille Gate. The security guard recognized him immediately.

"Mr. Vidor," he said, slipping a visitor's pass beneath

the T-Bird's windshield wiper. "It's good to see you. Are you going to be doing another picture with us?"

"I'm working on it," Vidor said with a smile and drove inside. He parked between twin Mercedes sedans in front of the directors' building. He wasn't sure what he would find, but he wanted to see everything in the studio's files on both Taylor and Mary Miles Minter.

Vidor made his way past a television crew shooting *Mannix* on his way to building L, where he had often used the Research Archives, known as the morgue, in preparing for a film. Inside, rather than the old musty, underlit warehouse filled wall-to-wall and floor-to-ceiling with file cabinets and bookshelves, he found a neat cluster of fluorescent-lighted offices.

"Can I help you?" another guard at a desk asked.

"I was looking for the archives."

"Oh. They've been moved. The studio needed space. So when Legal moved in here, the morgue, what was left of it, was moved to storage."

"Storage? Is it still available for use?"

"Sure, but as I say, there isn't a lot left to it. Most of the stuff hadn't been used in years, so they put the torch to it. It's a damn shame, if you ask me, but what are you going to do? Progress."

The guard gave Vidor directions to the morgue's new location. As he had said, there wasn't much left of it. Vidor found a file cabinet marked DIRECTORS and opened a drawer to the Ts. He found a folder marked TAYLOR, W. D. Though a typewritten notation on the folder's tab indicated that it had once been the first of ten folders on Taylor, it was now the only one. Its contents told Vidor nothing he didn't already know: a filmography, a thin publicity bio, a few posed photographs, and a handful of press clippings. He folded the material and stuffed it in his jacket pocket.

Then he found the files on actors and looked up Mary Miles Minter. Again, nothing of more than the most general biographical interest had been saved. Vidor wondered what his own file at MGM—an entire cabinet nearly bursting with material the last time he'd checked—would look like if that studio too found its own history a small sacrifice to make in the name of space-saving.

Outside, he walked back through the lot, past the Carson City exterior set, where *Bonanza*'s Cartwright family were saddling up to ride to the Ponderosa. In front of the white post-production building, teeming with activity from the Christmas releases, he saw an old friend, an attractive blonde, who worked in the film library. He complimented her miniskirt, then asked if he could take a look at some of William Desmond Taylor's films. He was particularly interested in Taylor's last production, *The Green Temptation*. She went to the office to see what she could do.

Over the years Vidor and Moore had seen many of their own films destroyed. In the early sixties, silent films were thought to have no commercial value. They were difficult to store, dangerous to handle, and a fire hazard. Vidor's had been destroyed in a Bekins Storage Company fire, and Colleen's entire collection had burned up in a fire at Warner Brothers.

Vidor's friend brought him the news of Taylor's films. What titles had not disintegrated by the fifties were in such bad condition that they were taken out of the vaults, cut into small pieces with a chain saw, then burned, to salvage the silver content of the film stock.

"Well," Vidor told his friend, his frustration growing with each new dead end he encountered, "thanks anyway. It was good to see you again."

He walked slowly back to his car, more sensitive than ever before to the changes that had overtaken the lot. Most of the studio production seemed to be for television, location shooting having come into vogue for features.

Vidor sat in his car and flipped through the pilfered Taylor file. One photograph showed Taylor with Hugh Walpole and Somerset Maugham; another, the director with George Hopkins, the art director whom Gloria Swanson had mentioned. A newspaper article mentioned the actress Claire Windsor and Fatty Arbuckle's wife, Minta Durfee. The journalist and Colleen Moore's best friend, Adela Rogers St. Johns, had written extensively on the murder and Mary Miles Minter. At least he might salvage a couple of new names to look up, Vidor thought. He locked the file in the glove compartment and left.

Dick Marchman lived near Hollywood in a residential development called Park LaBrea. His poker games were like Boys' Night Out for Vidor and any of a number of friends, including fellow director Lewis Milestone. Marchman was married to Vidor's sister Catherine (Cassie) and was a retired insurance executive who had spent many years as a fraud investigator. Vidor always looked forward to the poker games but was especially eager tonight. In light of his failure to turn up any useful information at Paramount, his desire to see the police files on the Taylor case grew stronger. And who would be better to ask for help in his endeavor than an old sleuth like Marchman? With his connections, he ought to be able to get to those files. That is—the thought struck Vidor as a somewhat fitting end to the kind of afternoon he was having—if the files were still around to be gotten to. The murder had been, after all, nearly a half-century ago. Vidor just hoped that in the years since, the Los Angeles Police Department hadn't, like Paramount Pictures, suffered a deadly shortage of storage space.

16

It had been years since anyone had attempted a full cleaning of the basement beneath the guest house. Thelma Carr refused even to set foot there, claiming the entire room, stacked randomly with dusty, unmarked boxes the contents of which only Vidor knew, was crawling with mice. Vidor had Western Exterminators rout out all subhuman species, but Carr still wanted nothing to do with the place. So Vidor attacked the job himself. His Taylor investigation was on hold for a while, until he heard back from a few people. He had made two lists of the principal characters in the mystery about whom information might be found. One contained the people thought to have played important roles in Taylor's life before his murder: Henry Peavey, Edward Sands, Howard Fellows, Mabel Normand, and Mary Miles Minter and her mother. The second listed those who played important roles just after the crime: Charles Eyton and his fellow studio executives who arrived at the scene of the crime before the police, and the three district attorneys who were in charge of the investigation—Thomas Lee Woolwine, Asa Keyes, and Buron Fitts. He hoped that the official police files, should Dick Marchman be able to get hold of them, would provide him with good information on the investigators and on just what went on in the bungalow after Taylor's body was found. For the others on the list, particularly Minter and Normand, he assigned some of his students "special projects"—to gather biographical information for him. Until he heard from them, he had time to attend to other business, like the cleaning of the basement.

He cleared a wooden table for a workbench and set about going through the room. Nearly every box contained something that Vidor took time out to read: old diaries, film treatments, correspondence with half-forgotten former colleagues, pictures of people he no longer recognized, bank statements, and binders stuffed with handwritten notes. The stacks of papers and scripts to be donated to UCLA grew only at the constant remindings from Carr that they were not being destroyed but simply transferred to a new storage place, and that they represented a substantial tax write-off. Vidor did little to lessen the quantity of memorabilia in the basement, but he was determined to compress it into a smaller area, stacking the boxes higher and making more space to move around in the room that he now decided would be the official headquarters of his Taylor investigation. He knew he was safe from intrusion in the room, and that he could spread his work across the table without Thelma Carr's asking what he was working on. At one end of the table he set an old steel strongbox. Inside he put all his Taylor notes and files to date, along with an old envelope and photograph he'd found pressed between the pages of a biography of Mack Sennett, the film producer. On one side of the envelope was a question, in his own handwriting; on the other, written in another hand, was the reply. When he'd come across the envelope and photograph, he'd sat down at the table and recalled a day he was surprised hadn't come to him earlier in his Taylor research.

It was February 23, 1930. Vidor had been called to MGM to discuss his film project *Billy the Kid* with production chief Irving Thalberg. Thalberg and Eddie Mannix, the executive in charge of *Billy the Kid*, met Vidor and screenwriter Laurence Stallings in a limousine near the studio gate.

"We don't have much time," Thalberg said. "Tell me about your story."

Used to this treatment from Thalberg (though never in a speeding car), Vidor quickly explained his and Stallings's plan to make the Kid a sympathetic victim of unfortunate circumstances rather than the cold-blooded killer most people thought of when they heard his name. He hadn't yet finished the pitch when the limousine stopped in front of a church where a large crowd was gathering.

"It sounds good," Thalberg said. "We'll continue after."

Assuming that Thalberg and Mannix were attending what appeared to be a funeral at the church, Vidor stepped out of the limo to hold the door for them. As they followed him outside, someone touched Vidor's shoulder from behind. It was Marshall Neilan, Mary Pickford's director and Gloria Swanson's intimate friend.

"How are you, King?" Marshall Neilan asked.

Vidor hadn't seen Neilan in some time. As he said hello, he saw other familiar faces getting out of other limos. Everyone started into the church.

"Aren't you coming?" Neilan said.

"What's going on?" Vidor asked. He looked at Stallings, who shrugged his shoulders, just as lost as Vidor was. "I'm not dressed for—"

"You look fine," Thalberg said. "They'll be expecting you."

Vidor shut the limo door and with Stallings followed the others inside.

An organ was playing. A flower-bedecked casket sat at the front of the aisle, just before the altar. In the pews Vidor saw Chaplin, Mack Sennett, Stan Laurel, Oliver Hardy, Buster Keaton, Minta Durfee, Fatty Arbuckle. Hollywood's comedians were crying. Vidor sat beside Thalberg and, as the organ stopped and a minister stepped into his pulpit, took an envelope from his pocket and scribbled "Who is it?"

Mannix was surprised at the question. He wrote "Mabel Normand. Don't you read the papers?" Vidor and Stallings looked at the name with shock. Ten years earlier she had been one of Hollywood's brightest stars. Then the Taylor scandal had sent her career into a decline. Now she was dead, and Vidor and Stallings hadn't even heard the news.

Though Vidor remembered the beautiful brunette hair, brown eyes, and the classic way she always posed for the camera, he had forgotten how small Normand was. She couldn't have stood over five feet tall, nor weighed over a hundred pounds. In the photo Vidor had taken during her Keystone Kops days, she had been smiling, as she always seemed to be doing, with her small feet pointed inwards, and her small fingers pointed outwards—the pose that made almost everyone who met her want to give her a great big bear hug.

Vidor put a padlock on the strongbox and hid the key in his wallet. He brought in a new comfortable chair for use at the worktable and continued methodically but slowly consolidating his boxes. After a week, he had gathered enough material for his UCLA donation and had just sent it off when the first of his student researchers presented him with her work. Coincidentally, she was the student he had assigned the task of delving into the background of Mabel Normand. So, with Normand's tragic end fresh in his mind, he sat at his basement table and, through a collection of notes worthy of an A+, put together an outline of her life from the beginning.

Mabel Normand was born on Staten Island, New York. Her father was a failed pianist, her mother a seamstress. She quit school when she was very young to join her mother's profession, but by the time she was fifteen she had become a successful model.

From modeling she turned to acting. One day on a motion picture set, she met D. W. Griffith's right-hand man, Mack Sennett. Though her parents opposed her association with the types of people they believed were involved with show business, she signed contracts with Biograph and, later, Vitagraph, the most important New York film studios. She learned her trade from those around her: Mary Pickford, Wallace Reid, Antonio Moreno, and the Talmadge sisters.

When Griffith's company moved from New York to California for winter shooting, she was among those left behind. But soon Sennett was back, with his own film company, Keystone, that he wanted Normand to join. He had been in love with her, he said, from the start. He offered her seventy-five dollars a week, twice the salary of what her parents made combined. Then, interpreting her speechlessness as dissatisfaction with the offer, he upped the ante to $100, and finally to $125. Normand signed and moved to Los Angeles, where her fellow players for Sennett would eventually include Gloria Swanson, Charles Chaplin, Harold Lloyd, W. C. Fields, and the man who would become her frequent on-screen partner, Durfee's husband, Fatty Arbuckle.

In 1915, just days before Normand and Sennett were to be wed, Normand discovered Sennett in his long johns and actress Mae Busch completely naked, rehearsing, according to Sennett, for a new picture. Before Normand could even react to Sennett's ridiculous explanation of their undress, Busch reportedly struck her with a vase. An hour later, she was found by Arbuckle and Durfee, lying on their porch with a bloody head wound.

Somehow, she and Sennett made amends, though their wedding plans were canceled and their relationship was never the same.

The next year Normand threatened to leave Sennett for good if he didn't give her a studio of her own. Her request was granted. *Mickey*, the first production, was a problem picture, fraught with delays, cost overruns, and bickering on the set. Normand fired three directors, the last of whom stole a portion of the film negative as insurance that he would be paid the money owed him. By the time the picture wrapped, everyone involved felt sure it was going to be a $150,000 flop—except Normand.

Normand angrily left the company. She signed a five-year contract with Samuel Goldwyn, with a starting salary of $1,000 a week increasing to $4,000. Then, just as her contract with Goldwyn had begun, *Mickey* was released and became a critical and box-office success, making her a full-fledged star.

With this unexpected career turn and change of studio came a change of personality. She suddenly became undependable, often showing up late or not at all. She demanded more money from Goldwyn. When he refused, she walked off the set. Fan magazines and newspapers reported that she was in Europe, where she engaged in lavish spending sprees, dropping $10,000 on a single dress.

Goldwyn didn't know how to handle Normand as Mack Sennett had. No sooner was she back working than he discovered that she wasn't cashing a single salary check. Investigating the situation, he discovered that she kept most of her money in a shoebox in her bedroom. He was amazed. Money meant nothing to her. She not only didn't cash his checks, but what other money she had she was known to give freely to her friends and, occasionally, perfect strangers. For her own good he decided to keep her on an allowance, the majority of her salary paid in the form of $1,000 Liberty Bonds automatically put into her savings. (Years later, at a time when she thought the studio was in financial trouble, Normand handed Goldwyn a thick envelope containing all the bonds she had accumulated, along with all the cash and real estate deeds in her name. Always the gentleman, Goldwyn refused the offer.)

Normand made sixteen films for Goldwyn before her popularity began to fade. In 1921, released from her contract, she returned to Mack Sennett, one of the few producers to offer her a contract. Her first picture for him, *Molly O*, was released just two months before the Taylor murder. It bombed. Sennett made two more with her, but with much the same results.

Then, on the first day of 1924, her career all but over,

she found herself involved in another scandal when her chauffeur shot a millionaire boyfriend of Normand's friend Edna Purviance with a pistol owned by Normand. The boyfriend lived and refused to press charges, but the chauffeur, who called himself Joe Kelly, was in fact an ex-con and cocaine addict named Joe Greer.

Even Sennett wouldn't use Normand after that. Unable to find any work in motion pictures—her name was popularly linked to censorship czar Will Hays's rumored Hollywood blacklist—she accepted an offer to star in a Broadway musical, *A Kiss in the Sky*. But by the time she arrived, the producer had changed his mind. Instead, he gave her a role in a road production of *The Little Mouse*, hoping her name would draw an audience to a play that had already flopped several times under different titles. The play ran less than a month.

By 1926, Normand was back in Hollywood, appearing in film shorts as she had at the beginning of her career. Though Mary Pickford welcomed her back with a full-page letter in *Motion Picture World*, most of her former friends and associates failed even to acknowledge her return. And to those who did, it was clear that Normand was not well. At some point in her dramatic decline, she had become a habitual drug-user.

At a party on September 17, to the amusement of everyone present, actor Lew Cody offered her an exaggerated, vaudevillian proposal of marriage. She accepted and, maintaining the whimsical mood of the proposal, the entire party drove to Ventura County for an impromptu ceremony at 2:00 A.M.

Though they actually were married, Normand and Cody kept separate residences up to the time of Normand's death. Her obituary named tuberculosis as the cause of death, but many who knew her suspected that it was a result of her addiction to drugs.

It was a sad, lonely ending to a story that had begun as a fairy tale. And clearly the Taylor scandal marked the turning point. But seeing her entire life outlined on the table before him, Vidor couldn't help but recognize the feasibility of Herb Dalmas's theory. Normand's popularity had indeed already faded before the Taylor murder scandal; the scandal merely accelerated her fall. And her later drug dependency suggested that perhaps she had, as many had theorized, been using narcotics during the time she was involved with Taylor. These were questions Vidor jotted into his pocket notebook, along with the names of the friends of Normand's who were still living, and who he felt would be best qualified to answer them: Minta Durfee and Claire Windsor.

He added the Mabel Normand file to his strongbox, pleased with the footwork he had saved by having his student do the research for him. Another should be giving him a file on Mary Miles Minter soon. But meanwhile there was work to do that only he could accomplish. He locked the strongbox, slipped his notebook into his back pocket, and made his way through the still unstraightened half of the basement. Then he turned out the light and walked back to his office.

17

V

idor paused in front of Minta Durfee's bungalow. A man was sitting on the front steps, pulling greeting cards from envelopes, looking at them with fascination, putting them back into the envelopes, then taking them out again. Vidor judged him to be not terribly younger than himself, early sixties maybe. But the innocent wonder on his face each time he reread one of the cards said that mentally he hadn't aged since childhood.

On the porch behind him, Durfee sat in a white wicker chair, watching him with loving matronly eyes. She was tiny, wrinkled, and wrapped in a tobacco-brown comforter. Her hair, though thin and wiry, was the color of orange soda. On a parsons table beside her sat a perfect arrangement of crustless sandwiches and an antique porcelain tea set. She looked up as Vidor walked up the steps.

"Happy Valentine's Day," he said, extending a bouquet of flowers to her.

Old age prevented Durfee from rising to greet him, but she reached out her hands and beckoned him forward.

"Thank you, King," she said, and indicating the man with the cards, "This is my brother."

The brother stood and offered Vidor a gentleman's handshake. "Valentines," he said, showing Vidor his envelopes. Then he sat back down.

"I've made some sandwiches," Durfee said, as Vidor took a seat across the table from her. "I hope you like tuna fish."

As they ate their lunch, they reminisced about the early days in Hollywood. Durfee spoke freely and animatedly, thoroughly enjoying the opportunity. Even when King broached the subjects of the Arbuckle and Taylor scandals—which he brought up with delicacy, wanting neither to tip his true hand nor touch upon uncomfortable subject matter—she spoke as frankly and openly as if they were discussing events that had taken place the week before.

About Mabel Normand she said, "We used to spend a lot of time together out in Fatty's pool house. We thought it was the only place we could talk without worrying about someone listening in. It seemed like for months after Fatty's trouble and Bill Taylor's murder, we couldn't take a breath without some reporter or detective asking something. We even thought they had our homes bugged. I don't know if they did or not, but it always seemed safer to talk out in the pool house."

"What did you talk about?" Vidor asked, refilling their cups with mint tea.

"Mostly the troubles. And why the press had it in for her. No matter what she said, they turned it around somehow. She would have laid down her life for Bill Taylor, and they kept saying she was the one that killed him."

"Did she talk about that night?"

"Of course."

"What did she tell you?"

"Just what she told the police and reporters. What she always told everybody: the truth. She went to see Taylor. They talked about books. He was teaching her about literature. She never had much education, you know, and hadn't read much more than the scripts of the movies she made. Taylor was opening up a whole new world for her." Durfee sipped her tea. She looked at her brother, who was now turned around, facing them, listening to their conversation.

"How are you doing, Paul?"

"Fine," he said, looking away as though embarrassed.

Durfee set her tea on the table. "Anyway, she left, went home, had her dinner in bed, and went to sleep."

"And the next morning?" Vidor asked.

"Well, she was getting dressed for work—I think she was making *Suzanna* at the time—when Edna Purviance called and told her the news."

"Did she go to the bungalow?"

"Not that morning. She went a couple of days later, at the request of the police."

"I see." Vidor recalled published accounts he had read of that morning. One of the facts he had taken for granted was that Normand had been at the bungalow when the police arrived, scrounging around for her letters to Taylor. "What about her letters?"

"What about them?"

"She didn't try to get them out of there?"

"She didn't have to. The studio got them. Then the police. Then when the press got wind of them, they made them seem like torrid love letters, like Mabel and Bill were spending all their free time behind locked doors. They even tried to make it out that Mabel and Mary Miles Minter were fighting over Bill. Mabel and Mary hadn't even met each other till after the murder."

"After?" Vidor said.

"Of course not. They traveled in entirely different circles. The murder came as a revelation to both of them. Afterward, that is, after the inquest, Mabel and Mary had a long talk about all of it. From that moment on they were the best of friends."

"Did they talk about their letters?" Vidor asked, remembering that Minter's letters were found along with Mabel's.

"Perhaps," Durfee said very quietly.

"Do you know what was in the letters?"

"If you mean did I read them, no. But I knew Mabel, and I'm sure they were just about books and movies and things."

"Were Mabel and Taylor lovers?" Vidor asked.

Durfee paused as though thinking about it. Finally she said, "Bill was like a father to her. He was probably the only man in her whole life—and that includes Mack Sennett, who was supposed to be so in love with her—who never took advantage of her, who really cared for her as herself and not as the movie star Mabel Normand."

"Then they weren't lovers?" Vidor said, still wanting her word on the matter.

"What difference would it possibly make now?" she replied.

Vidor carefully chose his response, deciding to throw her a curveball.

"Well, for one thing, it would mean that Taylor was not a homosexual."

Durfee wasn't fazed. "I suppose it would," she said, then laughed. She leaned forward, speaking softly as though she didn't want innocent Paul to hear. "Then again, I've heard tales of some men who went after anything, didn't care which sex it was."

She smiled naughtily. Vidor reciprocated, wondering if she were just being facetious or if there were a message behind her joke that he hadn't even considered before: that Taylor was bisexual? Either way, he had recognized Durfee's hesitance to address the question of Normand's physical relationship with Taylor. He turned her attention back to the night of the murder.

"Do you remember the telephone call everyone said Taylor was making when she arrived at his bungalow that night?"

She did.

"Did Mabel ever say anything about that?"

"She said it seemed to make Bill very ill at ease."

"Did she know who it was from?"

"Marjorie Berger. Berger was Taylor's accountant. She was also the accountant for Mary Miles Minter, and did work for Charles Chaplin, Mack Sennett, and Mickey Neilan."

"And the call bothered Taylor?" Vidor asked.

"It bothered him a lot. I don't know why the police never looked into it. When he walked Mabel out to her car to leave, the last thing he said to her was, 'I have the strangest, most ghastly feeling that something is going to happen to me.' "

Vidor quickly wrote the line in his notebook. He knew it was too hackneyed for his script, but he also knew that if Taylor had actually foreseen trouble after talking with Marjorie Berger, then Berger might be the missing link that held the whole mystery together.

"Did Mabel tell this to anyone else?"

"She told the police."

Then why was this the first time he had heard about it? Vidor wondered. He hoped Dick Marchman was faring well in his quest for the police files on the case.

"Did she say whether Marjorie Berger mentioned any of her other clients?"

Durfee was shaking her head almost before Vidor even finished the question.

"She said just what I told you. But you can forget about the whole Mack Sennett–jealousy angle. Mack and Mabel were finished well before Bill Taylor was killed."

"But he was with her the morning after the murder," Vidor said, checking Durfee's reaction before going on. "Some people have suggested that he was actually protecting his own interests when he appeared to be protecting her."

"There was hardly anything that someone didn't suggest," she said. Her sneering pronunciation of the word "suggest" embodied all the contempt she obviously held for the way the press had handled the Taylor affair. "They really do revere their copy above all else, including the truth. Like the time that one woman, the one Mack was seeing and Mabel walked in on them, the time she smashed a bottle over Mabel's head?"

Vidor remembered the story well.

"That wasn't how it happened. Mabel walked in on them, then walked straight to the Santa Monica pier and jumped off. She tried to kill herself. Some men saw her hit the pilings and fished her out of the water. One brought her to our house. It just made better reading to say that the hole in her head was caused by that other woman."

"So Mack Sennett stood by her to the end, even though they were no longer involved with each other?"

"There are other kinds of love than sexual," Durfee said.

"What about drugs?"

With that, Vidor thought he detected the first flinch in Durfee since they had been talking. She attempted to cover her reaction by reaching for her teacup, but Vidor was sure the question made her uncomfortable. She picked up her cup. It was empty.

"The District Attorney grilled Mabel for days. They turned her house inside out. Don't you think if she'd been on drugs it would have come out for sure, instead of a bunch of unfounded rumors?" She spoke with true emotion, but stopped before the point of tears. She gathered herself and continued as though she hadn't broken. "Mabel was lonely, King, and Bill Taylor was a true friend. That's all you, or anyone, needs to know about it."

The interview was over. Vidor thanked her for speaking with him and for the lunch. As he stood to leave, Paul stood again for another hearty handshake. When Vidor drove off down Coronado Street, he saw Paul standing on the step waving good-bye and Minta Durfee sitting silently in her chair, her empty teacup in her hand.

18

C ocaine."

Claire Windsor stood before an easel, studying her painting of the mission at San Juan Capistrano. Without looking at her palette, she smeared brown paint onto her brush and darkened the earth just below the mission. Even in her loose painter's smock she looked more voluptuous and attractive than Vidor had expected. He hadn't seen or spoken with her in nearly forty years, since he had directed her in *Show People* at MGM. Yet when she answered the door of her Spanish duplex on South Orange Drive, her powder-blue eyes, creamy white skin, and long blonde curls were just as he remembered them. Seeing her took him back to the days when Windsor, Mabel Normand, and other friends had been at the core of the legendary Hollywood crowd that gave the Cocoanut Grove, in the Ambassador Hotel, its reputation as the swingingest nightspot in town.

She stepped back from the easel, inspected it in the light from a row of windows.

"Cocaine," she said. "That's the only real drug I ever saw Mabel use. But she did use a lot of it. Gave a whole new meaning to the phrase 'powder room.'"

"Where did she get it?"

"Oh, here and there. It wasn't any harder to come by than alcohol, which as you know was just as illegal in those days."

She set her palette on a window sill and lifted her smock over her head. The tailored dress beneath, the same blue as her eyes, complemented her full figure. Vidor watched her step toward him and settle onto a low chair.

"But I don't think the cocaine killed her," she said. "Not alone. She did have tuberculosis, you know. Since she was a child. I think it was the combination that did her in."

Vidor asked her if Normand had any particular suppliers of narcotics who might have resented William Desmond Taylor's publicized attempts to get her off drugs and clean up Hollywood.

She shook her head. "I don't think so. It's possible, I guess, but I never really thought much of that idea. Bill and Mabel had known each other for something like six years. And the whole time I'm sure he knew about the drugs. Bill was someone you couldn't keep secrets from. You didn't want to. He was a good friend, always there to lend an ear or a helping hand. If one of Mabel's drug connections wanted to retaliate against Bill's concern for her, he probably would have done it a couple of years earlier, when Bill sent her to that sanitorium to dry out."

"When was that?"

"Nineteen-twenty, I think, somewhere up in New England. By the time Bill was killed, Mabel was back on her feet, making a new picture, not staying out all hours of the night. Why would one of her old pushers have waited until then to get back at Bill for something that happened so long ago?"

"You said the dope was part of what killed her. When did she start using it again?"

"I don't know. Later. But not, at least not as much, around the time of the murder. I think Mabel had been in New York up until a few months before the murder."

"The papers said she had a two-thousand-dollar-a-week habit," Vidor said.

Windsor laughed. "Do you know how much cocaine two thousand dollars would buy in nineteen twenty-two? A card cost around two dollars. That's how they sold the stuff, by the card. An entire deck was only fifteen or twenty dollars, and that's not even buying in quantity, which would make it even less expensive. For two thousand dollars you could have supplied the whole Ambassador Hotel for a week. It's ridiculous. The whole thing's ridiculous. If there were even the slightest chance that one of her drug pushers had anything to do with Bill's death, Mabel would have turned him in right away."

Vidor made a note that in yet another area—narcotics —the press had painted a picture that grossly distorted reality.

"Didn't anyone ever speak up about the newspapers' twisting of facts like that?"

"Twisting? More like a flagrant disregard." Windsor shifted in her seat, crossed one leg over the other. "As for speaking up, you know what it was like, King. We were all laboratory specimens, everyone in Hollywood was under such close microscopic scrutiny all the time that if we wanted to keep any secrets at all, we'd better just toe the line and keep our mouths shut. I started to defend Mabel —she was my friend—but the second I opened my mouth, my picture was splattered across the *Herald-Express* along with my given name and the fact that I had a three-year-old illegitimate son, which, never mind the circumstances surrounding it, was just the kind of scandalous information the papers loved printing about us. If I hadn't shut up, I would have been out of a job."

"Did the studio tell you that?"

"Not in so many words."

Vidor tapped his pencil against his notebook. The role the studio played in all of these events was growing rapidly, and Vidor began to wonder if the lack of storage space at Paramount had actually been the reason, as it had for so many other things, for the disposal of all records pertaining to Taylor; or if perhaps someone had decided long ago, and for entirely different reasons, to get rid of everything that might one day incriminate the studio in . . . what? A cover-up of some kind?

"If you had been able to speak up more," he asked Windsor, "what would you have said?"

She thought about it. "That we all loved Bill, I guess. And that Mabel was getting unjustly jerked around by the papers, while Tony Moreno and Jimmy Kirkwood and some others were the ones they should have been talking to."

"Why them?" Vidor said, jotting their names once again into his notebook.

"Because the Saturday night before the murder, I was at a party at the Ambassador with all of them."

"Oh, yeah," Vidor said. "Gloria Swanson mentioned that party."

"She did? How is she?"

"Fine."

"I wrote her last month, but she still hasn't answered. What did she say about the party?"

"Just that she was there. What happened?"

"Well, I'm not sure exactly, but Bill and Jimmy Kirkwood spent a lot of time talking, you know, privately, among themselves, and Bill seemed pretty upset about something."

"You don't know what they were talking about?"

"No, but it upset Bill enough that he didn't even want to talk to me or Mabel or anyone. I even went to the party with Bill and Jimmy, but Mabel had to drive me home. Bill went off somewhere with Tony Moreno. I don't know where or why, but when a couple days later he was dead, it all did seem pretty suspicious. And I never read one thing about that in any of the papers."

"And you have no idea where they went?"

"None. Well," she hesitated, then leaned forward, adopting a confidential tone. "We had one idea."

"Who?"

"Mabel and I."

Vidor watched her as she seemed to arrange her thoughts before expressing them.

"Mabel loved Bill for many years. So did a lot of us for that matter. But in all that time, Mabel never once slept with him."

"Are you sure?" Vidor asked.

"Just as sure as I am that I didn't sleep with him, either, or that any other woman I knew ever did."

"But what about all the stuff they found in his bungalow? Mary Miles Minter's nightgown?"

"I don't know about that. I just know that Bill never seemed very interested in women. If you know what I mean."

Vidor knew well. "Then when he left that party that night . . . ?"

"Well," Windsor said, "he didn't leave with a woman, did he?"

Vidor closed his notebook.

"Well," he said, "this has been very interesting. I appreciate your talking with me. It's really nice to see you again after all this time."

As Windsor walked him to the door, he marveled once again at her appearance, thinking that he and she were the two exceptions to the popular notion that men grow distinguished with age while women merely grow old.

"Oh." He had a final thought as they reached the door, something he had meant to ask earlier but forgotten.

"At that party at the Ambassador, was Marjorie Berger there?"

Windsor thought back. "I don't think so. Why?"

"Just curious," Vidor said, and kissed her lightly on the cheek.

19

In Hollywood, there was never time for yesterday's business, and yesterday's business was all that Vidor found himself occupied by. By the time the second of his student researchers had brought him a folder of information about Mary Miles Minter, he had converted his cluttered storeroom into a crowded but functional office. Old appliances hung from hooks on the ceiling. A megaphone, viewfinder, and riding crop were dusted and sat alongside his baseball glove, walking cane, and collection of hats. Even threadbare costumes from old movies that no longer existed had their place. Though the room still had the feel of a pack rat's den, it beat the cold sterility of the new morgue at Paramount. Vidor felt comfortable there.

He set the manila folder on the worktable and spread out its contents: newspaper clippings, Xeroxed copies, and typewritten notes. The clipping that first caught his eye dated from the early twenties and described the author's discovery in Mary Miles Minter's childhood Louisiana hometown of a tombstone with Minter's exact name and birthdate engraved upon it. A quick check of the public records revealed only one birth certificate on file under that name, presumably the birth certificate of the actress then living and well in Hollywood and certainly in no need of a tombstone in Louisiana. The article went on to explain that Mary Miles Minter had actually been born Juliet Reilly, but at a very young age, at her mother's insistence, had assumed the name (as well as "borrowed" the birth certificate) of a deceased cousin. The reasons for the name change illustrated clearly the one fact about Minter's life that no one, in print or in person, had ever challenged: that any examination of her life would have to include an examination of her mother's life. The two were, from Mary's childhood on, indelibly intertwined.

Lily Pearl Miles, the future Charlotte Shelby, mother of the future Hollywood actress, grew up on a large plantation near Shreveport, Louisiana. Her father, a physician, died when she was twelve. Her mother never remarried.

At the Virginia Female Academy, where a visiting thespian told her that her acting talents were worthy of Broadway, she announced her intention to marry one of her instructors, a man nearly three times her age. Then, for unknown reasons, she suddenly eloped to San Antonio with a visiting Texan named Homer Reilly and was not heard from until she returned to Shreveport less than a year later with a child, Margaret Reilly.

In 1902, a second daughter, Juliet, was born.

Why Lily Pearl had married Homer Reilly no one knew. No one in Shreveport had witnessed any indication that they had ever gotten along. The marriage ended in 1907 when Lily Pearl sent Homer packing.

Later that same year, Lily Pearl left home for Broadway, entrusting her children to their grandmother Julia Miles.

In New York, Lily Pearl almost immediately landed a starring role in a Broadway production and adopted the name Charlotte Shelby. Reporters looking back could never ascertain how she had come to that particular name, or even how she, with no Broadway connections or particular stage experience, had landed such a plum role, though there was speculation that a politician named Shelby may have helped her along, in exchange for whatever she might have had to give.

Soon, with a bank account and a career growing, she wired her mother to bring her children to New York. Julia Miles arrived with the girls, whom she had, again for reasons reporters could only speculate about, renamed Juliet and Margaret Miles. Charlotte Shelby, from then on the only name Lily Pearl would answer to, disapproved of her mother's changing her children's names, and immediately changed them again, to Margaret and Juliet Shelby.

Charlotte's producer, Charles Frohman, took an immediate liking to four-year-old Juliet and gave her parts in the plays *Cameo Kirby* and *A Fool There Was*. Margaret was given roles as well, but not as important as her sister's. Early theatre magazine photographs of Juliet at this time reminded Vidor of a rag doll his sister had played with as a child: rosy red cheeks, curly golden locks, big blue eyes.

For a time, the family became divided. Charlotte's mother, Julia, took charge of her favorite grandchild,

Juliet, while Charlotte saw to the career of her Margaret. This was why, in years to come, Mary would always refer to her grandmother as "Mama," and Charlotte as either "Mrs. Shelby," "Charlotte," or "Mother"—a source of great confusion whenever Mary was interviewed by the press.

By 1914, Mary's career had completely eclipsed that of both her mother and sister, and the entire family moved with their new breadwinner to Chicago, where she was to star in *The Little Rebel*. During rehearsals, the Gerry Society, which policed the use of children in theatre, demanded that Juliet be withdrawn from the production because she was not yet of legal age to work full-time. The Chicago producers, unlike their more powerful colleagues on Broadway, were unable to sidestep the rules. Charlotte Shelby, however, had an idea.

Eight years earlier, her own sister's child had died at the age of eight. Charlotte quickly traveled to Louisiana, borrowed her late niece's birth certificate, and within a week eleven-year-old Juliet Shelby was back on stage as Mary Miles Minter, age sixteen.

By 1915, Charlotte had decided that the stage offered only limited opportunities for Mary. The real money for a beautiful young actress was in the movies. So after a long series of heated negotiations with New York film producers, she signed Mary to a six-picture contract with Metro Pictures. The announcement was made in *Motion Picture News*:

> Filmdom's newest sensation becomes a permanent Metro star. The premiere juvenile star, little Mary Miles Minter, has been given a permanent place in the house of Metro stars by united request of all Metro Exhibitors and exchanges.

Spontaneity of achievement, extreme youth, beauty, grace, charm of manners, adaptability, realization, understanding, plus rare personal magnetism forecast that for Mary Miles Minter, the career of a great star awaits.

Metro's game plan, as was common in the industry, was to advertise Mary's films heavily, make Mary a star, and then, without having to advertise further, reap the profits as Mary's loyal fans all turned out to see her next series of films. But Charlotte, already the shrewd prototype for all future Hollywood stage mothers, hired lawyers to find a loophole in her contract, thus allowing her to pull away from Metro just when the public interest in Mary was at its height. Immediately after a loophole was found, Charlotte signed Mary to an exclusive contract with Flying A Studios in Santa Barbara, California.

Mary made headlines in California as she began making the first of twenty-six films Flying A had contracted to put her in. She also made headlines as an amateur pilot at Mercury Field, owned by Cecil B. deMille. Minter's flying lessons, it turned out, were her own idea, and not a publicity stunt thought up by zealous studio executives. She took to the skies with the greatest of pleasure until one afternoon Charlotte discovered what she was up to and had her grounded. But at Mercury Field Mary met a handsome new director named William Desmond Taylor, who was lining up shots at the same airfield for Jack Pickford's new picture, *The Spirit of '17.*

Though Charlotte continued to pursue careers for both herself and Margaret, Mary was clearly the star. When Mary Pickford suddenly announced that she was leaving Paramount, Charlotte saw the best opportunity for Mary. She immediately brought in lawyers to find a loophole in

Mary's Flying A contract, then negotiated a picture deal with Paramount, for the staggering sum of $1.3 million.

The family then moved into a mansion at Fremont Place, and from there to an even larger home down the road from Mabel Normand on Hobart Avenue. Charlotte was the perfect society matron, hosting teas and garden parties and commanding her staff of butlers, housekeepers, and chauffeurs. Eventually an even larger home was purchased, the grandest home any of Paramount's stars or producers had ever built—Casa de Margarita.

Vidor had heard stories about Casa de Margarita. Colleen Moore had told him of her own first visit to the mansion, in 1921. Marshall Neilan had asked Moore and her friend Thomas Dixon to double-date with him at the Cocoanut Grove nightclub. Neilan's own date was Mary Miles Minter. Moore hadn't met Mary before, but she knew the studio gossip about her. Mary was the young blonde Paramount was trying to transform into the next Mary Pickford, and a girl with an overbearing mother who would never let her little meal ticket out of her sight. Moore was surprised that the mother would allow Mary to go to the notorious nightclub with a reputed playboy like Neilan. But when they arrived at Casa de Margarita to pick Mary up, Moore realized that Charlotte had not granted such permission to her daughter at all. Mary introduced Thomas Dixon as her own date, pointing out that he came from the rich and important family of pencil makers, then told her mother they were all going to a large party that Neilan was throwing, a party that a lot of girls Mary's age would be attending.

Deceiving Charlotte was the only way Mary could maintain any kind of social life at all. Anything that would not meet with Charlotte's approval (which was nearly anything involving Mary with the opposite sex) had to be done on the sly. And the image that Charlotte insisted that Mary convey was the same image the studio wanted her to have. She was her public's virgin sweetheart—but not for long.

Mary's involvement in the William Desmond Taylor murder scandal came as a shock to virtually everyone who knew her. Before the murder, few had seen Taylor and Minter together in public except on official business-related occasions. The discovery of her love letters and her monogrammed nightie in Taylor's bedroom told everyone that little Mary was not the innocent sweetheart she seemed.

Mary made six more pictures after the murder, but neither the public nor the studio was interested in them. Just days before her twenty-first birthday, on April 25, 1923, Paramount paid off the rest of her contract for $350,000 and released her.

The only other information contained in the file concerned later years. One article from 1929 claimed that Charlotte Shelby owned a pistol similar to the one that killed Taylor and that her alibi for the night of the murder was not as solid as the District Attorney's office seemed to think. Her alibi was provided by a man named Carl Stockdale, an often unemployed actor who had starred in one of Mary's early Paramount pictures. Another article, from December of that year, with an Adela Rogers St. Johns byline, contained both Mary's and Charlotte's denials of wrongdoing, and demands that the police make public any evidence they might have linking either of them with the murder. The police said they had nothing, and Mary and Charlotte were officially exonerated from suspicion.

Another article, printed after Margaret's death in 1939, told of the family's ever-declining fortunes, of how they had fought legal battles against their accountant (who had replaced Marjorie Berger) to account for the money

Mary had earned during her career, and had been forced to spend much of their time in Europe, where the cost of living was lower than in the United States. Charlotte died in 1957. Soon after, Mary married her former Beverly Hills milkman, Brandon O'Hildebrandt. He died in 1965.

But the last article in the file was the one that intrigued Vidor the most. He read it many times, and though he wasn't sure exactly what it meant, or even if it was true, he knew it was exactly the sort of thing he needed for his screenplay. The article was written by playwright Leonard Sillman. One night in the late 1920s Sillman attended a party given by Mary Miles Minter in New York. Among the guests was a curious array of fortune-tellers, batik merchants, psychics, and spiritualists. At one point in the evening, with no apparent provocation, Mary stood in the middle of the room, clasped her hand to her throat, and screamed, "Each man kills the thing he loves!" Then she fainted.

Vidor had no idea what she might have meant by the statement, or that she had meant anything at all. And there was certainly no reason, given the time and place that the incident occurred, to suspect it had anything to do with the Taylor murder several years earlier. Still, it was such a powerful scene, so filled with mystery and (especially since it took place among such metaphysical company) foreboding, that Vidor wrote it immediately into his notebook. He wasn't sure it would find its way into his script, but he knew that if in any way the line Mary spoke at that party fit the ultimate solution that he would find for the Taylor mystery, the scene would be a natural. He might even open the picture with it.

He put everything back into the file. His next step would be to seek answers for the questions raised by Mary Miles Minter's capsule biography, just as he had done with

Mabel Normand. He had thought about talking with Florence, his first wife, who had been a friend of Minter's, but had hesitated, hoping the research done by his student would tell him everything he needed to know. Reluctantly, he concluded that he would have to talk to his ex-wife. Also, he decided as he locked the file into the strongbox, he might talk with Mary Miles Minter herself. She was apparently still alive. Finding her shouldn't be all that difficult. And it would be interesting to get her firsthand impressions of what went on so long ago. That is, if the thing that destroyed her career and drove her and her family out of Hollywood were something she would talk about.

20

The fog on March 15, 1967, reminded Vidor of Galveston. It enveloped the landscaped hills of Bel Air with a somber grayness that recalled mornings along the Gulf of Mexico. Only in the springtime, during the few weeks of its annual rainy season, did Los Angeles in any way resemble Vidor's childhood home. When working on a picture, Vidor often cursed such mornings; this was, after all, exactly the sort of weather his entire industry had migrated west to escape. But today he savored the cold dampness of the air rushing through him as he drove the T-Bird, top down, along the winding, westernmost stretches of Sunset Boulevard toward Pacific Palisades.

At the top of a long rise, he slowed the car, assured himself that no other vehicles were approaching through the fog, and eased across the left side of the road, stopping on a narrow summit that afforded an unobstructed view of the Pacific shoreline just north of Santa Monica. He turned off the car. The fog was thicker below him, like a low-lying cloud hiding the ocean. Vidor's earliest childhood memory was of a day that began with just such a morning and ended with a storm that completely washed away the city of Galveston. Vidor had used the memory as the inspiration for what some critics considered the single finest film sequence he ever directed: the Kansas twister that initiated Dorothy's magic adventures in *The Wizard of Oz*.

It was absolutely peaceful there on the summit as Vidor replayed distant moments from his own past. Lately, it seemed to take very little to send him into a reverie of old times. Every aspect of the project he was working on was tied in some way to a chapter of his own life. He had known many of the people he was now interviewing. And there was Colleen Moore. For forty-five years she had been a friendly ghost, a fond memory of the one true love that got away. Now she was his producer and, as a postcard he'd received from Cairo reminded him, his partner in every way. He had set out to solve the mystery of William Desmond Taylor's murder with purely professional intentions, not realizing he might pay an emotional price for the solution. He was now seventy-two years old; the fact struck him harder with each memory awakened by his investigation. His marriage to Betty, barely a consideration when he was first faced with the opportunity to revive his interrupted romance with Moore, filled more and more of his thoughts as it approached what he knew must be a confrontation. But he knew he wasn't going to let Betty stand in the way of a romance with Moore, or his investigation, so he drove back onto Sunset and headed down into the fog, to find more answers to the questions in his pocket notebook.

Florence Arto was Vidor's first wife. They'd left Texas in 1915, and worked together until Florence signed with Paramount and made pictures with both Taylor and Mary Miles Minter. Vidor and Florence had never lost touch with each other, and though their conversations through the years had grown less frequent and usually shorter, Vidor was always a welcome guest in her home. Today they sat in her living room overlooking the barely visible Pacific and talked about Minter.

"She and her mother were at each other's throats from the day I met them. They fought about everything. But her mother always won. Mary was like Charlotte's cute little puppet. I don't think she ever cared about acting too much, really, but Charlotte wanted her to be a star, so Mary did what she was told.

"One of the other girls, Alice Brady or Justine Johnson or somebody, I don't remember, made up a rhyme one day:

> 'Mary was a little lamb.
> Her heart was white as snow.
> And everywhere that Mary went,
> Her mother had to go.' "

"Did she have any boyfriends?" Vidor asked.

Florence laughed. "We didn't think so. The way she acted around the studio you'd hardly thought she ever knew what a boyfriend was. She was like a child. She must have been, what, at least seventeen or so, but for all we could tell, when she wasn't working she was playing with dolls or something."

"Then no one suspected she was having an affair with Taylor?"

"No one suspected she was having an affair with anyone. When would she even have time, with Charlotte always breathing down her neck?

"After the stories came out, about the love letters and the pink nightie and everything, we girls all talked about it and decided the only time they could have even been together without Charlotte was on the set, which Taylor always kept closed to stage mothers. So they might have had some kind of flirtation going on, which might explain the letters, but they certainly couldn't have done anything physical. Besides, unless there was a whole other side to Mary that no one I know ever saw, the whole idea of her even having grown-up silk underthings, monogrammed yet, was ridiculous."

"Maybe Taylor gave them to her," Vidor said.

"Could be," Florence agreed. "He wouldn't have been the only older man around with a yen for young girls. But you have to remember also that there was never what you would call a shortage of young girls around who were more willing to satisfy just such cravings; young girls far more experienced, not to mention available, than Mary."

Vidor nodded and stepped to the large picture window. Florence had further convinced him that there must have been two distinct, even opposite sides to Mary Miles Minter: the virginal little girl she wanted everyone (especially her overbearing mother) to see; and the precocious young woman who lied and sneaked around behind her mother's back with the likes of Marshall Neilan and William Desmond Taylor. The letters to Taylor and the nightgown were difficult evidence to dismiss, and yet one thing about them bothered Vidor. The police and the press saw them as evidence linking Mary or her mother to Taylor's murder. But, Vidor wondered, if either Mary or Charlotte had been involved in any way in Taylor's death, wouldn't something as damning as the letters and the nightgown have been the first things they would have removed from the scene of the crime?

21

The suspect list was shrinking. Vidor had eliminated Mabel Normand and he was now convinced that neither Mary Miles Minter nor Charlotte Shelby could have killed Taylor. And there was nothing suspicious in anything he read about Taylor's houseman, Henry Peavey, other than his arrest shortly before the murder on a morals charge. The fact that Taylor was scheduled to stand up for Peavey in court suggested that the two men were on good, friendly terms. It did raise again the question of whether Taylor himself was homosexual—and had perhaps more than a friendly relationship with Peavey—but Vidor didn't believe that Peavey was the murderer. In fact, he didn't yet have any prime suspects. It was far easier to surmise who did not kill Taylor than to guess who did. But it became more apparent with each new chapter in his investigation that there was a lot more to the case than he had expected. Every answer led to new questions; each solution opened up a new mystery. Who was Edward Sands, and where did he disappear to? Was he Taylor's brother? Whatever happened to the court-martialed soldier who promised revenge against Taylor? Or the hitchhikers with the gun and the story of "Captain Bill"? And what about the theories that revolved around narcotics and blackmail? The latter still seemed the only logical explanation for Taylor's withdrawal and redeposit of $2,300 the day he was shot.

All of these questions, and so many more, had been raised at some point in Vidor's investigation, as they had been by the police forty-five years earlier. Yet everything Vidor read, and everyone he talked with, seemed only concerned with the original list of suspects and theories that he—and the police—had started out with. It was as though, once raised, all subsequent questions were merely forgotten, dismissed without proper consideration. And Vidor was beginning to understand why. As with anything else that becomes a part of the public record, whether it be the private life of a celebrity or a historical event (and the Taylor scandal filled both bills), every detail of this mystery had been played out on the pages of newspapers and magazines. And yet, hungry as the press has always been for anything scandalous it could sink its teeth into—and there were scandals enough for a feast surrounding Taylor —all the newspapers and magazines kept returning to the original core of people who had been linked to the mystery from the beginning, the same people Vidor was now systematically eliminating from his own suspicions. Now

Vidor knew that celebrities made good copy, but why, he wondered, would the press continue to maul Normand and Minter and Shelby long after even the police had exonerated them from blame, while other possible leads to the solution to a capital crime were sloughed off like unneeded filler?

Obviously the press could print only what information it had. And Vidor thought it unlikely for the police to have investigated all the short-lived theories about the murder and neglected to tell the press about them. So its single-minded press coverage of the murder must not have come from a lack of other information but from a continual source that fed only stories concerning those people who had starred in the proceedings from the beginning. And Vidor knew of only two sources that could so influence what appeared in print: the police and the studios.

As Herb Dalmas had said, the press printed only what the studios wanted them to; and they might well have wanted these three women ruined and out of their hair once and for all. So every story about the murder was so filled with Normand, Minter, and Shelby that the real killer might have simply walked away unnoticed. Which would make the studios guilty of aiding a criminal's escape.

Vidor was excited. He felt he was onto something that might be even bigger than the murder itself: a large-scale inadvertent hindrance of a major criminal investigation. Perhaps the mystery could have been solved long ago if everyone's attention hadn't been continually diverted to Normand, Minter, and Shelby. Vidor wouldn't know for sure until he found out who the real killer was, but he had a new outlook on the press, something new to think about when he met with Adela Rogers St. Johns, who had been one of the most important reporters who covered the story.

St. Johns had once been among the most powerful of Hollywood journalists, the star reporter of newspaper tycoon William Randolph Hearst, and was still, in her seventies, an active novelist, columnist, and frequent guest on television talk shows. More than any other single writer, her work on the Taylor case seemed to Vidor to be fresh, alive, and most important, authoritative, as though her interest in it were more than simply exploiting the latest sensation. She met Vidor in her year-round bungalow suite at the Ambassador Hotel. She'd been waiting eagerly. Taylor's was indeed a favorite story of hers.

"Charlotte Shelby did it," she said.

Vidor hadn't expected such a matter-of-fact pronouncement. "A lot of people seemed to think that."

"A lot of people probably had good reasons."

"What are yours?"

She lit another cigarette with the butt-end of her last. "Where do you want me to begin? How about with the witnesses?"

"What witnesses?"

"Hazel Gillon and Faith MacLean."

"All they said was that they saw someone leaving the bungalow," Vidor said. "They couldn't even tell if it was a man or a woman. Faith MacLean kept going back and forth from one to the other."

"I read all that, too," St. Johns said, waving it off with her hand. "Both women had perfect views of Taylor's front door from their living rooms. Gillon told me she saw a woman leaving the apartment directly after hearing the gunshot. And Faith MacLean told me who the woman was."

"Wait a minute. Faith MacLean told you it was Charlotte Shelby who left the bungalow, dressed as a man?"

St. Johns nodded with such self-assurance that Vidor

knew she was not lying. What she was saying didn't corroborate anything he had already come up with, but he knew that St. Johns believed it to be true.

"Did she tell that to the police?" he asked.

"You would have to ask the police that."

"She couldn't have." Vidor was thinking out loud, trying to reconcile Faith MacLean's identifying Charlotte Shelby with everything he had read, learned from interviews, or surmised on his own. "Why wasn't she indicted? Why wasn't it in the papers?"

"I don't know, King. Obviously, someone didn't want her indicted, didn't want it in the papers. Or maybe they thought an eyewitness wasn't enough evidence for an indictment."

St. Johns laughed, coughed, then killed the cough with a sip of black coffee.

"But an eyewitness plus Mary's love letters and monogrammed nightgown should have been plenty of evidence," Vidor said. "If Charlotte did it, why did she leave all that stuff behind?"

"I don't know that, either. Maybe she wasn't aware that they were there."

"Or maybe they weren't there," Vidor said. He stood up and nervously paced the hotel carpet. "I've read hundreds of articles mentioning that nightgown, but never seen one picture of it. Maybe it never existed. That might explain why years later, when Charlotte and Minter demanded that the police make public anything they had tying them with the murder, the police said they didn't have anything. Even with Faith MacLean's identification, maybe they needed some hard evidence that they didn't have. There have been so many other things that I simply took for granted when I started researching this that I've learned weren't what they were made out to be—maybe that nightgown is another one. I haven't met one person who actually laid eyes on the thing."

"Yes, you have," St. Johns said. "Me."

Vidor stopped in his tracks. "You've seen it?"

"My husband Ike brought it home one night. He knew all the politicians. Apparently it went through a lot of curious, though unofficial hands. Kind of a hush-hush conversation piece."

Vidor sat back down. He had expected his talk with St. Johns to help him ascertain the plausibility of his theory of the studio's bungling of the investigation. Instead, she had him, once again, right back where he started. Just days ago, he had scratched Charlotte Shelby and her daughter from his list of suspects. And now, if what St. Johns was saying was true, he had another reevaluation in store.

"Are you sure it was the same nightgown?"

"M.M.M.," St. Johns said. "Mary Miles Minter. Or as I've always said, Millions, Murder, and Misery."

"What do you mean?"

"The story of poor Mary's life. The millions was money, and the fanatical need that Charlotte had for it. Everything she did centered on it. Did you know that she took thirty percent of every cent Mary ever made in her life? Called it her manager's fee. Not bad for a career that consisted of signing a total of four contracts for Mary. And the rest of Mary's money she invested, in her own name and that of her older daughter, Margaret. Mary finally had to sue Charlotte, and then only got a fraction of what she had earned. Charlotte didn't want anything to come between her and the millions she loved so much. Not Mary's own wishes—she never wanted to be an actress, especially later on, that's why her pictures started getting so bad: she hated acting, even tried to kill herself once, I've been told,

King Vidor and Colleen Moore on the set of *The Sky Pilot*, 1922.
King Vidor Collection

William Desmond Taylor in a studio publicity shot, 1920.
Courtesy Len Corneto

The Taylor bungalow before and after its demolition in 1966.
Art Ronnie

ABOVE: **The scene of the crime.** *Marc Wanamaker, Bison Archives*

BELOW, LEFT: **Coroner's photograph of Taylor on the morning the body was found.** *King Vidor Collection*

BELOW, CENTER: **The Taylor funeral, February 8, 1922. The service was held in Pershing Square, Los Angeles.** *Marc Wanamaker, Bison Archives*

ABOVE: Police detectives standing on Taylor's doorstep, February 4, 1922. *Michael Yakaitis Collection*

BELOW, RIGHT: L.A.P.D. detectives Thad Brown (left) and Leroy Sanderson came the closest to solving the crime. *King Vidor Collection*

ABOVE, RIGHT: Faith
MacLean, the eyewitness at
the scene of the crime.
*Michael Yakaitis
Collection*

ABOVE, LEFT: Mary Miles
Minter's love letter
to Taylor, which
was found by detectives
in Taylor's bungalow.
*Marc Wanamaker,
Bison Archives*

LEFT: Claire Windsor,
who was seen with
Taylor on the Saturday
night before his murder.
*Michael Yakaitis
Collection*

William Desmond Taylor starring in *Captain Alvarez*, 1914.
Michael Yakaitis Collection

Mary Miles Minter and King Vidor (far right) in *Faith*, 1916.
King Vidor Collection

King Vidor, his wife Florence, and daughter Suzanne at Vidor
Village, 1921. *King Vidor Collection*

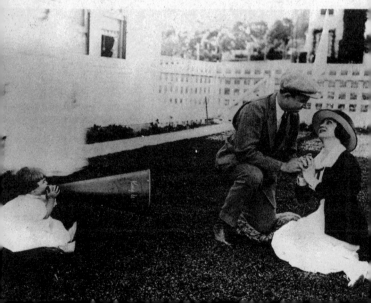

James Kirkwood (on right of camera) and Mary Miles Minter on the set of *Adventure*, 1916. *Marc Wanamaker, Bison Archives*

Mary Miles Minter and William Desmond Taylor, 1920.
Michael Yakaitis Collection

BELOW, LEFT: William Desmond Taylor and Mary Pickford, 1919.
Michael Yakaitis Collection

BELOW, CENTER: Left to right: Somerset Maugham, screenwriter Edward
Knoblock, actress Elsie Ferguson, and William Desmond Taylor, 1921.
Marc Wanamaker, Bison Archives

OPPOSITE: Art director George Hopkins (left), actress May McAvoy, and
William Desmond Taylor, 1921.   *Marc Wanamaker, Bison Archives*

BELOW, RIGHT: Left to right: King Vidor, producer Abraham Lehr,
and director Emmett J. Flynn at Goldwyn Studios, c. 1923. *King Vidor Collection*

OPPOSITE, TOP: The Shelby family at Casa de Margarita. Left to right: Charlotte Shelby, Mary Miles Minter, Julia Miles, and Margaret Shelby, c. 1919.
Courtesy Len Corneto

OPPOSITE, BOTTOM: Charlotte Shelby and Margaret Shelby, c. 1919.
Courtesy Len Corneto

ABOVE: William Desmond Taylor with his chauffeur, Edward Sands, 1920.
Michael Yakaitis Collection

LEFT: Dennis Deane Tanner, brother of William Desmond Taylor, c. 1909.
University of Southern California

Sincerely yours
Mary Miles Minter

LEFT, TOP:
Mabel Normand, 1914.
Michael Yakaitis Collection

LEFT, BOTTOM:
Mary Miles Minter, 1917.
Michael Yakaitis Collection

OPPOSITE:
Charlotte Shelby, c. 1920.
Courtesy Len Corneto

King Vidor and Colleen Moore at Willow Creek Ranch, 1971.
Courtesy Kevin Brownlow

to get out of it. And you know what she tried to kill herself with?"

St. Johns grinned at the irony.

"Charlotte's gun. The same one she killed Taylor with. So Charlotte personally escorted Mary to the studio every day and made sure she carried out her contract. Then at home, she often had to lock Mary in her room to keep her from running away or, worse, getting involved with some man. There was no way she was going to let Mary fall in love and get married and move off with all her money. I remember Jimmy Kirkwood, rest his soul, telling me horror stories about trying to go out with Mary. Charlotte threatened to kill him when she found out, and I don't think it was an idle threat. And I hear Monte Blue, that American Indian actor, had some stories of his own to tell."

"Do you think Charlotte suspected Mary and Taylor were involved?" Vidor asked.

St. Johns poured herself another steaming cup of coffee, sipped it immediately.

"Even better than that," she said with a smile. "I think Charlotte was interested in Taylor herself. What more could she want from a man? Good looking, sophisticated, good income. And when she found out that Taylor's designs were on her daughter instead of herself, it was a personal affront as well as a threat to her millions. So she solved the problem once and for all with the second M in the monogram: Murder."

This entire scenario was completely new to Vidor. In itself, forgetting everything else, it would make for a good screen story, but he knew he would have to weigh it heavily against all his other evidence and questions before he could know just how believable it was.

"What about the third M?" he said.

"Misery. That's what Mary's life has been since the murder. Her career died, she lost most of her money, her beauty. She was a virtual pariah in Hollywood. All because of that ogre of a mother, who for all we know is still haunting the poor woman. I read all about Charlotte dying a few years ago, but I wouldn't be surprised if that too wasn't one of her scams, trying to cheat even the devil out of his due. She's probably still alive, still making Mary's life miserable."

St. Johns stood up, stepped across the room to a small writing table. She took a book from a drawer, flipped it open, then set it back in the drawer. She quickly scribbled something onto a notepad, tore off the top sheet, and stepped back to the sofa.

"Still not convinced?" she said.

"I'll have to think about it," Vidor answered. "I've never looked at it quite this way before."

"Well," St. Johns said, "I didn't just make all this up out of the blue, about Mary and Taylor or the Shelby millions. It all came from a highly reliable source. Including the fact that Charlotte was really in love with William Desmond Taylor."

She handed Vidor the slip of notepaper. "Mary's done a lot of talking," she said. "This is her phone number. Why don't you give her a call? Ask her who killed the man she loved."

22

Vidor couldn't place the voice.

"Is this my dear boy?" it asked, sounding English over the phone, with perhaps the slightest Irish tinge.

No one had ever called Vidor "dear boy" but his mother, who had died ten years earlier.

"Don't you know who this is?" the woman said. "Emma said that you'd called."

It was Mary Miles Minter. Vidor had called her the week before, after his talk with Adela Rogers St. Johns, but had only spoken with her maid, Emma. She had informed him that Minter, who now answered only to the name Mrs. Brandon O'Hildebrandt, permitted no interviews.

Perhaps she had changed her mind.

"Mrs. O'Hildebrandt," Vidor said, reaching across his cluttered desk for his notebook. "How are you? I was sorry to hear about your husband. I hope everything's all right with you."

"Thank you, dear boy. I'm as well as can be expected, I suppose. But tell me about yourself. Are you making a new picture?"

"I'm thinking about it," he said. "Right now I'm just doing research. About the old days. It might turn into a movie, or a book, or something, I don't know. There aren't many of us left from the old silent picture days, you know."

Mrs. O'Hildebrandt giggled. "No, there aren't. And it's gratifying to see that those of us who are still around are still keeping themselves busy. I'm a writer, too. I bet you didn't know that."

"No, I didn't." All Vidor had seen of her writing were the love letters to Taylor reprinted in newspapers, and her denial of involvement in the murder.

"Oh, my, yes. I've been writing my entire life. Especially since Mother died. The poetry just pours out of me."

"I'd like to read some of it."

"Well, perhaps, if you're a very good boy. Now what was it you wanted to talk with me about?"

Vidor led her through a general discussion of early Hollywood, very slowly and carefully steering toward the subject of Taylor. He didn't know how willing she would be to talk about Taylor. But she surprised him with an eagerness to discuss her friend. It seemed as though she had been waiting for the opportunity.

"Do you remember all that trash they wrote after Mr. Taylor was killed? About how I did it? Or Mother did it?"

"I remember."

"It was all yellow-bellied muckraking trash. I should have sued every last newspaper that said it. Maybe I still will one day. Them and the police, too. They were the real criminals, all of them. They knew who really did it; they just had it in for us and Mabel."

"What do you mean they knew who did it? They knew who killed Taylor?"

"That's right."

"Then why didn't they arrest anybody?"

"They couldn't find him. So rather than look incompetent they went after us. And it was all lies. Guns! Silk underthings! I never had any such things in my life! My mother bought everything for me, and believe me, she wasn't about to buy silk underthings with my initials monogrammed on them! When we told the police to either show us this so-called evidence or leave us alone, they said they didn't have anything, and they cleared our names."

Vidor's immediate thought was of the nightgown Adela Rogers St. Johns claimed to have seen: if Mary never had such a thing in her life, where did it come from? But he kept the thought to himself.

"Who killed him?" he said.

She responded almost before he even finished the question.

"There was a petrol station down at the bottom of the hill on Alvarado. Right on Wilshire. I used to fill up the red roadster there that my mother gave me. The night Mr. Taylor was shot, three boys tried to rob it, but the owner pulled out a gun he kept in a cigar box and started firing. The boys scattered. One of them went running up Alvarado, and he must have seen Mr. Taylor outside talking to Mabel and sneaked inside to hide. He went upstairs, into the dark little bedroom.

"When he figured it would be safe to leave, he sneaked downstairs and tried to crawl past Mr. Taylor, who was at his desk doing his taxes. Mr. Taylor must have seen him, and the boy panicked. He pulled out his gun and *Bang!* He shot him."

She paused. She had gotten so involved in telling the story that she had to catch her breath. Then she concluded, "That's why the bullet traveled up instead of down. The boy was on the floor."

This was another entirely new scenario to Vidor. He jotted down enough notes to make a follow-up easy. If there had been a robbery the night of the murder, it would be a matter of public record.

He was about to ask another question when she spoke up again.

"It was really quite a shock, the whole thing. Mr. Taylor and I were going to be married. I hadn't known of course that he had been married once before. I guess he didn't tell me because he didn't want to hurt me. I was so innocent, you know."

So I've been told, Vidor thought.

"What about Edward Sands?" he said. "Did you know him?"

"Well, enough, I suppose. Certainly well enough to know he didn't look anything like the man the neighbor, Faith Cole MacLean, rest her soul, saw leaving the bungalow that night. She saw the boy from the robbery, thin and small. Sands was a big galoot."

"Was he Taylor's brother?"

Minter giggled like a schoolgirl. "He wasn't any more Mr. Taylor's brother than I am Emma's sister."

"Then you think," Vidor said, choosing his words very carefully, "that the whole thing could have been solved very quickly, but the police chose you and your mother . . ."

"And Mabel," she interrupted.

"And Mabel to implicate because they didn't want people to think they were baffled?"

"That's right. We were all close to Mr. Taylor, you know. And, if I do say so myself, we all had quite newsworthy names. But to think that we would have done anything like that was absurd. Why would I kill the man I was planning to marry? And then even if I did, why would I become friends with his daughter?"

"You knew his daughter?"

"I met her in New York a few years after the murder. She looked exactly like her father. It was amazing. And she knew right off I didn't kill him. Especially after I told her about the last time I saw him. It was at the funeral home. I gave an attendant a few dollars to let me see him, alone. I leaned over and kissed him good-bye, and left a rose with him. He was buried with my flower."

Vidor didn't know what to believe. Whoever was responsible for the crime, Vidor was now convinced, was cruel and powerful enough to pull off the most heartless, destructive scam in the history of Hollywood, and cunning enough never to get caught. And for the first time, Vidor asked himself if he actually thought he was any match for the killer.

He thanked Mary O'Hildebrandt for talking with him and made plans to meet with her soon, to continue their conversation in person. Then he hung up and sat at his desk, silent and motionless, for the rest of the day. He had a lot of thinking to do.

23

Vidor's favorite game was poker. He likened the game in many ways to his chosen profession. Betting a promising hand was like investing in a motion picture, always a risk, but carrying the possibility of great profit. He had in fact, as a teenager in Galveston, financed his first film project with winnings from a game at the Rice Hotel in which his own stake had been perhaps the greatest of his gambling career: he had "borrowed" his father's shotgun, his sister's typewriter, and a hidden stash of cash his mother was saving for a trip to Pike's Peak, and put them all on the line. Luckily, for both his hide and his future career, he had won. He no longer risked more than he could afford as he had in Galveston, and as he had in his early Hollywood days at the Sunset Casino, but he still enjoyed regular Friday night games at his brother-in-law Dick Marchman's house. Tonight, however, April 18, 1967, an off-night invitation, he wasn't sure he wanted to play. It had not been a good month for him, professionally or personally.

It had taken Vidor weeks to investigate the story Mary Miles Minter had told him of the night Taylor had been murdered, and what he finally learned just left him more confused than ever. According to real estate records he had finally been able to locate in a basement archive at the California State University at Northridge, there hadn't even been a filling station at the corner where Minter had said a station was robbed. The nearest station to Taylor's bungalow was Hartley's, whose owner, as Vidor had already known, had been interviewed at length about a mysterious stranger he'd claimed had asked directions to Taylor's.

Further interviews he had conducted with newspaper journalists who had covered the Taylor story didn't help clarify anything. One reporter, speaking from his bed in an Encino nursing home, claimed with no doubt whatsoever that Edward Sands had killed Taylor.

"I saw the pawn tickets," he said with an authority that made him no less believable than anyone else with a theory about the mystery. "They were signed by Sands and made out to William Deane Tanner. Obviously, Sands knew who Taylor really was and was blackmailing him."

Another reporter, who had later become an editor of a major San Francisco newspaper, was just as convinced that Mabel Normand was to blame. Citing officials of the Los Angeles District Attorney's Office as his sources, he claimed that Normand, an addict, regularly bought her dope from a peanut vendor, and that was what was in her peanut bag when she arrived at Taylor's for her short visit.

One man he talked with, a fellow film director, claimed that Charlotte Shelby's chauffeur had told him that he had seen Shelby remove her pistol from her car the morning after the murder, that Shelby had killed Taylor and then paid off the District Attorney's Office not to prosecute her. Someone else even spelled out a scenario that Vidor, who thought he'd considered every possibility by now, hadn't even dreamed of: that Taylor had been killed at Mabel Normand's house, wrapped in a throw rug, and then taken back to his own bungalow. Vidor didn't buy that theory, but knew that it was as possible as anything else he'd heard.

The only productive discovery he'd made in the last month was that it had been Allan Dwan who had informed the late Antonio Moreno that Vidor was investigating Taylor.

"I ran into him at a cocktail party," Dwan said over the phone. "I mentioned Taylor to him because I thought you might be interested in speaking with him."

"I wondered how he found out what I was doing," Vidor said. "It was really strange, his calling me in New York."

Dwan said, "Well, you know Tony and his imagination. I wouldn't put too much stock in whatever he said. Sounds to me like he wanted to indict all of Hollywood in some grand conspiracy or something."

"That's what it sounded like."

"The problem with those kinds of conspiracy theories," said Dwan, "is how are so many people going to keep so quiet about it for so long?"

All in all, Vidor's project was not exactly proceeding apace. And a call from Sam Goldwyn, Jr., had informed him that another project, a film that was to mark Vid-Mor's official debut as a production entity, was not going to work out as he had hoped, either. Vidor would still get to direct the picture, as Goldwyn had promised, but only if he directed the version of the script that Goldwyn chose, a version that neither Vidor nor Colleen Moore wanted to make. Since Colleen, who could have provided both professional and personal support, was still touring the Dark Continent, Vidor had declined the offer.

Another unexpected blow to Vidor's pride struck the very morning that Dick Marchman had invited him to the off-night poker session. In a new history of motion pictures written by one of America's best-known film critics, Vidor had read that not only was he a relatively unimportant director, but also that he was an unimportant *deceased* director. Vidor begrudged no critic his opinions, but he felt that calling him dead was beyond the critic's professional realm.

So he was not in the best spirits when Dick Marchman called. Betty had just returned from a shopping trip and, as was becoming her fashion, said nothing at all to Vidor though she walked directly past him in the kitchen.

"Not tonight," Vidor told Marchman. He thought about taking Betty somewhere, to try to make some domestic peace.

Marchman insisted. "There's a couple new players I want you to meet."

So Vidor packed his green visor and custom-made poker chips and drove to Marchman's, stopping along the way for a six-pack of Budweiser. When Vidor arrived, Marchman greeted him with a grin that told him he was up to something, then introduced him around. One of the new players was an expert gambler. Vidor didn't like this. He was in no mood to lose. But the other new player was Thad Brown, chief of detectives of the Los Angeles Police

Department. He was sixty-four years old, built like a box-car, and had one secret desire: to solve the William Desmond Taylor case before he retired in a year's time.

"It was one of the reasons I joined the force in the first place," he said. "Now I've been there forty-one years, and haven't made an inch headway. But from what your brother-in-law here says, you might be able to offer a little help. Of course, I just might be able to offer you a little help, too."

Vidor perked up. Dick Marchman had come through. Vidor would finally see the official police records on Taylor.

24

0n Friday morning, April 21, 1967, Vidor picked Dick Marchman up at eight and drove downtown. On the way, he filled Marchman in on the main things he was looking for in the police files. In addition to the obvious questions, which Vidor had been trying to answer for months now, there were the following points:

What was there about Taylor's distant past that had led investigators to think he was on the run?

What was the significance of Denis Deane Tanner, and what made investigators believe that he could have been Edward Sands?

What explanation had Taylor's wife, Ethel May Harrison, given to investigators to explain why he had vanished so suddenly?

What did investigators know about Taylor's relationship with Charles Eyton, Antonio Moreno, Marshall Neilan, and James Kirkwood?

What had the police not told the press that tied Taylor to Mabel Normand and Mary Miles Minter?

What was there about Taylor's relationship with Edward Sands that had led investigators to feel he was the number-one suspect?

What clues in Taylor's financial records had led police to believe Taylor was being blackmailed?

What was the final verdict about the keys that fit no locks, the handkerchief that appeared and disappeared, and the mystery doctor who claimed death by hemorrhage of the stomach?

Had pornographic photos actually been found? And what about the nightie and the collection of lacy panties?

Above all, why was it that so many leads—Mabel Normand, Mary Miles Minter, Charlotte Shelby, Edward Sands, and so many others, including hitchhikers, war veterans, and disgruntled studio employees—had all seemed so promising but then simply disappeared as though they had never existed?

Vidor and Marchman hoped that in a few hours many of these questions would be answered. The arrangement that Chief Brown had made for them would allow Vidor and Marchman to be left alone with the Taylor files in an assigned office. Rules were being bent to accommodate them, so they would have to keep a low profile, and would be allowed only this one chance to study the files.

Vidor knew that an enormous amount of material must exist on a case that had been open for so many years, and that one day would barely give him time to read it, let alone to make the kind of detailed notes that he would need for his investigation. So the day before, he visited a friend at a large Hollywood film equipment rental house. The friend was a sound expert who had worked on some of Vidor's films. When microphones had had to be hidden so that they would not be seen by the camera, this friend had found extraordinary ways to conceal them. Vidor knew he would never be able to copy the police records word for word—but he would be able to read them aloud. And if there were a way to conceal a microphone and tape recorder out of sight inside his briefcase, then he could make his own illegal copy of everything the police files contained. Asking no questions, Vidor's friend was more than willing to rig the briefcase.

Vidor and Marchman parked on the street and hurried up the granite steps to the Detective Bureau. The office that was assigned to them was small and on an upper floor. The documents were stacked neatly on a desk in the center of the room.

"Try not to lose anything and my conscience will be clean," Chief Brown told them as he left them alone in the room.

Vidor's hands began to shake as he opened the first yellowing file. EXHIBIT A. He carefully turned to page one and read the heading: DISTRICT ATTORNEY'S OFFICE, FEBRUARY 7, FIVE O'CLOCK P.M., PRESENT: MR. W. C. DORAN, DEPUTY DISTRICT ATTORNEY, MISS MARY MILES MINTER, JOHN G. MOTT, ATTORNEY FOR MISS MINTER, AND G. H. BOONE, SHORTHAND REPORTER. Vidor was excited. This was the real thing.

Vidor set his briefcase on the corner of the desk, with the handle facing Marchman. He pushed the right-hand latch on the case inward instead of outward, and the tape recorder inside switched on. Vidor nodded to Marchman to begin reading.

Marchman picked up a file marked CONFIDENTIAL. He began reading: "June twenty-eighth, nineteen thirty-seven, letter from Alfred A. Wright, 956 Sunbury Court, San Diego, to Chief of Detectives L.A.P.D., regarding Eddie Mason, who confessed to Wright that he had killed a man identified from pictures as Denis Deane Tanner. . . ."

Vidor could barely contain himself. The files contained letters, confessions, testimony, photographs, suspects, and notes by individual investigators. Typical of the paperwork and potential evidence that accumulated was a file that contained a lock of Taylor's hair; another that contained three different sets of ballistic reports; a file of fingerprints; one of discredited confessions; one of purported letters from Edward Sands; and another of so-called eyewitness accounts of the murder. And Vidor's heart skipped a beat when he saw the report by the detective who first entered Taylor's bungalow on that cold February morning.

The first order of business, he knew, was to get everything he could into the tape recorder. A thorough investigation, like a good film, was built on many small pieces, all intricately woven together and all significant. To miss one was to miss it all. He could analyze it all later, after a complete recording of everything was made and transcribed. And he knew just where he would do it. Colleen Moore was due back next weekend, and what better way to celebrate their reunion than to take her and his precious tapes to his ranch in Paso Robles, three hours north of Los Angeles? They could be alone together, catch up on lost time, and with luck, hone the rough edges off the story that would put them back into the mainstream of Hollywood.

25

Willow Creek Ranch was Vidor's dream retreat. Spread over twelve hundred rolling acres in Paso Robles, minutes from the Pacific Ocean, it offered the perfect escape from the bustle of Los Angeles. Though Vidor preferred to think of retirement as only a distant eventuality, he often imagined spending his later years overseeing the ranch's operation, living the quiet life of the landed gentry. The ranch contained a spacious three-bedroom house, two guest houses, and several outbuildings that Vidor planned one day to renovate into warehouses for his personal archives and perhaps a studio where he or any of his guests could write and develop projects in comfortable privacy.

When Vidor pulled the T-Bird off Vineyard Road and over the lead-pipe cattle barrier onto his property, the ranch looked dark and spooky. He employed a full-time caretaker, and for years after buying the ranch in the 1940s had visited it regularly, but somehow nearly five years had passed since his last visit, and the place reflected its owner's neglect.

"Looks like a ghost town," Vidor said to his passengers: Cassie and Dick Marchman in the backseat with Nippy, and Colleen Moore beside him in front.

It was midnight when they arrived at the house. Inside, the furniture had all been draped with sheets, and the beds stripped of their linens. But the caretaker had kept the place clean, and within an hour they were settled in for their stay.

Vidor slept soundly in his own bedroom the first night, then awoke early and walked Nippy outside, beaming proudly at his property and breathing deeply the cool air blowing in from the ocean. After an invigorating shower in cold well water, he walked into the kitchen where Cassie and Colleen were busy preparing a large country breakfast.

"Good morning," he said and sat at the table. "I'd almost forgotten just how nice it is up here."

"It's very peaceful," said Colleen. Standing beside Cassie at the counter, Colleen looked right at home, very much a part of the family.

After breakfast, Colleen, Cassie, and Dick made a list of chores that would occupy them for the day while King made his first intensive foray into the police files. He set a folding card table before a sun-filled window in the den of the house and pulled from his briefcase the entire typewritten transcript of the tapes he and Dick had made at the Detective Bureau. With his list of unanswered questions in his mind, he settled in for a long day's read.

King could see right away that the files offered much the same general information that the various media accounts had covered. But on many significant details, the files differed greatly from the version the public had been told by the press about the murder and its investigation. Some of the discrepancies could easily be attributed to the reliability of witnesses questioned, to the interpretations different interviewers gave to witnesses' statements, or to the zealous nature of the media scrutinizing Hollywood in 1922. But others, especially those discrepancies concerning what should have been matters of simple fact and not open to interpretation or supposition, made Vidor wonder why police officials had allowed the press to continue printing stories and theories that not only contradicted each other, but contradicted the police department's own, presumably definitive, findings.

Vidor made notes from the transcripts, re-creating chronologically the new version of the events of February 2, 1922. From the beginning the police story differed from the press version.

According to the police records, Henry Peavey discovered Taylor's body at exactly seven-thirty, only thirty minutes before the first police officer arrived at the scene. How newspapers could have varied as much as an hour in their reports of this easily documented fact Vidor didn't know. But it was a significant fact, because it meant that Taylor's friends and associates who were in the bungalow when police arrived had had less than half an hour to be roused from whatever they were doing (and some claimed to have been sleeping), hightail it to Alvarado Street, and start searching the bungalow.

When Peavey arrived that morning, according to his own testimony to investigating officers, the front door of the bungalow was locked—another "fact" that contradicted nearly every published report. And since the front door locked itself automatically whether it was shut from the inside or the outside, and all other doors and windows were sealed from the inside, the police knew that the killer had exited through the front door.

Peavey entered the bungalow, found Taylor's body in the living room, and immediately ran into the courtyard screaming for help. The first bungalow resident to hear him was E. C. Jessurum, the bungalow court's owner. He followed Peavey into the bungalow and saw the body. Seconds later they were joined by Douglas MacLean, who lived in the bungalow directly opposite Taylor's.

The most definitive description of the body had Taylor lying on his back, head to the east and feet to the west, with one arm outstretched and the other beside his chest. His left leg lay six inches under a standing desk chair. His right was pushed up against a rug, folding over a corner of the rug. Blood had dribbled from Taylor's nose, coagulated on his cheek, and stained the carpet beside him. What happened, Vidor wondered, to the perfectly laid-out corpse that had become accepted as one of the case's most mysterious "truths"?

The police reported no evidence of a struggle. From the body's position, as well as the position of the desk chair and bloodstains on the rug, police ascertained that Taylor had been shot while standing and facing the east.

Within five minutes of the body's discovery, Jessurum used Taylor's phone to call the police. Then MacLean used the same phone to call the studio. Later, before police arrived, Taylor's chauffeur, Howard Fellows, also called the studio from the phone. Police had no reason to believe that any of these men suspected at that time that Taylor had been murdered.

The police were unable to pinpoint exactly when the others began arriving at the bungalow, or even exactly how many people entered the bungalow before the police arrived. But they did positively identify ten people who were either inside the bungalow or milling about outside when police arrived, and they were sure that there had been at least three others there before them. Those identified were Verne Dumas, Charles Maigne, and Edna Purviance, all neighbors; Christina Jewett, the MacLeans' live-in maid; Neil Harrington, a resident of a building across the street; Howard Fellows and his brother, Harry, who was Taylor's assistant director; Arthur Hoyt, a friend of Taylor's from the Athletic Club and a studio producer; Julia Crawford Ivers, Taylor's screenwriter; and Jimmie Van Trees, who was Ivers's son and Taylor's cameraman.

One unidentified man was believed to have been a studio employee who disappeared before police could take his name. Another had told studio employees in the bungalow that he was a physician visiting the neighborhood and had asked if he might be of some assistance.

There was no mention in the files of anyone "ransacking the place" or of studio executives "burning documents." Nor was there any mention of Mabel Normand "searching the shelves for love letters." According to the police, Mabel Normand, as Minta Durfee had told Vidor, didn't visit the bungalow until two days after the shooting. And the only studio executive to visit the bungalow was Charles Eyton, who arrived well after the police and did nothing the slightest bit suspicious.

The neighbors of Taylor's who were at the bungalow

prior to the police were all questioned. Douglas and Faith MacLean, questioned separately, each told of hearing a "shot" or an "explosion" at approximately seven-forty-five the night of the murder. Faith MacLean also told of seeing a "stocky man with a plaid cap and a dark suit" leaving Taylor's bungalow shortly after the shot. She said nothing about a woman dressed as a man, or, as Adela Rogers St. Johns said she had, about Charlotte Shelby. Others claimed to have heard the shot, but no one else saw anyone leaving the bungalow. Hazel Gillon hadn't even been questioned.

Only one studio employee who arrived at the bungalow before the police seemed to have been questioned. Harry Fellows, assistant director and brother of Taylor's chauffeur, testified that he and others, including Julia Crawford Ivers and Jimmie Van Trees, entered the bungalow sometime between 7:35 and 7:50 A.M., and on orders from the studio (orders later corroborated by Charles Eyton) conducted a search for anything that might reflect negatively on Taylor or the studio. They removed from the bungalow bottles of bootleg liquor and a large number of letters from Mabel Normand, Mary Miles Minter, Neva Gerber, Claire Windsor, and Daisy Deane Tanner. Five days after the murder, police demanded that the letters be turned over to them, and in a private meeting Charles Eyton personally showed them to District Attorney Woolwine. The letters were not mentioned again in the files.

From the fact that only Harry Fellows and, privately, Charles Eyton were questioned from among the studio employees involved, Vidor assumed that the police saw little reason to interrogate the others. Still, the fact that Julia Crawford Ivers, Jimmie Van Trees, and at least one other unidentified studio employee were never questioned at all in a murder case that had never been solved struck Vidor as odd.

The man who identified himself as a doctor apparently arrived at the same time as the studio employees, made his cursory examination of the body, stated his diagnosis of Taylor's having suffered a stomach hemorrhage, and disappeared. No one other than Harry Fellows could even describe the man, and even Fellows, who observed the man in action, said nothing of his emptying Taylor's pockets or picking up a silk handkerchief anywhere near the body.

Detective Tom Ziegler arrived at the bungalow from the L.A.P.D.'s Wilshire Station at a minute or two before eight. Immediately following him was Charles Eyton. Ziegler was met at the door by Jessurum. Inside, he briefly inspected the body, took a statement from Henry Peavey, and ushered everyone outside. From this moment, the only persons permitted inside the bungalow in any nonofficial capacity were the MacLeans, the Fellows brothers, Henry Peavey, E. C. Jessurum, and Charles Eyton.

Ziegler called the coroner to pick up the body, then took statements from everyone present. Everyone assumed that Taylor had died of natural causes, though Ziegler did note two things that struck him as peculiar. One was the "shot" or "explosion" that the MacLeans and others claimed to have heard the night before. The other was the fact that Charles Eyton had disappeared upstairs while someone else was being questioned. Asked about this later, he said he was making a last-minute search for any incriminating love letters that might not have been found during the previous search. He said he found some and stuffed them into his pockets.

At about 9:20 A.M., Detective Ray Cato arrived with the deputy coroner. Ziegler had already written the words "natural causes" in the cause-of-death space of his preliminary report when the coroner turned Taylor's body over and discovered the pool of blood beneath it, and the bullet hole in Taylor's back. The body was immediately set back on the floor, and sketches were made. A routine death investigation had turned into a murder case. Other officers were called. By 10:20, the body was removed to the morgue, the bungalow sealed off to all nonpolice visitors, and word was leaking out that Taylor had been murdered.

A search of Taylor's pockets and body turned up a platinum wristwatch, a gold pocket watch, and a diamond ring. The police files contained no mention of a collection of mysterious "keys without locks"—another peculiar specific whose origin, since it obviously didn't come from the police, Vidor could only wonder about. The watches, ring, and wallet found in a nearby desk drawer containing $78.20 caused police to rule out robbery as the motive for the killing.

Taylor's body was delivered to the Los Angeles County morgue, where an autopsy was performed immediately. The autopsy report, filed later that day by Dr. A. F. Wagner, stated that Taylor was shot in the back, six and a half inches below his left arm pit. The bullet passed through his lungs and came to a stop just beneath the skin in his lower neck. Ballistics expert Spencer Moxely reported that the bullet was made of lead, weighed 144.83 grains, carried five land marks, and was fired, in all probability, by a .38-caliber Smith and Wesson revolver, the rifling of which was in fair condition. Though there was no indication that the bullet or the pistol was of an "ancient" or "old" variety as had been popularly reported, the press correctly stated that the bullet holes in Taylor's jacket and vest did not line up. Taylor had had at least one arm raised when he was shot.

By noon the bungalow complex was swarming with

detectives. Captain David Adams of the Central Station was put in charge of the case. He dispatched two detectives, Murphy and Cahill, to question Mabel Normand about the meeting that witnesses, notably the MacLeans, said she had had with Taylor the previous night.

In Taylor's bedroom, a pink nightgown was found, embroidered with the initials M.M.M., as well as a signed photograph of Mary Miles Minter. Here was one detail that jibed with newspaper accounts.

Captain Adams was going to send Murphy and Cahill to interview Minter after Normand, when Minter showed up at the bungalow asking to see the body. Apparently she had already heard, though the afternoon dailies had not yet hit the streets. Interested in her reaction to the news of Taylor's death, Adams broke his own orders that no one other than police be allowed inside, and Adams's report stated that Minter was in a state of shock. The report also stated that Minter—just as Murphy and Cahill's report would state about Normand—had an acceptable alibi for her whereabouts the previous evening.

Vidor was surprised to read that Minter had been at the scene of the crime that morning. That such an important fact about someone who was for so long considered a prime suspect in the murder had been ignored in so many reports was without precedent in Vidor's long experience with the media. And the bungalow court must have been crawling with reporters by the time Minter arrived.

But this was just one of many details that Vidor couldn't understand. Along with the mysterious keys, the unlocked front door, the ransacking studio executives, the monogrammed handkerchief, and the perfectly laid-out corpse of William Desmond Taylor were other details and "clues" that were mentioned in nearly every published account of the case but were curiously absent from the police files. Most obvious were the cache of photographs that had been supposedly discovered depicting Taylor having sexual relations with any number of prominent Hollywood starlets; and the locked closet that supposedly contained dozens of items of women's lingerie, all tagged with initials and dates.

The discrepancies between the two versions had a pattern: the press reported more than the police actually found. But there was one exception to the pattern, one instance in which the police found something in Taylor's bungalow that not a single newspaper or magazine that Vidor had read had even hinted at the existence of. And it was something that any reporter in the business would have jumped at the opportunity of publicizing, and something that seemed to Vidor the most glaring discrepancy of all.

The police reports stated that in examining Taylor's body, officers found three strands of blonde hair on the jacket Taylor was wearing when he was shot. The hairs were analyzed.

They belonged to Mary Miles Minter.

26

The next day, Vidor and Colleen finished their breakfast coffee on the back porch. Watching the sunrise over his own rolling pasture, Vidor wondered why he had allowed so much time to pass since his last visit. Everything at the ranch was calm and quiet and rooted to the earth with a permanence and a patience Vidor had never seen in Hollywood or Beverly Hills.

Dick and Cassie had driven to town for supplies, saying when they left that they might take a drive around San Simeon, William Randolph Hearst's celebrated kingdom, an hour's drive away, before coming back. Vidor decided this would be the best time to fill Colleen in on all that had happened during her African trip.

"Goldwyn passed on the project," he said. "He wants to do the other script of it."

Colleen set her coffee on the porch railing and took Vidor's hand. "I kind of thought something like that might have happened, when you didn't even mention the project all the way up here. Didn't he even offer you the directing job?"

Vidor evaded the question. "They turned down *Cervantes,* too."

Colleen knew what a blow to his ego these snubs were. She had once been an important part of the industry herself and knew what it felt like to be a victim of its selective, ever-shortening memory. But she had married, moved away from it, and established a more successful and more rewarding career for herself. Still, she understood perfectly what Vidor was feeling as he quietly told her of the latest series of setbacks his career had taken.

"It could work out for the better," she said. "You won't have to put aside the Taylor story, which, I must say, is getting more fascinating all the time. I don't see how Goldwyn or anybody for that matter could turn this one down."

The night before, he had told everyone over dinner about his day's work.

"Do you think Mary Miles Minter was the murderer?" everyone had asked.

"I don't know" was Vidor's answer. "But I do know that the story I've been pursuing these last few months and the story presented in those police records are two quite different and distinct stories."

"Why do you think that is?" Dick Marchman had asked.

"Well, obviously, the press all latched onto their version of things, which you have to admit contains some pretty juicy stuff, and that's the version that everyone has accepted as truth. And it may be the truth. But whether it is or not, it had to have originally come from somewhere, and it apparently didn't come from the police. They never found a closet full of underwear."

"Then where did it come from?" Cassie had asked.

"Herb Dalmas says the studios made it all up to get rid of Mary Minter and Mabel Normand."

"I wouldn't put it past them" had been Colleen's response to that. Hollywood's heartlessness no longer surprised her. She reached up and brushed a strand of white hair from King's forehead.

"I need a haircut," Vidor said. "I'd better call Frank as soon as we get back to Los Angeles."

"Why call Frank when I'm around?" Colleen said. "I'll cut your hair. I used to cut Homer's all the time. I'm a regular barber."

Homer was Colleen's late husband, a millionaire who hated paying barbers.

Vidor hesitantly agreed, and as he sat on the back steps with a towel across his shoulders and Colleen snipping away, he felt closer to Colleen than ever before.

Vidor liked what he was feeling, and imagined once again what might have happened if he'd been able to whisk Colleen away to this place forty-five years earlier. As she spoke of future excursions she was planning around the world, of investments she felt could make Vidor financially secure for the rest of his life, Vidor pictured the dapper director and the vibrant actress, whose passion had once burned through a mountain blizzard, spending the decades that had passed since that fateful winter living together in contented rural bliss at Willow Creek Ranch.

Then Colleen put her scissors down. She rubbed her fingers against Vidor's temples. Vidor could feel her breath on his face as she looked at him closely.

"These brown spots look like skin cancer," she said. "You should really get that taken care of. Do you want me to call a doctor when we get back to L.A.?"

Vidor was reminded of Betty, who had finally stopped asking him when he was going to call a doctor about the spots; who had, in fact, stopped saying much of anything at all to him. He shook his head.

"I'll call someone," he said.

Later that afternoon, he returned to the police files. Having chronicled their version of what happened the day Taylor's body was found, he wanted to see what they had to say about Taylor's life up to the time of the murder. Concerning Taylor's early life, as William Deane Tanner, Vidor was surprised to find that he had, with the help of Bob Giroux, Allan Dwan, Gloria Swanson, and Laurence Stallings, already gathered more information than the police files contained. Still, he discovered discrepancies between his and the "official" version.

Taylor's father, Sergeant Major Kearus Deane Tanner, had apparently not died during the First World War, as Vidor had come to believe. According to L.A.P.D. findings, he died in 1901, shortly before Taylor decided to abandon his life as a traveling actor and settle down to marriage and a career in antiques. His death also closely coincided with Taylor's renewed contact with and financial support of his family back in Ireland.

Taylor's mother, however, Jane Deane Tanner, did die during the war, during a London air raid a month before Taylor enlisted in the army.

That either of these facts would shed any light on Taylor's death Vidor doubted, but they did deepen his conviction that some strange power had been at play in 1922 and thereafter that saw to it that different investigators discovered different sets of facts.

Other discrepancies concerned Taylor's brother. Vidor had read press accounts of how Denis Deane Tanner worked in an antiques store across town from his brother. The press accounts Vidor had read failed to convey the fact that Taylor had once employed Denis, providing him with his start in the antiques business. Taylor and Denis were also members of the same athletic club and were known to have dined together on a regular basis. They were both close to their sisters in London, too, and gave no one who talked with the L.A.P.D. any reason to believe that they had in any way abandoned their British roots.

Taylor wasn't, however, close to Denis's wife, Ada Tanner. According to various entries in the police files, Taylor had only met Ada on three occasions in his life, twice in New York (as best man at her wedding and at her bedside when she gave birth to Denis's first child) and once years later in Hollywood, when she stormed his office at Paramount demanding financial aid.

Vidor found records of a police interview with Ada Tanner, but they implied that she was questioned only about how she had located Taylor in Hollywood. Her explanation of her final meeting with him was simply that a friend had told her where Taylor was, and that she had then gone to him for help. The questions of who the friend was and how the friend knew Taylor's true identity were not raised. (Vidor himself still preferred his theory that she had seen the film *Captain Alvarez*.)

The most surprising revelation in the files concerning Denis Deane Tanner was that the police had known from the beginning that he and Edward Sands were not the same person. That entire theory had been launched by an anonymous letter mailed to the police. Research eventually proved it to be a complete lie. Police had also found a snapshot in Taylor's bungalow that proved that Tanner and Sands didn't resemble each other in the least. Why, Vidor wondered, had police even bothered to waste their time running the lead down? And why had police allowed the theory to be bandied about in the press when all along they knew it was nonsense? Did they think they might have something to gain by swaying public thinking decidedly off the right path? And if so—why?

Vidor found no mention of Taylor's ex-wife or daughter having been questioned concerning the murder. Apparently police saw no tie-in between the crime and Taylor's disappearance from New York. Further evidence supporting such a conclusion was found in a series of letters the police obtained that Taylor and his daughter, Daisy, had written to each other. Though he had left them abruptly in New York by 1908, he was on good, open terms with her, writing regularly, sending Christmas and birthday gifts, as well as a sum of money amounting to over $7,000 to be used for Daisy's education and future dowry. These were not exactly the actions of a man hiding from an unsavory past.

Vidor found no mention of homosexuality in relation to Taylor. The subject appeared only in the file entries concerning Henry Peavey's arrest in Westlake Park on a morals charge. Howard Fellows had apparently bailed Peavey out, and Taylor was scheduled to appear in court on Peavey's behalf on the morning he was found dead. But no one questioned Peavey or Fellows about Taylor's reaction to the incident, though both were questioned at length about any number of other matters; hence the police records shed no light whatsoever even on Taylor's feelings about homosexuality. Though Vidor could read into certain moments described throughout the record, the majority of testimony suggested quite strongly that Taylor was actively and openly heterosexual.

Perhaps the most glaring discrepancy between the public and official reports of Taylor's life—most glaring because they should have been the most easily documented by any worthy reporter or investigator—was the detailed evidence found in the police files that Taylor was anything but penniless, as the press had consistently made him out to be, when he died. Dwindling bank accounts—one in New York containing only $18.20—had led to journalistic conclusions that Taylor was being bled by blackmailers.

Taylor had over $6,000 in his account at the First National Bank of Los Angeles. In a safety deposit box he had eight Liberty Bonds totaling $4,500 and over 18,000 shares of stock in petroleum and mining companies, stocks whose purchase value when they were bought was estimated at $20,000. These figures, coupled with Taylor's material possessions—a MacFarland Touring Car, a Chandler sports car, diamond and gold jewelry, furniture, hunting gear, piano, etc.—showed clearly that Taylor had died a wealthy man. (Adjusting the figures to the standards and inflation rates of 1967, Vidor estimated that Taylor's financial worth had been the 1922 equivalent of $1.5 million.)

The subject of blackmail, another favorite among both Hollywood and crime reporters, was also little supported by police findings. Taylor's financial records, both those he kept personally and those maintained by Marjorie Berger, were thorough and revealed nothing out of the ordinary. His monthly expenses were considerable, including regular checks to his daughter and sister-in-law, salaries and expenses of his personal employees, even the rental of a room nearby for Henry Peavey to sleep in when he worked too late to catch the trolley home. But Taylor still lent money willingly to friends and associates who needed it, displaying no evidence at all of any financial strain. The New York bank account containing only $18.20 was shown to be an account Taylor kept for his daughter, who had recently made a considerable withdrawal to pay tuition at her boarding school in Westchester County, New York. And Taylor's withdrawal of $2,500 from the First National Bank of Los Angeles the day before the murder and redeposit of a sum nearly as large the day he was killed—actions that reporters everywhere pointed to as evidence of blackmail—were in fact just as innocent. Taylor had taken the money from the bank to buy an expensive gift for Mabel Normand. He shopped at Robinson's department store, where a jeweler he had dealt with many times would help him choose the appropriate gift item. Unable to find exactly what he wanted, Taylor put the money back in the bank for a later time.

The police pieced together this sequence of events very early in their investigation, yet like so many other things that would have altered the very flavor of the mystery as reported in the press, it never found its way to the public.

Just as blackmail now seemed an unlikely factor in the story, so did the notion, as purported by Gloria Swanson and others, that Taylor might have sensed that he was in imminent danger. His activities during the final days of his life, meticulously documented by police investigators, were in no way inconsistent with the way he acted at any other time.

On the morning of what would be his final day, Taylor rose early and swam his regular laps at the Los Angeles Athletic Club pool. After a normal day's work he stopped at the B. H. Dyas Sporting Store and bought a dozen golf balls, a dozen rubber tees, and a pair of fingerless putting gloves. As he did every week, he sent arrangements of flowers to various friends and associates, including two dozen roses to Mabel Normand and three "fireflames" with three bunches of Scotch heather to Mary Miles Minter. He had also just taken delivery on a newly purchased overcoat and blue-serge suit. On the morning Taylor was found dead, Henry Peavey had stopped at a local pharmacy on Taylor's behalf and picked up for him a bottle of milk of magnesia, bought a box of mints, and had Taylor's razors sharpened.

Neither the police nor Vidor believed these to be the actions of a man who even remotely suspected he might be in danger.

The single event that the police seemed to have thought most likely connected with Taylor's murder was the July 15, 1921, robbery of Taylor's bungalow by Edward Sands. As Vidor had already learned, Taylor had returned from a trip to Europe to find that Sands had stolen about $2,400 in petty cash and had also forged checks, along with borrowing and then abandoning Taylor's sports car. Taylor had then fired his chauffeur, Earl Tiffany, and hired a new one, Howard Fellows, whom he sent to the police to secure a warrant charging Sands with grand larceny.

The volume and detail of the file entries on this robbery betrayed its importance to the police, and yet the one man who logic said might have been able to shed some light on exactly what happened the day of the robbery—Edward Knoblock, Taylor's house guest at the time—was never questioned for the official record.

The next mention of Sands had him identified as the man who had pawned some of Taylor's stolen jewelry at the Capitol Jewelry and Loan Company in Fresno, California, on December 12, 1921, signing the name W. D. Tanner to the tickets. Twelve days later, more jewelry was pawned for ten dollars at Zemansky's Loan and Jewelry Company in Sacramento. Again, the man signed his name W. D. Tanner, and again was identified as Edward Sands. But by this time, Taylor had decided against continuing the fruitless search for his former employee; Sands had disappeared for good.

Vidor paused in his notetaking. He had wanted to set aside any mention he encountered of two specific evenings that he wanted to study very closely: the Saturday night before the murder and the night of the murder itself. But by now it was quite obvious that the police files were going to be of very little help with the former. They did contain a summary report telling of Taylor having attended the party at the Ambassador Hotel, but that was apparently the extent of police interest in the affair. Even though interviews with Claire Windsor, Mabel Normand, and Mary Miles Minter all indicated that Taylor had had more than a passing contact with Marshall Neilan, James Kirkwood, and Antonio Moreno, among others, that night, none of these men was questioned about the party or anything else.

Concerning Taylor's last night, the files were of little more help. They confirmed in detail the visit to Taylor's bungalow of Mabel Normand, the last person other than the murderer to see him alive. She arrived at 7:00 P.M., driven by her chauffeur, Bill Davis. At 7:15, Henry Peavey left for the night, speaking briefly with Davis on the street on his way out. About this time, Douglas and Faith MacLean's maid, Christina Jewett, heard someone walking along the path behind the MacLeans' bungalow. At 7:40, Taylor walked Normand out to her car, then returned to his bungalow alone.

At 7:45, residents of the bungalow court heard the

"shot" or "explosion." Faith MacLean hurried to her front window and saw a stranger close Taylor's front door, then walk off toward the rear of the building complex.

At eight o'clock Howard Fellows rang Taylor's door-bell to ask him when he would be wanting the car the next morning. Though lights were on inside the bungalow, no one came to the door. Fellows rang again, then left.

There was nothing in this account that was new to Vidor. However, the police investigators had found out something that had happened a bit earlier in the evening that Vidor found quite interesting. Taylor had met Marjorie Berger, not in his bungalow but in her office downtown. During their meeting, the telephone rang. It was Charlotte Shelby, who asked if her daughter, Mary Miles Minter, was with Berger working on her own taxes.

"No," Berger said. "I haven't seen her. I'm working with Bill Taylor now."

Shelby thanked her and hung up, and no one, including police investigators, gave a second thought to the seemingly innocuous call.

But Vidor was intrigued that Charlotte Shelby had been making phone calls looking for Mary at a time when Mary, according to her own testimony to the police—testimony completely corroborated by her sister and mother—had been right at home, sitting by the fireplace reading a book aloud to her family.

27
V

idor had trouble sleeping that night. He lay on his bed, a single sheet covering him from the steady breeze rustling the trees outside his windows, as pages from the police file transcripts flashed over and over in his dreams like flipping calendar pages marking the progression of time on a movie screen.

He finally sat up, put on his terry-cloth robe and leather slippers, and walked into the den. The house was quiet except for the breeze and an occasional muffled crackle from the last ash-buried embers still glowing in the fireplace. Empty wine bottles sat on magazine coasters on the hardwood floor along with the Monopoly board still lined with the hotels, houses, and cash that Colleen had amassed while taking the others to the Parker Brothers bank. Vidor added fresh wood to the fire and took one of his guitars from its case. He sat directly in front of the fire, holding the guitar but not playing it. Nippy walked in without making a sound and curled up at Vidor's feet.

In a couple of hours, the others would be up, preparing for the picnic they planned to have on Moonstone Beach while Vidor finished his examination of the police files. Vidor thought of Colleen, of the decision he knew he had to make. He and Colleen could not continue to see each other, to speak of any kind of future together, until he did something about Betty. Likewise, the future of Vid-Mor Productions—perhaps, Vidor was beginning to feel, his only promising connection to Hollywood—seemed to depend on his decision about his marriage. He didn't know if he could continue a professional partnership with Colleen if he couldn't make a commitment to a personal one. And he desperately wanted Vid-Mor to succeed, to show the powers that were running the motion picture industry that two old veterans could still pack a powerful creative punch.

But, over four months into his research, Vidor had yet to write one page of his William Desmond Taylor script.

Vidor decided not even to try to sleep again. He set his guitar down and went to the kitchen, where he brewed a pot of coffee. Then he returned to the living room, shut the door quietly behind him, and settled in for another day's work reading the reports of each successive district attorney, this time paying particular attention to every mention of Mary Miles Minter and her mother.

Once again, he was surprised at what he found. During the entire first year after Taylor was murdered, Minter, known nationwide as the girl with the pink nightgown, was questioned only once, while her mother was never questioned at all. Five years later, Minter and Shelby became the prime suspects, with police gathering such circumstantial evidence against them as the items that now so bothered Vidor. But once again, just as logic seemed to dictate that an indictment would be brought against them, they were officially exonerated from any blame. Vidor knew that circumstantial evidence—personal items at the scene of the crime, blown alibis—wasn't necessarily enough to produce a conviction. But he also knew that these leads ought to be more than enough to inspire further investigation. Yet Minter and Shelby were declared innocent without a trial, and the investigation was focused away from them.

Vidor wanted to know why. He combed the transcripts chronologically, rereading even those pages he had read so many times that he could recite them by heart. During the first two months of the original investigation, police had already discovered more about Minter's relationship with Taylor than even the most muckraking of journalists had suspected. They had no doubt that Minter was in love with Taylor. Mary admitted as much during her only interrogation. She wrote Taylor love letters and poems, sent him small gifts through the mail, even though, she said, Taylor didn't exactly return her love. In trying to paint a complete picture of the absolute gentleman she was in love with, Minter even said that on many occasions Taylor rejected physical advances from her. He would not make love to her.

Though Mary shyly refused details of these rejections, other friends and associates of Taylor told of Minter's chasing him around the studio, begging for affection while Taylor merely treated her like a "little girl." Arthur Hoyt, a friend from the Athletic Club, told of Minter arriving unannounced at Taylor's bungalow and "threatening to make a scene" if Taylor did not respond to her overtures. Another Athletic Club member said Taylor himself told of Mary's once bursting into his bungalow, undressing, and begging to be made love to. Taylor again turned her down.

Early in their investigation, police had learned of the meeting Minter had had with Marshall Neilan the Friday night after the murder, the same meeting Gloria Swanson had told Vidor about. According to Swanson, Neilan had attended a meeting at the studio, then rushed to Minter's to discuss matters of utmost importance to both Minter and the studio. Minter told the police that Neilan had informed her that the studio had in its possession the letters she had written to Taylor, and that executives were in the process of feeding them to the *Examiner*. Neilan told Minter he wanted to help protect her from bad publicity but, in order to do so, he needed her to tell him everything she knew about Taylor's personal life. He said he and others, including Antonio Moreno, had heard "ghastly things about Bill" and needed to know that they were not true. Minter told Neilan she didn't know what he could be talking about, and the matter was dropped.

Vidor wrote the phrase "ghastly things about Bill" in his notebook, along with the one-word question, "homosexual?"

Despite these early findings, District Attorney Thomas Woolwine apparently saw little reason to press Minter for more details about her relationship with Taylor or about her meeting with Neilan. (Neilan himself was never questioned at all, nor was Antonio Moreno.) Similarly, Minter was not asked to explain how, if as she claimed she'd never had a physical relationship with Taylor, her nightgown came to be found in his bedroom, or how hair from her head had found its way to Taylor's jacket collar. Apparently, Woolwine bought her statement that she hadn't seen

Taylor since the previous December and that on the night of the murder she had been reading the *Cruise of the Kawa* to her family. Minter was dismissed from official attention until three years later when Asa Keyes, who replaced Woolwine as Los Angeles district attorney, reopened the investigation.

The wealth of the new information discovered under Asa Keyes made Vidor question further D. A. Woolwine's investigation. Further circumstantial evidence tying Minter and Shelby to the murder appeared in Keyes's files, evidence even more damning than that which Woolwine had seen fit to dismiss. Almost immediately, investigators uncovered the fact that Charlotte Shelby owned a .38-caliber Smith and Wesson breaktop revolver, the exact type of gun that police ballistics experts believed shot Taylor. They were unable to produce the weapon, but had a sworn affidavit from a Nick Harris Security patrolman that he had given the pistol to Shelby in the summer of 1920, and statements from several witnesses who saw the gun in Shelby's possession around the time of the murder. Two of the witnesses also claimed knowledge that both Shelby and Minter knew how to use the weapon.

Shelby's personal secretary, Charlotte Whitney, providing testimony during the Asa Keyes investigation, said that one night in the summer of 1920 Minter came home late from a date, whereupon Shelby accused her of having been sexually intimate with Taylor. Mary denied the sexual charge and, after being physically struck by Shelby, ran upstairs and locked herself in her mother's bedroom. Shelby's chauffeur, Chauncey Eaton, heard the commotion and ran inside. While he, Whitney, and Shelby all stood outside the locked bedroom door, they heard three gunshots from inside. Eaton broke the bedroom door down, and the three rushed in to find Mary holding the pistol. She said she'd held the gun to her head to kill herself, but the gun wouldn't fire. Then it had fired as she pointed it around the room trying to get the safety off.

Asked why this incident was never mentioned during the original Taylor investigation directed by Woolwine, Whitney said she imagined it was because neither she nor Chauncey Eaton had been questioned.

Whitney also told of Shelby's having spent time practicing firing the pistol during the months prior to Taylor's murder, and of Shelby's actually threatening Taylor and others with it. Among the others threatened was actor Monte Blue, whose name, Vidor noted, had come up on several previous occasions. Whitney said that Shelby was extremely jealous of any man who paid attention to Minter, especially William Desmond Taylor, with whom Shelby had many verbal altercations. One particular argument, witnessed by several Paramount employees questioned, ended with Shelby's screaming, "If I ever catch you hanging around Mary again, I will blow your goddamned brains out!"

One witness said that Shelby was "livid with rage, and shook her fist in [Taylor's] face and swore dozens of times."

Another night, Whitney stated, Minter was out late, and Shelby, believing her to be with Taylor, went out looking for her with her pistol in tow. "I will take my gun," she told Whitney, "and if I find her there, I am going to kill her."

Whitney begged her to leave the gun behind, but Shelby refused. She put on a coat with sleeves big enough to conceal the weapon and insisted that Whitney drive her to Taylor's bungalow. There Whitney was ordered to stay in the car.

"Mrs. Shelby took the gun," Whitney told police, "but

I don't think she had any intention of using it on Mary."

Shelby didn't use the gun on anyone that night. Mary hadn't been there.

The more he read and reread, the more Vidor questioned the entire investigation directed by Woolwine. Everything that Asa Keyes and his investigators were able to find out four years later should have been that much easier to discover immediately after the murder. But Vidor was also bothered by the fact that even in light of Asa Keyes's findings, it was not until a full four months after Charlotte Whitney's testimony that Keyes decided to question Shelby.

Vidor heard movement in the house. The others were getting up. Nippy scratched at the door to the living room, but walked away as Vidor heard Colleen ask the dog if he wanted to go outside. Vidor decided to face the others now, when their intrusion into his workday wouldn't interrupt a thought. He walked out with his empty coffeepot.

"What time did you get at it this morning?" Colleen asked after "good mornings" in the kitchen.

"Early."

Vidor wished the others a fun excursion to the beach and returned to his table, to the first official mention in the files covering Asa Keyes's investigation of Charlotte Shelby's other daughter, Margaret.

The night of the murder, Margaret said, was a night she remembered quite clearly, because her grandmother, Julia, had prepared a special meal for the family at their Hobart Avenue house, and Charlotte had not shown up for dinner. After dinner, Margaret and Julia and Minter sat in the living room, where Minter read to them from a book called *The Cruise of the South Sea Islands*.

The next morning around nine or ten, Margaret said, Charlotte arrived at the Hobart house and announced to everyone, "Marjorie Berger tells me that Bill Taylor has been murdered." She also claimed to have had dinner the previous evening at the family mansion, Casa de Margarita, with family friend Carl Stockdale and Jim Smith, the night watchman.

Vidor was fascinated with Margaret's testimony. It blatantly contradicted both Minter's and Shelby's long-standing versions of that evening, from the general circumstances—Minter and Shelby claimed the entire family was together all night—down to the minor details, such as the name of the book Minter was supposed to have been reading.

Marjorie Berger categorically denied that she called Charlotte the morning Taylor was murdered. In fact, she swore it was Shelby who called her with the news of Taylor's death.

"I arrived at my office between seven and seven-thirty on the morning of February second, nineteen twenty-two. My telephone was ringing. I answered the phone. Mrs. Charlotte Shelby said, 'Marjorie, I have something terrible to tell you. The man that was in your office yesterday afternoon is no more. He is dead.'"

Between seven and seven-thirty, Vidor thought: Shelby was telling someone that Taylor was dead at about the same time that Henry Peavey was first discovering the fact himself?

Berger went on to tell of Shelby's having called her the night before the murder looking for Minter, then ended her testimony with another statement that gave Vidor pause to think.

In claiming never to have withheld knowledge or information from the police, Berger said that two days after Taylor's death, she had filed a complete report with the police, covering these very same points. The man who took her report was District Attorney Thomas Woolwine himself.

Charlotte Shelby was interrogated on April 9, 1926, by which time any informed detective should have known exactly what to ask her. She denied any involvement in the crime. She denied having known of any love affair, or even friendship, that might have been going on between Taylor and her daughter Mary. In fact, she claimed to have been quite upset when she, along with the rest of the world, first learned about Minter's love letters when they were printed in the press. She denied any but the highest regard for Taylor, and denied having ever had harsh words with him. She said she never once threatened Taylor or any other man. Though she did admit visiting Taylor one evening while Charlotte Whitney, her secretary, waited in the car, she denied having a gun with her at the time. She denied having ever owned a weapon at all. (Later, upon cross-examination, she confessed to having once, years ago, owned a gun that her mother, Julia Miles, threw away. She said she'd practiced firing the gun, but was not pleased with it. "The thing was too short. I can shoot a long pistol. I wouldn't mind shooting a shotgun.")

Asked about Minter's failed three-shot suicide attempt, she said the incident occurred when, for reasons she didn't know, Minter suddenly ran up the living room steps screaming, "I'm going to end it all!" then locked herself in Shelby's room and fired the pistol twice. It was this incident, Shelby said, that made her give the pistol to her mother for disposal. "I never saw it again," she insisted.

Later, when the subject turned to Taylor's murder, Shelby's answers grew quite specific. She said that a little after 9:00 A.M. on the day in question, Carl Stockdale called her from the studio and told her about the murder. A few minutes later, she said, Marjorie Berger called, and Shelby relayed the news to her.

Shelby was then asked whether anyone had ever accused her of the murder, and whether District Attorney Woolwine had ever taken a statement from her.

"No, no one ever questioned me," she said.

And the only person who ever accused her of murdering Taylor, she said, was her own daughter Mary: "Mary said around the house, freely, 'Mrs. Shelby killed Taylor.' Not only once, but many times. She was always saying that."

Vidor then moved on to the final papers filed on the Taylor case. After Asa Keyes left office, his successor, District Attorney Buron Fitts, inherited the case, calling in only one new witness to provide testimony.

Chauncey Eaton, Charlotte Shelby's chauffeur, added two facts that further sealed Vidor's suspicion that Shelby was involved in Taylor's death.

On the morning of the murder, Eaton said, he was called by Shelby to bring the car to Casa de Margarita, on New Hampshire Avenue, where Mary and Margaret were. He arrived at approximately 8:00 A.M. and was told by Shelby that Taylor had been murdered. Once again, Shelby had told someone about the murder before Shelby herself, unless she had had knowledge of it prior to Henry Peavey's, could have known.

The second new detail that Vidor culled from Eaton's testimony was that Eaton claimed to have seen and examined Shelby's pistol immediately after Minter's suicide attempt. Shelby told him to unload the weapon and hand it to her. He did so, then hid the shells on a beam in the basement, where he said they might very well still be. He said he wasn't certain, but he thought the pistol was a .25-caliber automatic, not a .38.

Vidor wondered whether this testimony might have caused the D.A.'s office to balk at indicting Shelby. Subsequent to taking Eaton's statement, perhaps investigators had found the bullets on the beam in the basement and concluded that, even if Shelby had threatened to shoot Taylor, it hadn't been her gun that did it—so why prosecute her?

Vidor closed the file. As he pondered Charlotte Shelby's testimony he realized that if he decided she had killed Taylor, and wrote his screenplay based on all the evidence supporting the notion, he would be immediately slapped in the face with the one question he couldn't answer: if all this evidence existed against her, why hadn't anyone accused her before?

It was midafternoon. The others would still be gone for a while. Vidor quickly made himself a sandwich, not wanting to be caught outside the sanctuary of his workroom should they happen to return early. Then he opened the files again, starting once more at the beginning.

It was clear that District Attorney Woolwine had had his hands full at the beginning. Possible leads popped up everywhere, then disappeared as though they had never existed. Vidor remembered figures from newspaper reports; leads and confessions poured into police headquarters as many as ten in a single day, totaling over three hundred within the first five weeks of the investigation. There were not nearly that many contained in the police files, though there were quite a few, all of which had to be at least looked into. Among them was an anonymous letter addressed to L.A.P.D. Captain David Adams:

You people are all wrong in regard to W. D. Taylor. The bastard is in hell where he belongs. I could put you wise to a lot of dope that would set you right. I have a sister that went to L.A. and met Taylor and that was the end of her. Savvy? Well, nuff said. He is where he belongs and should have been there sooner. That dope about the cigarette at the rear of the house was bunk. Peavey dumped it there. I did not have to stand there two hours to get into that dump either. Another thing. Doug MacLean's wife did not see anyone if she was laying down in the living room and apparently asleep. She wants notoriety. You are all as far as you will ever get as I am in possession of all the dope. Another thing, them hop heads around there all turned in or they would have seen where my car was parked. Taylor was the shits and was due to be bumped off long ago although no one had the guts.

(signed) A Brother

P.S. The papers taken from the desk will be mailed to you as soon as things quiet down.

A sample confession read:

To Whom It May Concern:
William Desmond Taylor, going by the name of W. D. Tanner some years ago in New York State, stole my dear wife. The next time I laid eyes upon her she was dead. I have hunted Taylor for years and my vigilance has been rewarded. I have made him pay DEARLY. By the time you get this, as well as the confession I have made to the Examiner, my body will be floating in the ocean.

(signed) W. R. Hansen

Most of the confessions and letters were obvious hoaxes that were easily dealt with. But others demanded more attention: statements from Walter Kirby, the man identified as one of the two hitchhikers picked up by the Santa Ana rancher; statements from Otis Heffner, a Folsom inmate who claimed to have been a witness to the murder. A man named Harry Fields, a.k.a. Harry the Chink, said that he and fellow dope peddlers Jimmy Moore and the Lee brothers had tried to kill Taylor for killing the drug deals they had going with Mabel Normand. And there were dozens more, none that proved fruitful, but all of which cost the D.A.'s office man-hours and money. But this hardly excused overlooking such obvious backyard leads as Charlotte Shelby's public threats to Taylor or Mary Miles Minter's leaky alibi.

Vidor read through the confessions and leads, noticing for the first time that four statements he had read many times over in countless newspaper articles about the mystery were completely absent from the police files. Nowhere was there any mention of the owner or operator of the Hartley Service Station, or the conductor and motorman of the Third Street Red Car line, four men who had been presented in the press as the most promising witnesses at the beginning of the investigation.

Vidor began to wonder if some mistake had been made, if Captain Thad Brown had accidentally given him access to incomplete files, though that too seemed unlikely since the files he was given did cover the various investigations from the beginning through that of Buron Fitts. They just didn't seem to cover them as fully as they should.

Next in the files Vidor encountered Edward Sands, the man Woolwine said the police most wanted to capture, and the only suspect for whom a warrant had ever been issued. Nothing in the Sands papers shed any light at all on anything other than the fact that Sands himself was a mystery. He disappeared suddenly after robbing his employer and was never seen again. Certain facts, such as his knowledge of Taylor's true identity, made him too suspect to be dismissed entirely, but there was nothing against him like the kind of evidence against Charlotte Shelby and Mary Miles Minter.

The same was true of Mabel Normand. Though she had visited Taylor the night he was killed, there was nothing to suggest any wrongdoing on her part. Every detail of what she told police about that evening was checked out and proven, from the smudge of lipstick on the rear window of the passenger side of her car where she had pressed a farewell kiss to Taylor, to the man sitting in a window in the far end of the courtyard who Normand said watched Taylor walk her out to her car.

Vidor jotted these details down in his notebook. He found it interesting that Woolwine had investigated them with such diligence while not even bothering to interview Charlotte Shelby.

Illicit drugs also played a large part in Woolwine's investigation. Though no drugs had been found anywhere connected with Mabel Normand, a number of known pushers claimed that both she and Taylor had long been regular customers. In exchange for having peddling charges dropped against them, they promised to lead police to the dealer who shot Taylor. So many such claims were made that the police had to institute a quiz to be given to all drug pushers claiming knowledge of the Taylor murder, in order to separate self-serving liars and cranks from worthwhile informants. Not one drug-related lead—in fact nothing at all related to Mabel Normand—led anyone a single step closer to finding the killer. And yet, for reasons not evident in the police files, but well-documented in print, Normand continued to be considered a suspect long after she was proven not to have been involved. The end result of this public suspicion was the destruction of her career.

Vidor was considering once again Herb Dalmas's theory about Normand and Minter when he heard the others returning from their outing. He looked up and noticed for the first time that it was dark outside.

He leaned back and waited until, on cue, the door behind him opened and Nippy bounded in with a playful bark. Then Vidor heard Colleen's voice, speaking from the doorway.

"Are you still at it?"

"I'm about to call it a day."

"I should think so," Colleen said, stepping inside and putting her hands on his shoulders. Vidor welcomed her loving touch. "You've been at it all day long. You'll wear yourself out. You should take a break now and then, King. It's only a screenplay."

Vidor closed the files in front of him, thinking, "You're wrong, it's not only a screenplay. And it's not only a mystery either. It's three mysteries, all unsolved, and all entwined. And who killed William Desmond Taylor is the least of the three. Beyond that is the mystery of where all the information printed about the case came from. Most important is the third mystery: why the Los Angeles Police Department seems to have directed its investigation of the case in every imaginable way except the one that would have led them directly to the killer."

28

Vidor arrived back in Beverly Hills shortly before midnight. The drive from Paso Robles had taken nearly five hours, including a short stop in Buellton for a bowl of Andersen's pea soup—a treat Vidor gave himself on every trip to or from the ranch—and another twenty minutes seeing Colleen off on the red-eye to Washington, D.C. After dropping Cassie and Dick at their home and buying dog biscuits for Nippy at the all-night Hollywood Ranch Market on Vine Street, he could think of nowhere else to go but home, where he knew Betty would still be awake after a Sunday night bridge game.

As he turned up his steep tree-lined driveway, he

could see Betty in the living room apparently cleaning up from the game. She did not look up as the T-Bird's headlights hit her through the large picture windows.

Vidor parked, took his briefcase from the trunk, and walked Nippy to the kennel behind the house. Just as Vidor was reaching the chain-link kennel gate, Nippy began snarling.

"What is it, boy? Ghosts?"

Then Vidor heard a bark and turned to see an unfamiliar German shepherd eyeing Nippy from inside the kennel.

"Oh," Vidor said, taking Nippy by the collar and leading him back around the house. "Betty's bought herself another Toby."

He put Nippy in the garage for the night, then walked into the house through the kitchen door.

Betty was standing on a stepladder putting her silver serving bowls into the hall closet. She ignored Vidor's entrance.

"I see there's been an addition to the clan," Vidor said.

Betty stepped down from the ladder and back into the living room, out of sight.

Vidor put his briefcase down. He opened the refrigerator for a cold drink. He had expected his homecoming to be uncomfortable, but he hadn't expected Betty's silence. A confrontation of some kind he was prepared for, but not this.

Soda in hand, he walked into the living room. Betty was seated at her bridge table, separating two decks of cards.

"How was the game?"

No answer. Vidor sighed.

The cards separated and shoved into their boxes, Betty stood up. She walked to a desk and took a postcard from a leaning stack of mail. She handed the postcard to Vidor and walked back into the hallway.

The postcard pictured black natives posing before a collection of ivory tusks: *Welcome to Nairobi.* It was from Colleen and had obviously arrived while Vidor was at the ranch, postal service being slow from Africa to the United States. Vidor knew the confrontation with Betty could be put off no longer.

He found her in the kitchen.

"We'd better talk about it," he said.

"Okay," Betty said, sitting at the kitchen table. "Where do you want to start? New York? Paris? San Francisco? The ranch? Or somewhere else I don't even know about yet?"

Betty looked at him for the first time since he walked in the door, her eyes burning into him with a fire he hadn't seen in some time.

"We're working on a project together," he said. "It's only a screenplay." Only a screenplay. He nearly laughed to hear himself repeat Colleen's words from earlier in the evening.

"Come on, King," Betty said. "Give me more credit than that, would you? 'Only a screenplay.' If you're not going to be honest with me, then we have nothing to talk about."

Betty's eyes remained on Vidor, adding to his discomfort.

"What do you want me to say?"

"Just tell me what's going on. Are you in love? Are you just having a fling? Are you ever going to direct another movie, or are you just going to spend the rest of your life 'working on projects' like this 'screenplay' of yours? Are you ever going to be King Vidor again, the man I married, the man who was a vital part of this house and Hollywood, or are you just going to go on being this stranger who spends his time staring into mirrors and picking through all his old papers, and running around God knows where with God knows who all, trying to act like he's not seventy-two years old and like all the people out there in Hollywood even remember who he is?"

Vidor could see Betty's lips trembling, but not a single tear formed in her burning peppercorn eyes. He didn't know what to say. This could be the moment he'd been imagining since his fateful reunion with Colleen, the moment he would make up his mind once and for all what he was going to do about his marriage and about Colleen. But he was at a loss for words.

"Do you ever intend to stop this galavanting around the world, trying to prove whatever it is you're trying to prove to yourself? And settle down and just be King Vidor?"

"I don't know," Vidor said softly, truthfully.

Betty stood up. "Well, when you do know, tell me. Because I'm here, and your home is here, and we'll still be here if you decide to come back to us. But until you decide, I think you'd better find a new home."

Vidor sat perfectly still, staring at his soda as Betty's final words sank in. Then he looked up at his wife, whose eyes, still fixed upon his own, had lost their heat, becoming the cold, vacant eyes of someone deeply hurt.

Vidor packed a suitcase, took Nippy out of the garage, and walked down to his office to spend the night.

There, as Nippy slept on the floor beside him, he lay on a cot thinking long into the night, finally reaching his decision just as the first hint of dawn gave shape to the shadows outside his window.

He sat at his desk and with a ballpoint pen began to write on a yellow legal pad:

Dear Betty—

Let me begin by saying that I have a tremendous affection and admiration for you. But there is an obvious lacking in our relationship. I love the ranch and the country around it; you love the comfort and security of Beverly Hills. I like to travel; you do not. I need to be around creative people in a creative atmosphere, while my creativity and the recognition it affords me have long been a source of discomfort, perhaps even resentment and jealousy, for you. The list goes on and on, and I'm sure you could add considerably to it yourself. So what do we do? A temporary separation? What would that accomplish? Neither of us, at our age and station in life, would change. We are two separate and distinct individuals, who could probably remain the closest of friends if we would just put an end to the charade we've been calling a marriage. This is not a rash decision, and has not been reached without extensive, painful thought on my part—and I'm sure on yours. We should do this now, before our differences destroy the feelings we still have for each other.

When he finished, he put the letter unsigned into an envelope and addressed it to Betty. He would mail it or deliver it himself to her tomorrow before calling Thad Brown about the police files. Lying back on his cot, he felt none of the relief he had long imagined he would feel when he finally made his decision about Betty and Colleen. He stared at the ceiling trying to turn his thoughts to the Taylor case, but couldn't concentrate. He'd been awake nearly forty-eight hours. In three more, Thelma Carr would arrive and find him on a cot, the first to get the news. But Vidor couldn't even think about that. He just slipped his letter to Betty under his pillow, closed his eyes, and fell immediately to sleep.

29

Thelma Carr brought lunch from Hamburger Hamlet. When she had arrived for work that morning, Vidor, unshaven and still contemplating the letter to Betty, had immediately sent her off on errands. In her absence, he had shaved, showered, dressed, hidden his suitcase—though Thelma must already have guessed from his appearance that he had slept in the guest house—out of sight in a closet, and decided that the letter was too impersonal a way to put an end to thirty years of marriage. Though the letter was honest and straightforward, Vidor had begun to feel cowardly for having written it instead of telling Betty how he felt face-to-face. Now, as Thelma returned with the hamburgers, he put the letter aside and opened his pocket notebook.

"Thanks, Thelma," he said, accepting a paper sack. "Would you get the L.A.P.D. for me, please? Captain Thad Brown."

"Right away."

Thelma shut the door behind her as she stepped back into her own office. Minutes later, she had Brown on the line.

"Hang on a minute," his gravelly voice told Vidor. "I want to take this in my office."

On hold, Vidor looked over his notes from the ranch.

"I was wondering when I was going to hear from you," Brown said. "Learn anything from those files?"

"Even more than I'd anticipated," Vidor answered. "I walked in with a set of questions and walked out with more questions."

Brown laughed. "I hope it didn't cool your interest any."

"Cool it? Quite the contrary. This isn't even the same case I'd come to think I knew inside out."

"I know what you mean," Brown said. "My partner and I had the same reaction when we first read those files. I was hoping you'd feel the same way. What do you make of them?"

Vidor underlined entries in his notebook with a ballpoint. "Well, they raise some obvious questions, the most important one concerning Charlotte Shelby and Mary Miles Minter. Now I'm no expert on our legal system, but there certainly seems to be a lot of evidence pointing toward them, and yet nothing was done about it."

"I know," Brown said. "You'd think there was enough by nineteen-twenty-two standards in Woolwine's files to indict one or the other of them."

"But they were hardly even questioned," Vidor finished Brown's thought. "Then they were completely exonerated. It doesn't make sense. Unless something happened that isn't contained in those files. Are you sure you showed me everything the L.A.P.D. has on the case?"

"Everything I've seen in the police files, you've seen. When I first inherited this case I wondered the same thing. But as far as I've been able to find out, that's it. Which means that through the years, something has obviously been lost or stolen or misplaced or something, because it just isn't there. Now a lot of hands have gone through those files in the last forty-five years, both police hands and district attorneys', so I couldn't say which might have been sticky, but it seems that just as the physical evidence that might have convicted Shelby and Minter disappeared, so did whatever reasons Woolwine had for not indicting them in the beginning."

"That sounds awfully suspicious to me."

"Damn right it's suspicious," Brown growled. "But what can we do about it? Something must have happened that made Woolwine leave Shelby and Minter alone, something that outweighed all the evidence against them. If I had that evidence now, the famed M.M.M. nightgown or the hairs from Minter's head, I could reopen the case and even if I couldn't indict anybody, maybe I could turn up some of the old reasons that they weren't indicted before. But even that evidence has disappeared."

Vidor thought about something for a moment, then double-checked his notes. Finally he said, "Whatever happened that convinced Woolwine of Shelby's and Minter's innocence disappeared from the files before Asa Keyes took over Woolwine's job. Otherwise, why would Keyes have, all those years later, re-suspected Shelby and Minter?"

"Go on," Brown said.

"Which could mean that Woolwine or someone in his administration didn't want subsequent investigators to know why they turned blind when it came to Minter and Shelby."

"You mean a conspiracy of some kind to suppress evidence?"

"Either that or all the evidence just disappeared accidentally."

Now it was Brown who thought in silence.

"What do you think?" Vidor asked anxiously.

"Why would they suppress evidence?"

"To hinder the investigation seems the most logical answer," Vidor said. "I'm not sure why they'd want to do that, but it does seem possible. I mean, they certainly undermined any help they might have gotten from the press or the public by allowing so many rumors and theories they knew were groundless to dominate everyone's understanding of the case."

"Do you think they also originated those rumors and theories?"

"I don't know. I've always assumed they came from the studios, who have always had the ability to spread whatever rumors they wanted. And they did have employees at the scene of the crime, apparently tampering with possible evidence. But two things bother me about that. One, if the studios were out to protect Shelby and Minter, why would their people leave behind the most damning piece of evidence of all, the nightgown? And why would they themselves publish Minter's letters to Taylor? The other thing that bothers me is, if, as someone has suggested to me, the studios were out to dump on Minter, why wouldn't her nightgown being found in Taylor's bungalow have been enough? I mean, add those transgressions of logic to the fact that so many of the rumors and theories printed by the press couldn't have had any effect whatsoever on anyone's opinion of either Shelby or Minter, and the studios look less and less likely to have started the rumors. Yet they had to come from somewhere."

"Well," Brown said, "there's no evidence that they came from Woolwine or any of his men."

"That's just it. There's no evidence they came from anywhere. The only evidence that exists at all says that Shelby and Minter were involved one way or another in Taylor's death, and that Woolwine knew this and did nothing about it."

"So what are you going to do next?"

Vidor had been waiting for this question. He hoped Brown would be able to help him. "I thought I might try to talk with some of the investigators on the case, some of the names mentioned in the files."

Vidor heard Brown's deep laugh again. "Good luck with that one. Most of the original investigators are dead. Bill Cahill's out in Arcadia. Ray Cato's still alive, the one that turned over Taylor's body and first saw the bullet hole. Of the D.A.s, only Buron Fitts is still around, lives in Hollywood."

"That's all of them?"

"Except for maybe some of the cops from later years, Fitts's administration. Leroy Sanderson's around somewhere. He'll probably talk with you. There are others from the Fitts administration but who knows if they'll say anything. It was all kept very quiet. In fact, I don't know if you know this, but days before Fitts was going to announce his Taylor investigation findings someone tried to gun him down in his driveway. I couldn't say there was a connection between the Taylor case and the shooting, but Fitts hasn't mentioned the case since."

Vidor thanked Brown for the information, then listed the names Brown had mentioned on a fresh notebook page. He circled Buron Fitts.

"You wouldn't happen to have any of their phone numbers, would you?"

"As a matter of fact," Brown said, "I have them right here."

30

At 10:00 A.M. on May 1, 1967, Vidor turned off Santa Anita Avenue in the Los Angeles suburb of Arcadia and found a small house at 27 Magna Vista Street. In the front yard flew an American flag, the only one in the neighborhood.

Bill Cahill met Vidor with a toothy grin and a hearty handshake that belied his eighty-one years. A retired L.A.P.D. lieutenant and Arcadia chief of police, Cahill still had the physique of a much younger man.

"I appreciate your seeing me on such short notice," Vidor said.

"Think nothing of it," Cahill replied, leading Vidor into the backyard.

They sat on lawn chairs, completely hidden from neighboring houses by rosebushes that climbed trellises nearly as tall as the houses themselves.

"So you're making a movie about William Desmond Taylor."

"Right now I'm just trying to get the story together," Vidor said. "Which isn't exactly easy. There are so many versions to choose from."

"How can I help you?"

"Well, there was so much written about the case, and so much of it obviously untrue, that right now I'm trying to weed out what was real and what wasn't, and even more importantly, trying to find out where everything that was printed that wasn't real came from. Did newspapers just make it up? Or was somebody planting stories?"

"Who could have been planting stories?"

"I'm not sure yet," Vidor said. "But it seems unlikely that some newspaper reporters could invent things like a set of mysterious keys or a monogrammed handkerchief or a couple of hitchhikers in Santa Ana, and the police would simply allow them to do it."

"In the first place," Cahill said, leaning forward and punctuating his words with hand gestures, "I imagine that police were more concerned with finding the killer than keeping tabs on what was said in the newspapers. And in the second place, why are you so sure those things were invented? How do you know there was no set of keys, or no handkerchief?"

"I don't," Vidor answered quickly. "Those are just examples that came to mind of the many things written about when the case first hit the press. It's become obvious in my research that many of those things, not necessarily

---

the ones I just mentioned, either led nowhere or were simply dropped later as though they had never existed. And I'm wondering if the reason may be that they were false from the beginning."

"I see," Cahill said, looking directly into Vidor's eyes. "So once again, how can I help you?"

"As I understand it, you headed up District Attorney Woolwine's investigation of Mabel Normand."

Cahill nodded.

"She was formally interviewed twice," Vidor said. "The first time by you and Detective Murphy on the afternoon after the body was discovered."

"That's correct."

"She told you that she arrived at Taylor's bungalow the night before at about seven o'clock and left at seven-forty-five. This was confirmed by her chauffeur and a neighbor who saw her leave and then heard Taylor return to the bungalow alone."

Cahill said nothing, just continued looking at Vidor with a stare Vidor imagined had dampened the collars of many suspects in Cahill's long enforcement career.

"The second time Normand was questioned was a week or so later, February tenth. She repeated exactly what she'd told you and Murphy. And yet the press continued to report that she had been at the bungalow the morning they found the body, that she had been searching Taylor's shelves, that she was a drug addict, all kinds of things that were never brought up either time she was questioned."

Cahill finally allowed his eyes to drop from Vidor's. He looked around the yard. "You've certainly done your homework, Mr. Vidor," he said. "I mean, you seem to know every word said during Miss Normand's two interrogations. Funny, I don't remember any transcripts of those sessions ever reaching the press."

"As you say," Vidor said, "I've done my homework. And the question I was hoping you might be able to help me with is why, after Normand's story was accepted by the police, the press was still permitted to present her as a prime suspect for the next six months."

Cahill replied quickly, "She was completely exonerated."

"Not until her career was shot out from under her."

Vidor thought Cahill was growing nervous. He no longer looked Vidor in the eye. He stood up, pulled on a pair of work gloves from a redwood table, and picked up a pair of garden clippers. As he stepped to a wall of rosebushes, he spoke, his back to Vidor who followed.

"I joined the police force in nineteen-nine. Los Angeles was a rough place in those days."

Vidor said, "I know. I came here myself not long after."

Cahill started clipping his roses. "We never would have guessed it, but it got even rougher years later, during Prohibition. Those days were something else. Brothels, speakeasies, dope. It was impossible to keep tabs on all the criminal activity going on. The best we in the department could do was to do what we were told. If they said to raid one joint and ignore another one, that's exactly what we did. Maybe someone had an arrangement with the owner of the place we ignored, or maybe they just chose our targets out of a hat—we didn't ask questions. Because if we did, and believe me I knew a lot of good officers who asked the wrong questions, we were told to find another line of work."

"Are you saying someone told you to back off the Taylor case?" Vidor asked.

"I'm just saying I did what I was told." Cahill stopped clipping and faced Vidor again. "I don't know what all went on concerning that case. All the high-level meetings went on behind closed doors."

"Woolwine's doors?"

"He was in charge."

"Could all the information leaked to the press, false or not, have come from behind those doors?"

"I couldn't tell you."

"What about Mary Miles Minter?" Vidor asked. "Or Charlotte Shelby? What about the investigation of them?"

"Surely you know that from all your homework, Mr. Vidor," Cahill said. "Just like Normand, they were both exonerated, and just like Normand, they remained suspects in the press."

"I know that," Vidor said, choosing his words very carefully, trying to suggest without disclosing outright that he knew information contained only in the official files. "I'm just wondering if the stories the papers printed about them differed as much from what really happened as they did with Normand. Or if maybe the police also knew more about them than they told the press."

Vidor felt that Cahill got his unspoken message. They stepped back to the chairs. Cahill set his clippers on the ground.

"Well," he said, "I didn't question Minter myself. And I never even met her mother. So I can't really give you any firsthand information about them. But I recall hearing that the mother, Shelby, was a friend of Woolwine's. Of course, I don't know that for a fact."

Vidor grinned. "Of course." Vidor knew now that Cahill hadn't been nervous before. He had just been feeling Vidor out.

"All I really know is Mabel Normand, and I guess you're already aware of everything I know about her that didn't make it to the press. So you know we had no reason to suspect she had anything to do with killing Taylor. Her alibi was airtight. But there was that one thing that didn't seem to ring quite right about her testimony. At least five times she told the story of how when she arrived at Taylor's bungalow that night the door was open and Taylor was talking on the phone. She said she waited outside until Taylor hung up and didn't hear any of the telephone conversation. But each time she told this story she said that Taylor had *received* the call. Now if Taylor was already on the phone when she arrived, how did she know Taylor received the call? How did she know he didn't make it? Only two ways. Either she heard some of the call, or Taylor told her something about the call—both of which she adamantly denied."

Vidor remembered what Minta Durfee had told him: that Mabel Normand had told her that Marjorie Berger had called Taylor that night. And from Marjorie Berger's own testimony, Vidor knew that no more than an hour before Taylor received his call, Charlotte Shelby had called Marjorie Berger looking for Minter.

"And another thing." Cahill interrupted Vidor's line of thought. "What about the fact that Taylor's door was open when Normand arrived? We know he wasn't expecting her. And it was cold that night, far too cold to stand around with the front door open. So he must have been expecting someone else to arrive right about the time Normand arrived. Either that or someone had just left the bungalow or just entered the bungalow, and was there the entire time Normand was."

"It could have been Minter," Vidor said. "That could be when her hairs got onto Taylor's jacket."

"Hairs?" Cahill said. "What hairs? I don't remember any hairs mentioned in the papers."

Cahill smiled and Vidor smiled back, caught in his

playful deception. He immediately re-covered his tracks.

"Just another rumor I have to run down."

"I see," Cahill laughed. "Well, speaking of Minter, shortly after Taylor's inquest, Normand ran into Minter in the lobby. They whispered briefly, then walked off together. I followed them upstairs, but they locked themselves in the ladies' washroom and turned all the faucets on so no one could hear whatever they were talking about. Now I don't know of any other time when these two were together—they were not exactly known as friends. But they sure had something they wanted to talk about in private that afternoon."

Vidor thought about this. What could Normand and Minter have talked about? Did Normand know more than she told anyone about other things besides Taylor's phone call? Or could it have been the phone call itself they talked about? Vidor was trying to arrange a logical scenario, tying Charlotte Shelby's call to Marjorie Berger, Taylor's mysterious phone call, and Mabel Normand's and Mary Miles Minter's carefully concealed conversation in the ladies' room, when Cahill stood up again. Picking up his clippers, he said, "Are you married, Mr. Vidor?"

"Yes, I am," he said. "Why do you ask?"

"I just thought you might like a few roses to take home to the missus."

Cahill walked away, the conversation obviously ended. Vidor watched him clip a rose from a bush, then stood up himself. He declined Cahill's offer of the roses and walked back around the house to his car.

31

Ray Cato stood before a wall covered with plaques, citations, and other awards for distinguished law enforcement and public service. Most of the awards were signed by Woolwine, Asa Keyes, or Buron Fitts.

"I rode to the bungalow in the coroner's truck," he said. "They told us to park around back so we wouldn't draw any undue attention to the place. Can you imagine that? The place was already crawling with people and they didn't want us to draw attention."

He laughed heartily and showed Vidor to an easy chair.

"Do you think anyone there already knew it was murder? Charles Eyton or anyone?" Vidor asked.

Cato sat across from him. He shrugged his shoulders. "I don't know. Somebody must have known something; they'd turned that bungalow inside out before we even got there. But whether it had anything to do with murder I couldn't say. I tend to doubt it, though. Eyton seemed to be in charge of the studio contingent at the bungalow, and I remember he seemed as shocked as I was when I turned the body over. His mouth fell open, and he shot out of there like a jackrabbit."

"He left?"

"Not for good. He'd been in and out all morning, as a matter of fact. That's why, once we found out it was murder, it was so tough to find any usable clues. With people like Eyton going in and out, leaving fingerprints on everything in the place, fobbing off with who knows what all, it was hard to trust anything we found that might have been good evidence. We couldn't even be sure whose cigarettes were in the ashtrays."

"But you knew whose love letters were found, and whose nightgown."

"Whose," Cato agreed. "We did, it's true, know whose those things were. But what we couldn't be certain of was whether they bore any importance to Taylor's being killed, or whether they were even in the bungalow before Taylor was killed. It would have been just as easy for something to have been put into the bungalow before we arrived as for something to have been taken out."

"Planted evidence?" Vidor said, thinking out loud. It hadn't occurred to him before that Eyton and the others hadn't merely overlooked the nightgown in their search of the bungalow, but might have purposefully placed the nightgown there. That possibility would certainly be consistent with a studio effort to hide Taylor's having been homosexual. By filling the bungalow with women's underthings, and then publishing love letters written to Taylor by women, the studio could have ensured that anyone looking into Taylor's death would have naturally assumed Taylor was not only heterosexual, but quite a ladies' man.

"It's possible," Cato said, pulling Vidor from his reverie. "Of course, we didn't know anything was planted, but by the same token, we didn't know anything wasn't. Which was just one of the things that made this such a difficult case."

Vidor consulted the list of questions he had written in his pocket notebook. "What about the mysterious doctor who said Taylor had had a stomach hemorrhage?"

Cato nodded enthusiastically, as though Vidor had said exactly the correct thing. "Another stick in the spokes of justice, and another supposedly unexplained mystery. But let's think about it. I pull up in the coroner's truck. We go inside, see all these people, and then discover a bullet hole in the body. Eyton takes off, comes back a few minutes later and says, 'Hey, we didn't know he was murdered, this doctor who was here just a few minutes ago said he had a stomach hemorrhage.'

" 'What doctor?' I ask him.

" 'I don't know,' he says. 'Just some doctor.'

"Just some doctor," Cato said to Vidor. "Some doctor who just happened by, whom no one claims ever to have seen before, who takes a quick look at the front half of a fully clothed body, says 'Stomach hemorrhage,' and then disappears forever."

"I thought the doctor came after the police arrived," Vidor said.

"Uh-uh," Cato said. "No policeman saw him. No policeman even heard about him until I turned over the body.

Then all of a sudden we got this story about this doctor who was here just a few minutes ago!"

Some of the pieces of the puzzle were starting to fall into place. Paramount Pictures didn't know Taylor had been murdered, simply that he was dead. They were informed by a phone call from Taylor's own bungalow, and wanting to ensure that no one find out about Taylor's having been homosexual, they dispatched Eyton and a crew to strip the bungalow of evidence. But then the police arrived and discovered that Taylor had been murdered, which made the studio's presence in the bungalow doubly suspicious. So Eyton walked outside when the bullet hole was found, then came back with the story about the mysterious doctor, a story that made the studio employees' being in the bungalow less suspicious. "We were told he died of a stomach hemorrhage."

Obviously, there never was a mysterious doctor.

"So," he said to Cato, "do you think the questionability of the evidence found at the scene of the crime was the primary reason this case was never solved?"

Cato didn't have to think to answer the question. "It was a good enough reason we didn't jump to any immediate conclusions about who killed Taylor. But the deeper the investigation went, obviously, the less bearing this questionability, as you call it, would have on things. By the time I was taken off the case, I had a feeling there were other reasons that kept this case on the books."

"What were those reasons?"

Cato grinned. "Just conjecture. Nothing I could really tell you." Cato stood up, began walking around the room. Late-afternoon sun sliced through the blinds on the windows in bright, dust-filled strips. "I'd been running down leads on Edward Sands. You see, Sands was a pretty good suspect. Had already robbed Taylor, knew all about Taylor's secret past, and was also obviously on the run. I found a girlfriend of his down around Forty-sixth and Figueroa. I was also the one who dug up the details of Sands's military career."

"Military career?" Vidor said.

"Didn't read much about that anywhere, did you?" Cato asked.

"No," Vidor said, thinking, Not even in the police files.

"Well, I found out about it. I also found out that, despite what all the newspapers and everybody was saying, there wasn't any evidence at all that Sands had been blackmailing Taylor. In fact, there wasn't any evidence at all that Sands had had anything at all to do with Taylor's death. He certainly didn't fit the description that what's-her-name, MacLean, gave us of the person she saw leaving Taylor's place the night he was killed. Yet, for some reason, Sands was given top priority as a suspect."

"By Woolwine?" Vidor interjected.

"Woolwine gave the orders," Cato said. "And when I asked him one time why we were putting so much time and effort into chasing someone who didn't seem to have anything to do with the murder, the next thing I knew I was taken off the case. After that, we stopped looking for Sands altogether, though according to all the papers, Sands was still Suspect Number One."

"Is Woolwine the one who kept telling the press Sands was the main suspect?" Vidor asked.

Cato raised the window shades, filling the room with light. "I don't know what Woolwine told anybody," he said. "But I know what he didn't tell anybody. He didn't tell anybody that just before he took me off the case I saw a report in his office from a police department in Darien, Connecticut, that said that a body was found in the Connecticut River with a self-inflicted bullet wound in the head, and that the body had been positively identified as that of Edward Sands."

Cato turned to face Vidor just as he finished the sentence. Vidor could barely respond.

"Sands was dead?"

"Six weeks after Taylor," Cato said. "And Woolwine knew about it. But that didn't stop us from carrying on a nationwide manhunt for him, in the press at least, for months afterward."

"Why do you think Woolwine hid the fact of Sands's death?" Vidor asked.

"Why do *you* think he did?"

Vidor stood up and seconds later realized that he was pacing the floor like a movie detective. He wondered if he'd ever done that before without noticing it.

"He obviously wanted everyone to believe he was still searching for Sands, to draw their attention away from whatever he was really doing," Vidor said.

"Which was?"

"I don't know. But whatever it was, wouldn't the truth about Sands have done an even better job of distracting public attention? I mean, a man linked to a murder killing himself would have been quite a story."

"Yes, it would," Cato said, "but as I just told you, there wasn't really anything linking him to the murder. If something as definite and real as Sands dying were found out, and Woolwine were, as you suggest, using Sands to distract attention from himself, then Woolwine would have had to find something else for the press and the public to latch onto. That is, if there is anything to this theory of yours."

"What do you mean, theory of mine?" Vidor asked.
"You must have a theory of your own. You can't tell me

your superior, a high-ranking public official, just sitting on important information relating to a scandalous murder case was something you didn't give a second thought to."

"I told you," Cato said coolly. "I was taken off the case. At that point, any theories I might have had concerning it became irrelevant."

"Why were you taken off the case?" Vidor asked rhetorically. "Because you knew too much, that's why. Because you found out that Sands was not only innocent, but he was dead. Because you knew that Woolwine was up to something. Surely you must have given some thought to what that something was."

"And surely you, Mr. Vidor," Cato said, "must realize that I am in no position even to be discussing this case with you. It is an open case, and I have already told you more than I should have."

"Taylor was killed forty-five years ago," Vidor said. "Wouldn't you like to see this case solved?"

"I'd love to see it solved. But I don't see how my theorizing about something my superior may or may not have done nearly half a century ago is going to do that."

"Then how about if I theorize?" Vidor said.

Cato opened his arms in a be-my-guest gesture.

Vidor continued pacing. He said, "Woolwine had good strong evidence against two people, Mary Miles Minter and Charlotte Shelby."

He looked at Cato, whose stone expression betrayed nothing at all.

Vidor continued, "Yet he did nothing with that evidence. I believe the reason he did nothing was that he discovered more, stronger evidence—evidence that superseded what he had on Minter and Shelby. I don't know what that evidence was, but I believe that Woolwine kept the supposed manhunt for Sands alive to hide what he was really investigating. How's that theory sound?"

"Okay, I guess," Cato said, after a hesitation. "Of course, it makes me want to ask you one question."

"What's that?"

"What's this strong evidence he was investigating? Without that, your theory will never be any more than that, a theory."

Vidor was impressed with Cato. Just like Cahill, he had mastered the art of conveying information without really saying anything. Covering his tracks. By not questioning Vidor's cold statement that Woolwine had had evidence against Minter and Shelby, Cato had silently, innocently, corroborated it. And now, he had not denied Vidor's theory about his former superior, but had simply told Vidor what Vidor already knew: that there were still holes in his story.

Vidor thanked Cato for his time. As they walked to the front door, he turned to the former detective as though one final thought had just occurred to him.

"I wanted to ask you," he said. "Was there any talk or anything in those days of Taylor's having been homosexual?"

"Homosexual?" Cato said, following it once again with his boisterous laugh. "Hell, you wouldn't think so from all that stuff about nightgowns and panties and everything, would you? But who knows? I'm all the time surprised to learn someone I never suspected is a queer. He could have been, I guess. But who could really say for sure?"

32

Vidor knew he should have come to George Hopkins earlier. The idea had crossed his mind many times since it first occurred to him in New York, but he had always set it aside, hoping something would turn up in his research that would make it unnecessary. He feared the interview would be far more uncomfortable than any he'd ever conducted, and also that it might prove to be a complete waste of time, but sitting in his T-Bird on a quiet Hollywood side street, he could think of no one else who might be able to answer his question about William Desmond Taylor's sexuality.

It was Gloria Swanson who had told Vidor that George

Hopkins had been a close friend of Taylor's. "Taylor gave him his first big job in pictures," she'd said. And Vidor, who worked with Hopkins in 1949 on *Beyond the Forest*, knew well that Hopkins was homosexual. He also knew that Hopkins's having been close to Taylor was not evidence that Taylor himself was homosexual, but he hoped their friendship had been such that Hopkins would know one way or the other.

But how was Vidor going to go about asking him? With no clear plan in mind, he walked to Hopkins's apartment.

"King." Hopkins welcomed Vidor with a friendly hug. "It's good to see you again. Come in. I have some wine on ice."

Hopkins's apartment reflected his years as a set designer. There was no unused space, and yet no feeling of clutter. Over a living room mantel were his three Academy Awards for set decoration and art direction—*A Streetcar Named Desire, My Fair Lady,* and *Who's Afraid of Virginia Woolf?* —along with a total of nine framed announcements of Oscar nominations. Atop a brightly polished piano sat a collection of silver-framed photographs, each perfectly in its place. Judy Garland, Marlon Brando, James Dean. Set apart from the others in a magnificent enameled art deco frame was a portrait that drew Vidor's attention immediately. The inscription on the photo read: TO MY FRIEND GEORGE HOPKINS, WHOSE FRIENDSHIP I VALUE AND WHOSE WORK I ADMIRE, SINCERELY, WILLIAM D. TAYLOR.

"The victim," Hopkins said, as he stepped up beside Vidor with a bottle of wine and two glasses.

"I'm sorry?" Vidor said, missing Hopkins's meaning.

Hopkins indicated the Taylor photograph. "The victim. Of this mystery you're writing."

"Oh, yes," Vidor said, accepting one of the wine-glasses.

"A great Sauvignon blanc from Mendocino County," Hopkins said, pouring. "Like to sit down?"

They sat facing each other over an ornately hand-carved coffee table. Hopkins set the wine on an otherwise empty silver serving dish.

"So tell me about your story," Hopkins said.

Vidor tasted the wine, found it precisely to his liking. He set the glass on the silver dish and told Hopkins more than he had intended to tell him, including his theory about the studio's having actively engaged in a cover-up of some kind—he specifically did not mention the word "homosexual," wanting to draw Hopkins into his trust before dropping that bomb—and Woolwine's having not acted upon the evidence against Minter and Shelby.

Hopkins sat silent when he finished. He poured himself a second glass of wine. "Well," he said, "I certainly knew nothing of this evidence, but I'm certainly not surprised by it. Hardly anything would surprise me about those two. Especially the mother."

"Why do you say that?"

"I think she dreamed up the whole idea of the stage mother. Wouldn't let little Mary out of her sight. I don't think Mary even existed, for all practical purposes, without Charlotte stuck to her side. Charlotte was like a vampire bat, sucking her life right out of little Mary's veins. I never did put it past her to kill Bill. Mary really loved him, and just like everything else—acting, stardom, money—everything Mary got, Charlotte had to have for herself."

"You mean she wanted Taylor for herself?" Vidor asked.

Hopkins finished his second glass of wine. He offered a second glass to Vidor before pouring his third.

"I don't know if she was actually in love with Bill, or if it was just a matter of wanting him so that Mary couldn't have him. Most of that stage-mother mentality does seem to stem from basic jealousy. I mean, Charlotte might not have hovered over Mary the way she did if she'd ever been able to become a star herself."

"Do you think," Vidor said, asking himself as much as he was asking Hopkins, "Charlotte could have killed Taylor because, not only was he paying attention to Mary, but because he was not paying the sort of attention she wanted him to pay Charlotte?"

Hopkins responded with a tentative nod. "There's very little you could ever accuse that woman of that I would tend to doubt. I even heard she wasn't even dead like all the papers said, and, hell, I'd believe it. Vampires don't kill easily. She could still be sucking blood out of poor little Mary."

Vidor stared blindly into his wineglass. This was the second time someone had said that Charlotte Shelby might not have died when she was supposed to have. When Adela Rogers St. Johns had said it, Vidor had dismissed it as a joke illustrating Shelby's character. Now he wondered if such a rumor really existed. He asked Hopkins as much.

Hopkins shook it off. "That's something I heard. Probably nothing to it. But as I say, I wouldn't put anything past her."

Vidor wondered how to turn the conversation toward the true reason he was there. He changed the subject as offhandedly as he could.

"When did you first meet Taylor?"

"My mother introduced us. She was head set decorator at Paramount for ten years. I started working with her when I was sixteen. Her office was right below Bill's. He and Marshall Neilan, Charlie Eyton, Jimmy Kirkwood, Dennis, all of them would come down all the time."

"Denis?"

"Tanner," Hopkins said. "Bill's brother."

"Denis was at the studio?"

"Until his wife showed up looking for him. Then he disappeared, changed his name, and moved to Riverside. That's probably why people thought he and Sands were the same person, both of them vanishing like that."

"Why did he take off?" Vidor asked.

"You tell me."

But Vidor had no answer. He steered the talk back to Taylor.

"So your mother introduced you?"

"That's right. Then when Lasky decided to give Bill his own company, Realart they called it, she said she was too busy to do all their design as well as the rest of the studio's, and suggested me for the job."

Vidor recalled Taylor's first picture for Paramount with Minter. "You worked with him right from *Anne of Green Gables* on?"

"Thirteen pictures, one after another, the first bunch all with little Mary."

"Why did you stop using her?" Vidor asked.

Hopkins finished his third glass of wine. He looked at the bottle, but made no move to reach for it again.

"She wasn't doing such a good job. She was great at first, a fine little actress, but after a few pictures, she seemed too nervous and so upset all the time she couldn't concentrate on what she was doing. The studio decided to drop her. Against Bill's wishes, I might add. He knew what was going on, that it was her mother that was doing it to her, but the studio didn't care about the reason, only the results, so they let her go."

"Did Taylor ever have words with Shelby?"

"Oh, yes," Hopkins said, emphatically. He topped off Vidor's glass, then emptied the bottle into his own.

"How well did you know Taylor?" Vidor asked.

"Very well," Hopkins said. "Work that closely with someone for that long, you can't help but get to know them."

"His death must have come as quite a blow."

Hopkins nodded, and Vidor hated the course the interview was taking: why couldn't he just come right out and ask what he wanted to know?

"He was a nice man. And would have gone on to make many great pictures. You know his last one? *The Top of New York*? Monte Katterjohn, the writer, was so drunk when he was working on it that I ended up writing most of the screenplay myself. Bill didn't live to see it screened."

Hopkins set his glass down and stood up. "I'll get us some more wine," he said and walked out of the room. Vidor sat, his own glass still half filled, and looked over at the framed photo of Taylor on the piano. Even from across the room it seemed set apart from the other pictures, seemed to occupy a space of reverence.

"Here," Hopkins said, returning. "Ice cold." He filled his own glass once again and sat down. "Now, where were we?"

"Taylor's death," Vidor said. "It seems like the minute they found his body all the rumors started. And all the stories about the things supposedly found in his bungalow. Nightgowns, handkerchiefs, mysterious keys, pornographic pictures."

To Vidor's surprise, Hopkins began to smile for the first time. "They did go a little overboard, didn't they? But it served their purpose. Until now, at least."

"What do you mean?"

"You yourself said all those rumors were started by the studio, by all of us at the bungalow that morning."

"All of us?" Vidor could feel his heart beating. "You were there?"

Hopkins slumped back in his chair, wineglass in hand. "I figured you already knew that."

Vidor shook his head. "No. You were the unidentified studio employee?"

"I guess so. Charlie Eyton called and said Bill was dead and to get there as fast as I could. I was the first one there from the studio. I didn't even know Bill'd been murdered until I was already back at the studio. I just ran upstairs and gathered every scrap of paper I could find and got the hell out."

"What exactly were you looking for?" Vidor asked, the tension at its peak. He knew this was why he was there.

Hopkins looked him in the eye, punctuating his nervousness.

"I figured you already knew that, too," he said.

"Taylor slept with men." It came out of Vidor's mouth as a statement, not a question.

Hopkins responded with affirmative silence.

"So the studio sent you and the others to destroy all the evidence and then planted contrary evidence, like the nightgown, and made up the existence of even more evidence like the pornographic pictures, the closet full of underwear, the mysterious keys—"

"The keys weren't made up," Hopkins said.

"There's no mention of them in the police files," Vidor challenged.

"That's because the police never saw them," Hopkins said. "But enough other people did that someone, probably Eyton, decided to make up a story about them, and said they were keys that fit no locks, just another dead-end clue."

"So what were the keys, then?" Vidor asked. "Why would they be so important Eyton had to cover up for them like all the other evidence? Unless it was the locks they actually fit that had to be covered up, unless they opened doors Eyton didn't want anyone to know Taylor would ever open? Is that it?" Vidor sat forward, excited. "Were they keys to Taylor's lover's house? Taylor's male lover?" He downed his wine and helped himself to another glass.

"You should have been a detective, King," Hopkins said.

"So who was it? Sands?"

Hopkins laughed. "I spoke too soon. Sands wasn't homosexual. He did know about Bill, though. Why do you think Bill didn't press charges after Sands robbed him the second time?"

"Sands was blackmailing him?"

"Sands threatened to expose Bill if he went to the police. That's why I had to take Sands's letters out of the bungalow that morning."

"And that's why the police had no blackmail evidence against him," Vidor said, realizing a great irony: if the studio hadn't taken the letters in their attempt to cover up Taylor's homosexuality, the letters—along with Sands's suicide six weeks after the murder—would have been enough for District Attorney Woolwine to have convicted Sands and closed the case before the arrival of whatever secret evidence it was that turned him away from the evidence against Mary Miles Minter and Charlotte Shelby.

"So if it wasn't Sands," Vidor said, "then who was it? Peavey? He was homosexual, and he had a room near Taylor's place. Taylor paid the rent on it!"

Vidor felt he was getting close. Then Hopkins said, "How do you know Peavey was homosexual?"

"Simple," Vidor said. "Right before the murder, he was arrested in Westlake Park on a morals charge. Soliciting young boys. Taylor was planning to stand up in his behalf."

"But he didn't stand up in his behalf," Hopkins said. "Did he?"

"Of course not. He died."

"So what happened at Peavey's trial?"

"I don't know," Vidor said. "But what does that matter? What matters is whether Peavey and Taylor were lovers. And Peavey was obviously homosexual, or why would he be in a public park soliciting young boys?"

"I couldn't imagine why," Hopkins said.

But suddenly Vidor could imagine why.

"Unless," he said, "he was soliciting them for Taylor."

Hopkins raised his glass in salute. "I was right in the first place, King. You should have been a detective."

"And the room Taylor kept for Peavey was really a secret hideaway where Taylor took the young boys Peavey found for him." Vidor pulled his notebook from his pocket to record this revelation while it was fresh in his mind. "That explains why the studio had to get rid of the keys, and why Eyton had to come up with a cover story about them for all the people who saw them before they were disposed of: to make sure no one found out about that room!"

Vidor quickly jotted notes into the book, mentally checking them against the incomplete theories he had walked into Hopkins's apartment with. When he looked up from the notebook, Hopkins was watching him over the rim of his wineglass.

"May I ask a question?" Hopkins said.

"Of course."

"Are you really going to tell this whole story?"

"When I know the whole story," Vidor said. "Why?"

"It all happened so long ago, I just wonder why you want to tell it now?"

Vidor put his notebook back into his pocket, preparatory to leaving. "Because it's a good story. And people love to see good stories. Especially true stories. And this is one of the greatest, most scandalous true stories ever to come out of this town, filled with behind-the-scenes dirt and deep, dark secrets that actual, real people tried so hard to hide. Don't you think so?"

"Of course I do," Hopkins said. "That's exactly why I wonder why you want to tell it."

33

Vidor left George Hopkins's apartment feeling he had a new, clear understanding of the Taylor case. What everyone, himself included, had thought for forty-five years to be an unsolvable convolution of mysteries and motives had in fact been a series of insidious fabrications that, while successfully concealing the facts of Taylor's life from the press and the public, also concealed the facts of his death.

What could have happened to cause Woolwine's behavior? This was Vidor's primary concern when he met on May 3 with former district attorney Buron Fitts.

Thad Brown, Bill Cahill, and Ray Cato had all warned

Vidor about Fitts. He was a hard, tough-skinned man, a former combat lieutenant and veteran public administrator with a wooden leg and a die-hard dedication to his work. He might not be willing to talk about the Taylor case, Vidor had been told. The case was still open, and could very well be a thorn in Fitts's side; he had once been about to make an announcement concerning it but, after an assassination attempt against him, had changed his mind. He had remained silent about the case since. But he had at least agreed to meet with Vidor, so Vidor was hopeful.

Vidor arrived at the Bel Air Country Club a little before noon. He sat at his favorite table, looking out on the seventeenth green and, through the trees beyond the green, toward his own home. Minutes later, the maitre d' showed Fitts to the table. Vidor stood and shook his hand.

"So you know who killed William Desmond Taylor," Fitts said as he sat down.

Vidor was slightly taken aback; he hadn't expected Fitts to get right to the point like that.

"I have an idea," he said.

"Oh," said Fitts. "An idea. Well, I hope you don't take this as an insult, but everybody's got ideas who killed Taylor. I've been hearing ideas for thirty years. What I'd like to hear is some good hard evidence."

A waiter stepped to the table to take their orders. Vidor ordered trout, Fitts sirloin steak, "blood red." As the waiter walked away, Fitts continued.

"You see, Mr. Vidor, I've heard every theory imaginable about Taylor, and they all amount to the same thing: nothing without evidence. From our telephone conversation I got the impression you might know something more . . . substantial."

"Well, I know Edward Sands didn't do it," Vidor said, deciding to reveal his hand and see how "substantial" Fitts found it. "And I know Thomas Woolwine knew Sands didn't do it, although Woolwine kept insisting he was looking for Sands even after he knew for a fact that Sands was dead."

Vidor could tell by Fitts's facial expression that the man was surprised by Vidor's knowledge.

"And I also know, as did Mr. Woolwine, that not only did Mabel Normand not kill Taylor, but she wasn't at the bungalow the morning after, as all those newspaper reports that put an abrupt end to her career said she was. She was no more guilty than, say, the mysterious doctor who showed up the next morning, who, by the way, I know never even existed. Does any of this strike you as the least bit . . . substantial?"

Fitts hesitated as the waiter served their drinks, then said, "I assume there's more?"

"Plenty," Vidor said. "I know that all the evidence found in Taylor's bungalow, evidence Woolwine said he hoped would lead to Taylor's killer, either never even existed, or was planted in the bungalow not to lead anywhere, except to the conclusion that Taylor was having affairs with Normand and Mary Miles Minter, and other women you might care to name. And I know that Woolwine, while paying public lip service to all this evidence, also knew it was bogus. Taylor wasn't sleeping with Normand or Minter or any other woman you might care to name. Young boys were more to his taste, a fact, too, that Woolwine was well aware of."

Vidor sipped his drink. Fitts, pouring his martini over the rocks, said, "This is very interesting, Mr. Vidor, your attributing so much knowledge to one of my predecessors, a man I don't believe you ever met yourself, did you?"

"No, I didn't," Vidor said.

"I see. Well, what else did Mr. Woolwine know?"

Vidor decided this was it. "He knew that neither Mary Miles Minter nor her mother, Charlotte Shelby, had alibis for the night Taylor was killed. He knew that Minter was in love with Taylor, and that Shelby had threatened Taylor unless he left Mary alone. He knew that Taylor, even though he did leave Mary alone sexually, went out of his way to help the girl, who—God knew, as well as Mr. Woolwine—needed help, with her crazy, jealous mother haunting her like a living nightmare.

"He knew Shelby didn't believe for a second that Taylor's attentions to Mary could be anything but lustful, a situation that doubly angered her because she was attracted to Taylor herself and could think of no other reason for Taylor to have snubbed her advances than that he was already having an affair with her daughter."

Vidor realized this last statement was still conjecture, but it made sense to him, and he voiced it to see if it sparked any different reaction from Fitts than anything else he was saying. Fitts's expression remained fixed, fascinated.

"Woolwine knew," Vidor continued, "that Shelby, though she claimed the whole family had been at home together all night, was actively looking for Minter the evening Taylor was shot. And Shelby certainly knew enough to look for her at Taylor's, because Mary had told her that she was going to marry Taylor. It wasn't true, of course, just something Mary said in retaliation for Shelby's ordering her never to see Taylor again. But Shelby didn't know this; as far as she knew, Taylor was actually going to take her daughter away from her. Or should I say her meal ticket? And Woolwine must have known how this would make Shelby feel—the man she'd told her friends was in love with her turning around and marrying her daughter."

"Must have known?" Fitts said, his trained prosecutor's ear picking up the speculation in Vidor's speech.

Vidor conceded the point by tipping his glass.

"I guess I'm attributing intelligence as well as knowledge to your predecessor," he said. "Either way, Woolwine knew of Shelby's, shall we say, ambivalence toward Taylor, calling him a class-A gentleman on the one hand while threatening his life on the other. And he also knew that Shelby owned a gun, and knew how to use it, as well as the fact, substantiated by her own secretary, that she had had the gun with her and had sworn her intentions to use it one night when she stormed Taylor's place only to find Minter not there.

"So you see, Woolwine knew there was both motive and opportunity for Shelby to have killed Taylor. When she couldn't find her daughter that night, she started making calls. She called Marjorie Berger, Minter—and Taylor's—accountant. Minter wasn't there. So later, after Shelby stopped at Berger's place, still looking, Berger knew she was on a rampage. So Berger called Taylor to warn him. And she called Marshall Neilan to tell him what was going on, which was why he later asked Minter if she knew about the murder.

"Then Shelby went to Taylor's place, but instead of Minter, she found Mabel Normand there, and thought Taylor was sleeping with Normand as well as Minter. So Shelby hid behind the bungalow until Normand left, at which time Minter came downstairs from where she'd been hiding in Taylor's bedroom. That's why Taylor's door was open when Normand arrived: Minter had just arrived also, and didn't want Normand to find her there.

"So when Shelby saw Minter come down the stairs, all her suspicions were confirmed. She had caught Taylor and

Minter together. So she walked inside and made good on her threat to kill Taylor if he didn't leave Minter alone."

Vidor stopped. Fitts said, "And you say District Attorney Woolwine knew all this?"

"He knew all the evidence that supports it," Vidor said.

"How do you know this?" Fitts asked.

Vidor was prepared for the question. He answered it indirectly, covering his tracks like Cahill and Cato.

"The same way I know that he pulled Ray Cato off the job when he started closing in on what was really going on. The same way I know there never were any pornographic pictures. The same way I know Woolwine had in his possession three hairs taken off the jacket Taylor was killed in, hairs Woolwine knew came from Mary Miles Minter's head. Should I go on?"

Fitts shook his head. "I get it," he said. "You've been talking with Sanderson."

Vidor hoped his face didn't reflect his absolute wonder at Fitts's casual statement. He decided immediately, though, that if everything he'd just said to Fitts made Fitts think of Sanderson, then Sanderson would be the next person he would try to talk with.

"I've talked with lots of people," Vidor said, still covering his tracks. "But there's one question no one's been able to answer for me, and I thought you, having been district attorney working on this case yourself, might be able to help."

"What's the question?" Fitts asked.

"Just this. Woolwine had the goods on Shelby and Minter. But he didn't indict them. He barely even questioned them. I want to know why."

Fitts signaled a passing waiter for another martini.

"What makes you think I can answer that question?

You're the one who seems to know so much about Wool-wine."

"Yes," Vidor said. "But you're the one who took over his job, who put his immediate successor Asa Keyes behind bars, the district attorney who raised the office's conviction rate to eighty-two percent, and you're also the man who once claimed to have new developments in the Taylor investigation but never mentioned them again after being ambushed one night in your driveway."

Fitts looked away, and Vidor knew he had hit a nerve.

"What were those developments?" Vidor asked. "What's the one missing link in my story? Were Shelby and Minter innocent? Did someone come forward with new evidence that I don't know about? Why has this case remained unsolved after all these years despite all these apparently uninvestigated loose ends?"

Fitts continued looking past Vidor into the dining room, as if looking anxiously for the waiter to bring their food.

"As I told you at the beginning, Mr. Vidor, I have heard a lot of theories concerning this case. And yours is certainly interesting. No doubt it would make a wonderful movie. But as I also said at the beginning, theories are worthless. Only proof has any value."

"Absolutely," said Vidor. "And that is exactly what I'm asking if you can provide me with. You must know something that would help me. I don't imagine you were gunned down for nothing."

"All I can say is what I've already said. You give me proof," Fitts said, "and I'll see that it is dealt with accordingly. But I can't give you anything. As long as this case is on the books, I am sworn to reveal nothing about it to anyone. I'm sorry."

Fitts sat back as lunch arrived. His exaggerated attention to the waiter told Vidor he had said all he intended to say. But as far as Vidor was concerned, the interview had been successful. Fitts might have been sworn not to give out information on open police cases, but he had given Vidor a name, Sanderson. Vidor didn't know how much Sanderson knew about the case, but he apparently knew as much as Vidor. But whether he would talk was one question; and what Vidor would tell him was another.

Vidor picked up his knife and fork. While cutting the head off his pan-fried trout, he looked out the window just as his wife Betty stepped onto the seventeenth green, putter glistening in the sun. He watched her line up a long putt as her partner, with whom she played regularly, manned the flagpole. Vidor watched her putt but turned away without seeing whether she had sunk it or not. William Desmond Taylor aside, he had a lot of thinking to do.

34

A month had passed since Vidor had moved into the office. Most of his clothes and necessary belongings were there, crammed into what little storage space yet another rearranging session had created, though he still had to make the occasional walk up the driveway for things, usually when Betty was out. Thelma Carr had accepted the arrangement without comment, but Vidor still felt uncomfortable about displaying personal habits and items in the office. He rose, showered, dressed, and concealed the evidence of his full-time occupancy of the office before she arrived each morning, and conducted business as though things were as they had always been.

This morning, two days after his lunch with Buron Fitts, Vidor sat on the back porch of the guest house and watched as Betty walked her new Toby from the backyard and loaded her into her white Lincoln Continental. He knew she was taking the dog to the Hollywood Dog Training School; Betty had slipped the bill through the mail chute of the office just before Vidor had stepped outside. She got into the car and drove slowly down the driveway, her twenty-year habit of waving to Vidor as she passed his office already broken. Colleen Moore was due in town in just a few days, and Vidor knew he had to do something quickly about the wall of silence that had sprung up between himself and Betty. They hadn't spoken since she had told him to move out, and yet, though he still had the letter he'd written to her in the top drawer of his desk, he couldn't bring himself to give it to her. He would have to face her soon; he didn't want Colleen to arrive and find him still indecisive.

As Betty's car disappeared between the pines down La Altura Drive, Thelma Carr's voice rose from inside the office. "I've got Leroy Sanderson on the line."

Vidor stepped inside. He shut the door between his office and Carr's and sat at his desk. "Mr. Sanderson?" he said into the phone. "This is King Vidor calling from Los Angeles."

"Ah, Mr. Vidor," Sanderson's voice said with an almost "Aha!" tone of discovery. "The man making the movie about William Desmond Taylor. Thad Brown said he gave you my number."

"Yes, he did. I was wondering if I might take a few minutes of your time, ask you a few questions about the case."

"Of course, though I'm not sure I could be of any

great help. From what Brown told me I'd say you're already one of the experts on it."

"I have been doing a lot of research," Vidor said. "And a couple of days ago, Buron Fitts mentioned your name, and I thought I'd give you a call."

"You talked to Fitts, huh?"

Vidor could detect a note of distaste in Sanderson's pronouncement of the name Fitts.

"I'm sure if Fitts mentioned my name it wasn't complimentary."

"You two don't get along?" Vidor asked.

"You could say that. What did Fitts say about me?"

"Nothing. He just mentioned your name, led me to believe you might be able to help with my research."

"Well, I'd be more than happy to talk with you, Mr. Vidor, and help in any way I can, though I can't imagine why Fitts would mention my name in relation to the Taylor case. Fitts personally took me off that case."

"Why did he take you off the case?"

"He didn't like the direction my investigation was taking."

Another vague, evasive answer from another former law-enforcement officer, Vidor thought. Their training must never wear off.

"Did that direction," Vidor said, "lead you to whatever it was Fitts had been planning to announce before the attempt was made on his life?"

"What do you mean, 'planning to announce'?" Sanderson said.

"Fitts was going to make an announcement about the case, but changed his mind after being ambushed by gunmen in his driveway."

"No," Sanderson said with conviction. "Fitts wasn't

going to make any announcement. Or if he was, I never heard anything about it, and to tell you the truth I can't imagine what it would have been. When he took me off the case, it was because he knew I was looking into some, let's say, odd things that seemed to have been going on in the D.A.'s office. Not just Fitts's own office necessarily, but back in the Keyes administration, and the Woolwine. And to my knowledge, which I trust more than anything that ever crossed Buron Fitts's lips, no one else was actively pursuing any other avenues of investigation in relation to the case. So the only announcement he could have made was either that nothing new had turned up in umpteen years, or that he had decided to stop me from what I was doing before I got a little too close to home. Besides, announcement or not, Fitts's getting shot didn't have anything to do with the Taylor case. He was shot by a bunch of angry union members for a riot he and some of his henchmen had become involved in."

"Are you sure about that?" Vidor asked.

"Look it up," Sanderson said. "It's a matter of public record. Fitts had his own private army of union busters and anticommunists he ran during the Red scare. That's what the union members were aimed at stopping."

This altered Vidor's thinking about Fitts. Perhaps Fitts hadn't been merely covering his tracks during their one-sided conversation but had been trying to lead Vidor astray, as though he were hiding something other than merely classified information.

"What sort of odd things seemed to have been going on in the D.A.'s office?" Vidor asked, adding before Sanderson could answer, "Did they have to do with Charlotte Shelby and Mary Miles Minter?"

"That was quite a family, wasn't it?" Sanderson said. "Always taking each other to court and everything. I've never known a family that loved to sue everybody so much. If it wasn't their accountant, it was each other."

"They sued Marjorie Berger?" Vidor asked. This was the first he had heard of this.

"No, Charlotte's Shelby's accountant, Les Henry. Marjorie Berger was Minter's accountant. Shelby said Henry was misappropriating funds. But even that one wasn't as crazy as when they started suing each other."

"What did they sue each other over?"

"Oh, this and that," Sanderson said. "It's all on the public record, too. I thought you were interested in Taylor."

"I am interested in Taylor," Vidor said. "When I asked you if what was going on in the D.A.'s office concerned Shelby and Minter, what I really wanted to know was whether you discovered the reason Woolwine didn't indict them. And whether that might be the reason Fitts took you off the case, because you found out something that would reflect badly on the D.A.'s office."

"Why Woolwine didn't indict Shelby and Minter," Sanderson said very slowly, as though thinking it out as he spoke.

"Right," Vidor said. "It couldn't have been just because Woolwine and Shelby were friends. The evidence he had against her and Minter, circumstantial though it might have been, wasn't exactly something he could just sweep under the table. It was in the police records, and should have at least been investigated. But as far as I've been able to learn, it wasn't. So something must have happened. And I was hoping that that might have been what Fitts's announcement might have been about: that Woolwine had discovered something new, or that some surprise witness had appeared with testimony that blew the evidence against Shelby and Minter right out of the water. And I was hoping that maybe that was what you found out that inspired Fitts to take you off the case. Something that would allow Woolwine to ignore damn good evidence, and something that, for whatever reasons, has eluded investigators since. Do you know what that thing is?"

"Well, someone did come forward," Sanderson said.

Vidor held his breath. For a brief moment he thought he had reached his journey's end.

"Who was it?" he said.

He waited as patiently as he could for Sanderson to respond. It wasn't easy. Finally Sanderson said, "I have no proof, Mr. Vidor."

"You have more than I do."

"Not really."

"You have a name," Vidor said, his patience slipping away. "And you must know what this person came forward with!"

"But it means nothing without proof, Mr. Vidor. You know that. If you didn't know it you wouldn't be talking with me. You know more than enough to make a movie about this case already, and I believe you'd get the story just about right, too. But I don't make movies. My job was to solve crimes, and for that, it isn't good enough to get the story just about right. You have to hit it square on the nose."

"Wait a minute," Vidor said. "You said I'd got it just about right. Are you saying that Shelby and Minter are guilty? What about this person that came forward?"

"I just said this person came forward, not, you'll remember, that this person saved Shelby and Minter."

"This person didn't save Shelby and Minter," Vidor said, as if repeating it might help him understand its meaning. "That doesn't make sense, Sanderson. If this person had such strong evidence, how can you say it didn't save them? They were exonerated. Now why was that?"

Vidor stood up from his desk and walked nervously around it, as far as the telephone cord would allow.

Sanderson said calmly, "This person's evidence was indeed strong, Mr. Vidor. If anyone had such evidence right now, this case could be closed forever. No one does. But I believe it's out there, and if anyone can find it, you're the one. I have a phone call to make right now, business to attend to, but keep in touch. Bring me that proof, and we'll give Fitts a little prize for mentioning my name."

Sanderson hung up. Vidor thought of calling him back immediately, but decided against it. Sanderson was obviously not going to tell him who it was that came forward with new evidence. But two things Sanderson did tell him stuck in his mind: that Vidor had the story of the murder "just about right" and that the evidence that Woolwine discovered was out there for Vidor to find.

Vidor tore a page from his pocket notebook. With a ballpoint pen he printed the word FACTS boldly inside the left-hand margin. Beside it he filled in the "facts" he had concerning Woolwine's treatment of Shelby and Minter:

1. Evidence against Shelby and Minter.
2. Someone comes forward with new evidence.
3. New evidence supersedes old evidence, yet—
4. New evidence does not save Shelby and Minter.
5. Shelby and Minter never indicted.

This sequence did not make sense to Vidor. One fact did not stem logically from the preceding one. How could new evidence supplant the old evidence and not save Shelby and Minter from indictment? The only explanation Vidor could think of was that the new evidence, rather than clearing Shelby and Minter from suspicion, nailed them, proved once and for all that they killed Taylor. Evidence such as that would certainly take precedence over the circumstantial evidence Woolwine already had. But the fact remained that Shelby and Minter were exonerated. So that theory didn't work either.

Vidor tried looking at these five facts from every possible angle, and in every possible order. Any four of the five could be fit into a logical sequence, but the five together made no sense at all. Vidor had convinced himself some time ago that two separate and distinct series of activities had been going on after Taylor was murdered, one involving the studio, and the other involving Woolwine's investigation. But he had not considered that the latter might have been just as underhanded and self-centered as the former. Now he felt that that must have been the case: Woolwine hadn't prosecuted because, for whatever reasons, he didn't want to prosecute. And in covering his own tracks, Woolwine had seen to it that nothing reached the police files that might incriminate him. No wonder there were holes in the files. No wonder the evidence that had originally existed—nightgown, hairs—had disappeared through the years. No wonder no one after Woolwine had ever been able to crack the case. And no wonder Sanderson had been taken off the case—he found out exactly what Vidor had: that the true villains of this story were not only whoever pulled the trigger that killed William Desmond Taylor, but also the studio that distorted facts in an effort to hide Taylor's big "secret," and the district attorney, who ignored evidence, hid evidence, probably destroyed evidence, so that the killer would go free.

Vidor's next step was to check into all those lawsuits. That would be easy enough to do, and they might reveal something that would give him clearer understanding of what the Shelbys were like. Adela Rogers St. Johns might have been right when she had summed it up, using Minter's initials: Millions, Murder, Misery. Charlotte Shelby loved her Millions above everything else, and committed Murder when she feared that Taylor was a threat to them, sending Mary into Misery.

35

South Hill Street was jammed. Construction and the lunch-hour rush had traffic stalled for blocks in either direction. Near the corner of Sixth Street, Vidor got out of the car. He walked to the Sugarman Building and waited in the lobby while Dick Marchman found a place to park. The Sugarman Building was one of many buildings in the downtown neighborhood that housed various offices of the Los Angeles County government. On the third floor were the county archives, where the records were kept of all lawsuits filed with the Los Angeles County Courthouse. When Dick Marchman walked in, Vidor pressed an elevator button and watched the clockhand floor indicator start its descent.

In the archives all criminal and civil suits were indexed by dates and the names of the principal parties involved. Vidor pulled two volumes, starting with 1922, from the shelf and handed one to Marchman.

"Remember," he said, "everything will be listed under their legal names—not Charlotte Shelby and Mary Miles Minter, but Lily Pearl Miles and Juliet Reilly."

Within minutes, they had found page after page of case numbers, all cross-referenced so many times they could have filled an entire ledger themselves. Between 1922 and 1943, Lily Pearl Miles and Juliet Reilly appeared in court nearly 150 times, with seven separate ongoing lawsuits and over a dozen various court injunctions. The first suit began only three months after the Taylor murder, with Mary suing her mother for money she said Charlotte owed her, and the final one over twenty years later, with Charlotte suing the estate of her recently deceased daughter Margaret. Each case in between also concerned claims against family members and their accountants over disputed amounts of money. Marchman and Vidor had not anticipated such voluminous files concerning one family's legal problems. What they had thought would be an easy afternoon's read became a two-day delve into twisted tales of Millions and Misery that to their surprise also shed light —to those who could recognize its illumination—on the other M, Murder.

The case of *Lily Pearl Miles vs. Les Henry* and the brokerage firm of Blythe Whitter began in 1931 and was settled two years later. Charlotte Shelby sued for $750,000— claiming her accountant, Les Henry, had stolen the amount from family accounts between 1918 and 1931.

Henry was convicted of falsifying the Shelby books and making improper financial transactions—but not of stealing the three quarters of a million dollars.

The case began when Shelby received a statement from the Internal Revenue Service demanding she pay $198,000 in taxes owed from a figure of $750,000 that Shelby had failed to claim as income. Shelby denied any knowledge of the $750,000 and accused Les Henry of stealing the money from her and her daughters.

Called to the floor by Blythe Whitter executives, Les Henry admitted to having made improper transactions with Shelby's money. But, he said, everything he had done had been done with Shelby's knowledge and consent. On a regular basis beginning in 1922, he had transferred sums from Minter's account into negotiable bonds and stock certificates that he had then given, minus his own fee, to Shelby. Asked for records of the transactions, he said that Shelby had insisted there be nothing in writing.

Henry could not understand why Charlotte Shelby, with whom he had long done mutually profitable business, would turn on him like this. But he knew he looked bad. That night before leaving the office, he left a suicide note on his secretary's desk.

The next morning, the secretary discovered the note and phoned Shelby to tell her about it. "Serves him right," Shelby said. An hour later, when Henry, having changed his mind, arrived for work, the secretary called Shelby again. Shelby said, "I had a lot of respect for him when I thought he was going to make good on my losses by killing himself, but I have no respect for him now."

At noon Henry called Shelby himself, to tell her he would fight her in this matter. Shelby calmly gave him "until two to go through with the letter" or she would "lay the cards on the table."

But when they met in court, it was Henry who dealt the decisive hand; his plan of defense was to prove that he and Shelby had worked hand in hand with the Shelby family monies, manipulating them in Shelby's favor since the day in 1918 when Henry had replaced Marjorie Berger as Shelby's personal accountant. In establishing proof, Henry revealed that he had been personally involved with Shelby —intimate both professionally and physically—from the beginning. He testified that he had witnessed Shelby's relationship with Minter grow strained in the Flying A Studio days in Santa Barbara, grow physically and emotionally violent at Paramount, and finally disintegrate entirely following the murder of William Desmond Taylor.

He claimed that Shelby had once put a sudden stop to an affair Minter was having with James Kirkwood, and that Minter's 1921 suicide attempt had been spurred by an argument with Shelby over Taylor. Both stories were corroborated by subsequent witnesses.

The Taylor murder, Henry said, caused a complete separation between the mother and daughter, with Minter moving to New York. Minter's only correspondence with Shelby from New York was a series of letters begging for some of the money she had earned and entrusted to Shelby for investment. Shelby refused every request.

Then, based on a complete disclosure of all his own personal financial records, Henry showed that the amount of money Shelby was accusing him of stealing had never found its way into his possession. He admitted that he had taken money from Minter's accounts without Minter's knowledge, but said that the money had been transferred to Shelby and to others upon Shelby's orders.

Did he know what Shelby was doing with the money? he was asked.

Henry answered that Shelby was using the money to

buy protection from the police and the press during the Taylor murder investigation. Whenever there was a flare-up in the investigation, he said, Shelby asked for more money.

One specific incident he related was a conversation in 1923 when Shelby asked him to transfer an unusually large amount of money into negotiable bonds because the new district attorney, Asa Keyes, would require "a great deal more money than Woolwine" had.

On another occasion, in 1926, Shelby had asked him to transfer more money because she "feared indictment" in the Taylor case. Shortly after the transfer, Shelby had gone to Europe, where she remained until the Keyes investigation subsided.

Each time Henry offered to submit hard evidence supporting these claims, Shelby's lawyers blocked him, claiming it was Henry who was on trial, not Shelby.

Henry did, however, manage to introduce into evidence certain items that gave his stories credence. A large flowchart of Shelby family finances showed particular activity—withdrawals, transferrals—occurring at times that corresponded directly with documented flare-ups in the Taylor investigation. Letters written to Henry by Shelby and Margaret made cryptic references to "a secret" that the family and he had to guard; other letters, written from Europe during the Asa Keyes investigation, asked equally cryptically whether it was yet "safe to return home."

Henry also submitted documentation of monthly two-hundred-dollar payments Shelby had been making since 1922 to a man named Carl Stockdale—one of the two men who had provided Shelby's alibi for the night of the Taylor murder.

By now Vidor felt he knew where Shelby's $750,000 had gone. She had bought herself freedom from prosecution with it. That was why Woolwine had never indicted her. And Asa Keyes, as well. They were being paid off. Though no conclusive evidence of this was presented in the trial—because the trial was not concerned with anything other than Les Henry's handling of Charlotte Shelby's finances—Henry's testimony answered perfectly the third of Vidor's three questions: why Shelby had not been indicted.

Further proof was contained in the transcripts of *Reilly vs. Miles,* in which Minter attempted to secure the money she had earned at Flying A and Paramount studios.

After the termination of her Paramount contract in 1923, Mary Miles Minter moved to New York, where she lived on West Fifty-sixth Street until 1926. During this time, she repeatedly wrote to Shelby demanding she send money. Shelby refused, claiming Mary's money was tied up in complex tax shelters and real estate development deals that couldn't be tampered with. Finally, Minter turned the matter over to a lawyer. A court hearing resulted in Minter and Shelby slinging accusations at each other, blaming each other for an unnamed "tragedy" that had predicated their estrangement.

Minter estimated the value of her estate at $1,345,000, less the thirty percent due to her mother for handling the finances. Shelby did not dispute the sum, simply her ability to turn it into ready cash.

The judge who heard the trial was about to hand down his decision when Minter and Shelby announced that they had reached a settlement out of court. Mary had agreed to take $25,000, to be delivered a year later. The judge, surprised by what he considered a ridiculously unfair settlement, asked both parties to explain how it was reached. Minter said simply that she and her mother had reached an understanding that she was "incompetent to handle larger sums" and that were she to persist in her legal actions against Shelby, she would "disrupt her mother's plans."

Shelby merely repeated what she had said all along, that Minter's money was being carefully tended to until Minter herself was responsible enough to assume control.

Vidor found Minter's acceptance of the settlement just as unreasonable as the judge did. There must have been considerations other than the money, he thought, that led her to it. Could Minter's reason have been that Shelby had explained to her that the money she had tried to sue for was the only thing that had kept them out of prison since Taylor was killed? It seemed to Vidor not only possible but quite likely. Charlotte, with her love of her Millions, was certainly not one to use her own money if she could get away with using Mary's.

In another case, *Miles vs. Minter*, Shelby and her Louisiana relatives fought over the estate of Julia Miles, Mary Miles Minter's grandmother. Julia had died at Casa de Margarita in 1925, leaving behind the family plantation in Shreveport. Shelby immediately set into motion a plan to sell the plantation, though her sister's family was still living there. When her sister's family found out what was going on, they took Shelby to court. They easily won control of the plantation, but the trial served to reveal that, along with denying Mary Miles Minter her own money, Charlotte Shelby had seen to it for years that Minter had no contact whatsoever with her grandmother, who had always been partial to little Juliet. Minter and her grandmother had regularly written letters to each other, and Charlotte had intercepted every one of them, jealous apparently of Minter's receiving attention even from her grandmother. Marjorie Berger found out about this situation and wrote to Minter about it, but not until Julia Miles lay on her deathbed. Upon learning of her mother's cruel and inexplicable deception, Minter immediately left for Los Angeles to see her ailing grandmother. Eddie Rickenbacker, famed World War I flying ace, donated his plane and services. Minter arrived three hours after Julia Miles had died.

Charlotte Shelby was clearly as ruthless and heartless a human being as Vidor had ever encountered. Furthermore, this story provided Vidor further evidence that Shelby had killed William Desmond Taylor. In the letters that Marjorie Berger wrote to Mary Miles Minter in New York, she mentioned a couple of people who were living at Casa de Margarita with Shelby. Vidor knew the names well: Carl Stockdale and Jim Smith—Shelby's two alibi providers for the night of the murder. Vidor had just learned that Stockdale was receiving monthly payments from Shelby; now he learned that Jim Smith, who had always been identified in the press and the police files as Shelby's night watchman, was also an employee of District Attorney Woolwine. And they were both living under the same roof as Charlotte Shelby.

Remaining doubts about Shelby's guilt disappeared when Dick Marchman handed him the file of a 1937 civil case, *Fillmore vs. Shelby*. Fillmore was daughter Margaret, who had married in 1926, and who sued her mother for $48,000 and a home in Laguna Beach that she claimed her mother owed her for services Margaret had provided in 1921, 1923, and 1926. Asked before a jury what those services had been, Margaret said she had provided false testimony during the William Desmond Taylor murder investigation, and had further protected her mother from suspicion by aiding her in private conferences with D.A. Woolwine, and by acting as a barrier between her and the press.

The judge, aghast at this testimony, awarded the settlement to Margaret, and ordered her to appear before

District Attorney Buron Fitts along with the transcript of her testimony, and to answer any further questions Fitts might have about Shelby and the Taylor murder.

The reasons Margaret had decided to make public this information now seemed to be rooted in trouble that had begun between her and Shelby in 1926, when Margaret met Hugh Fillmore, the grandson of U.S. president Millard Fillmore. After a whirlwind secret courtship, Fillmore had proposed to her. Charlotte opposed the marriage, saying that Margaret, who was then twenty-seven, was not prepared for such a step. But before Charlotte could do anything to stop it, she suddenly decided to go to Europe (for reasons Les Henry made clear in his own trial in 1931).

Charlotte sold Casa de Margarita before she left, taking all the family's fortune with her. Margaret, completely cut off from Charlotte financially, married Fillmore.

A year later, they were divorced. Margaret wired Charlotte for funds, then sailed to Europe to join her. When they returned in 1929, they went into business together, developing real estate in Los Angeles and Culver City. The business failed. Charlotte blamed Margaret but, caught up in her suit against Les Henry at the time, took no legal action against her. They seemed to be getting along fairly well.

Then in 1937, Margaret fell in love again, with film director Emmett J. Flynn. Again, Shelby opposed her daughter's romance. But despite her protests, Margaret and Flynn eloped to Yuma, Arizona. Shelby went after them. Days later, Shelby and Margaret returned with Margaret's marriage annulled.

Immediately after arriving back in Los Angeles, Shelby had Margaret confined to the psychopathic ward of a mental hospital.

Mary Miles Minter found out about this and after a

month-long effort managed to have her sister released. A team of doctors from the hospital examined Margaret and announced her perfectly sane, declaring that Charlotte's confining her there had been unnecessary and cruel.

It was shortly after her release that Margaret took Shelby to court and openly accused her of murdering William Desmond Taylor.

Why Shelby had Margaret committed was not in the records, but Vidor suspected it had been to keep Margaret quiet. Another thing not mentioned in the file for *Fillmore vs. Shelby,* but that Vidor had learned for himself earlier, was what later became of Margaret's second husband.

In 1937, at the age of forty-four, not long after his marriage to Margaret, director Emmett J. Flynn was found dead in his Hollywood apartment, rumored by some to have been killed by a blow to the back of the head. His murderer was never found.

Vidor set the file on the table, stunned. Had he just discovered a second murder committed by Charlotte Shelby fifteen years after she killed Taylor? The similarities between the two crimes were frightening: two Hollywood directors, roughly the same age, killed under mysterious circumstances after being involved with a daughter of Charlotte Shelby's.

Relieved as he was to have finally answered all three of his big questions, Vidor still felt confounded by a brand new question that presented itself.

With a fully detailed account of Charlotte Shelby's guilt in the murder and subsequent cover-up, why hadn't District Attorney Buron Fitts closed this case once and for all? Could Shelby have gotten to him, too? Was that overbearing, amoral, money-grubbing murderess powerful enough to buy yet a third Los Angeles District Attorney all those years after the crime she was, in her own diabolical way, paying for?

Vidor suspected he already knew the answer, and feared that when he found out for sure, yet another obstacle would present itself. Was Vidor willing to lock horns with Buron Fitts? Vidor had to know the truth.

And before he and Dick Marchman even reached the car, three blocks away, he had decided where he was going to look.

ix dollars?"

Vidor shoved the parking ticket into the pocket of his blazer. Colleen Moore's flight from Chicago, on June 16, 1967, had arrived five minutes late, just long enough for the time to run out on Vidor's parking meter.

"How do they give out tickets so quickly?" he asked. "Does an alarm go off when your time runs out or something?"

"At least they didn't tow the car away," Colleen said as Vidor opened the passenger door for her.

They pulled out onto Century Boulevard, then headed north on the brand-new 405 freeway.

"So, are you going to tell me now?" Colleen asked. "What's this big realization you mentioned in your telegram?"

Vidor checked the rear-view mirror for Highway Patrol, then eased the T-Bird smoothly above the 70 mph speed limit. He said, "I'm not sure the Taylor murder is the story we should tell."

Eyes on the road, Vidor could feel Colleen looking at him.

"Why not? New snags in the investigation?"

"No," he said. "I know who did it."

"Who?"

"Just who I suspected. Only the story's a lot more involved than that. The deeper I get into it the more sordid the whole thing is."

"I should think that would make the story all the more interesting."

"Oh, it's interesting," Vidor said. "But the story we should be telling is the Charlotte Shelby story, or Lily Pearl Miles story. Bill Taylor getting killed is only a part of it. A small part."

Vidor then spelled out the principal turns in the story: Shelby's early ambitions for herself and her daughters, her abandonment and subsequent reclaiming of them. He told Colleen of Shelby's preference for Margaret over Mary, and her domination over both of them. He outlined Shelby's growth as the prototypical stage mother, living off of Mary's earnings and attacking anything that seemed even remotely threatening to her parasitic existence—the most shocking examples being the mysterious deaths of Taylor and of Emmett J. Flynn. Vidor listed Shelby's cruelties to her daughters—bleeding them financially; starving them emotionally; refusing them private lives; undermining Minter's loving relationship with her grandmother; committing Margaret to a mental ward; and her attempts to make others—accountants, chauffeurs—appear culpable for her own deeds. And he listed the accomplices to her wickedness that she had bought over the years with her daughter's money: Thomas Woolwine, Jim Smith, Carl Stockdale, Asa Keyes, and, quite possibly, Buron Fitts.

"It's Fitts I want to find out about today," he said.

"And you think this detective will be able to tell you?" Colleen said.

"I hope so."

Vidor pulled off the freeway in Oxnard, some fifty miles north of Los Angeles. He followed the detailed directions he had written in his pocket notebook, through large strawberry and celery fields to a quiet shaded street where he parked in front of a newly built white frame house. Two Doberman pinschers surveyed the car without barking from behind a chain-link fence.

Vidor let himself out, then opened Colleen's door. They stepped to the gate in the fence. From the house a voice said, "They won't bite."

A man stood in the shadowed door frame. He called a single command to the Dobermans, who happily backed away. Vidor opened the gate, and he and Colleen walked toward the house.

The man in the door frame stepped onto the porch. He was a big man dressed in coarse chinos and a lumberjack's flannel shirt, the sleeves cut well above the elbow. Vidor looked at him, then stopped in his tracks. On the man's thick left arm was a familiar tattoo.

"You're the man I met the day they tore down Taylor's bungalow," Vidor said.

The tattooed man was just as surprised to see Vidor.

"And you're the man with the doorknob," he said. He stepped off the porch to greet his visitors. "It's nice to finally meet you, Mr. Vidor. I'm Leroy Sanderson."

"Call me King," Vidor said as they shook hands. He introduced Colleen, then marveled with Sanderson at all that had happened since the day they had made strangers' small talk over the rubble of Taylor's bungalow.

"I could have saved myself five months' work," Vidor said with a laugh, "if I'd known who you were that day."

"I wondered who you were that day," Sanderson said, leading them inside. "You didn't look like just a souvenir hunter."

Sanderson's wife, Rosalie, had prepared a cold-fried-chicken lunch for them. They sat at the kitchen table, trading stories of Hollywood and criminal investigation. Many of Sanderson's stories covered both topics, involving such names as Jean Harlow and Errol Flynn. The subject of William Desmond Taylor came up only after they had moved to the living room for coffee.

"After I talked with you," Vidor told Sanderson, "I looked into some of the things you said were matters of public record. You were right, the Shelbys were quite a family."

"Yes, they were. Did you find what you were looking for?"

Vidor noticed that both Sanderson and his wife were staring at him, as if equally interested in his answer.

"I found out it was Margaret who spilled the beans that her mother murdered Taylor. But I didn't find out why Buron Fitts didn't go after Shelby."

"And you think I can answer that for you," Sanderson said.

"Well, I thought that might just be what you were

looking into when Fitts took you off the case. Those odd things you said were going on in the D.A.'s office."

Sanderson picked up a humidor from an endtable. He offered his guests a cigar. They passed. He lit one himself, then spoke.

"When Margaret came to us, we didn't know what to think at first. But she had so many details, so many little facts that fit so perfectly with what other people—the chauffeur, the secretary, others—had told us, that we had to believe she was telling us the truth. Even though some of it was pretty fantastic. Do you know, for example, about Minter and Kirkwood?"

"Jimmy Kirkwood?" Colleen Moore said.

Sanderson nodded, puffed his cigar. "He was Mary's first love. She was fifteen, he was thirty-five. One day he took her into the hills outside the Flying A Studios up in Santa Barbara and performed a mock wedding ceremony. He said that that made them officially married in the eyes of God, so there wasn't any reason not to consummate their relationship. Mary got pregnant."

"Pregnant?" Neither Vidor nor Colleen had ever heard even a suggestion of this.

"Did she have the baby?" Colleen asked.

"No. Charlotte figured out what was going on. Mary was gaining weight, feeling sick all the time. Shelby finally intercepted a letter from Kirkwood and figured it out."

"And she threatened Kirkwood," Vidor guessed. "With the pistol."

"That was one of the reasons she bought the pistol. The first of many of her threats. Hell," Sanderson began to laugh, the laugh turning into a cigar-smoke cough, "she even threatened to kill a dog once that sniffed around Mary too much. But after she threatened Kirkwood, she immediately got Mary an abortion and then gathered all of Kirkwood's and Mary's letters together and put them in a safety deposit box."

"To blackmail Kirkwood?" Vidor asked.

"And Mary, whenever Mary started to get out of hand."

Vidor thought of something he had learned from Gloria Swanson and Claire Windsor about James Kirkwood. The Saturday night before Taylor was killed, Kirkwood and Neilan had had a secret conversation with Taylor at the party at the Ambassador Hotel.

"Did Kirkwood know about Minter and Taylor?" he asked.

"Everyone knew about them."

"So," Vidor said, "Kirkwood, knowing all he did about Charlotte Shelby, might have warned Taylor to be careful."

"It's very possible," Sanderson said. "Of course, that's something we may never know for sure. But we do know that Margaret was telling the truth about him and Minter. We checked out Shelby's safety deposit box. Kirkwood's letters were all there. And Mary's. Along with such other interesting items as canceled checks written to Carl Stockdale."

"What did Margaret say about Taylor?" Colleen asked.

"That Minter was in love with him, just as she'd been with Kirkwood. She had to sneak out of the house to see him, and whenever Charlotte found out about it, or even suspected something, she locked Minter in her room. That's why Minter tried to kill herself that time. The day Taylor was killed, Shelby overheard her talking to Taylor on the phone, saying she wanted to run away. Shelby thought she and Taylor were planning to run away together so she locked her up."

"How'd she get out?" Vidor said.

"The grandmother. And as soon as she was out, she hightailed it to Taylor's. She was there, near as we could figure, before Mabel Normand even arrived."

Colleen and Vidor glanced at each other. Vidor had been right about Minter's being in the bungalow during Normand's visit.

"You know another sad thing," Sanderson said, then added to Vidor's dossier on Charlotte Shelby's wickedness. "For the rest of the grandmother's life, Shelby blamed her for Taylor's death. Her own mother! Said if she hadn't let Minter out of her room, it never would have happened."

Vidor helped himself to a coffee refill. "So Shelby went looking for her," he said.

Sanderson continued his story. "She made some phone calls first. Marshall Neilan, Marjorie Berger. Then she went off looking for Mary. Her first stop was Berger's office. Mary wasn't there."

"Then Berger called Taylor," Vidor said. "That's who he was talking to when Mabel Normand arrived."

Sanderson nodded, flicked the ash from his cigar. "Meanwhile, Margaret said her mother went to the basement and came up with her long coat and muffler, and her pistol. Then she took off. An hour later, Minter came home hysterical. She climbed into bed with Margaret and told her what had happened, even though the two sisters rarely even communicated. After Normand left the bungalow, Minter walked down from the bedroom, and Shelby was already there. She had waited back behind the MacLeans' place for Normand to leave."

"That's who their maid heard," Vidor interjected.

"Right. Shelby walked in while Taylor was walking Normand to her car. Chances are she had no idea Minter was even there until she came walking down the stairs. That was all the proof Shelby needed that something was going on between Minter and Taylor. So when Taylor came back, she killed him."

Just at that moment something occurred to Vidor that he had not thought of before. "You know," he said, "this explains the different descriptions eyewitnesses gave of the person they saw leaving the bungalow. The woman dressed as a man that Faith MacLean saw was Shelby in her long coat. And the other neighbor, Hazel Gillon, who said she definitely saw a woman, must have seen Minter. Both their descriptions were right on target; they were just describing two different people."

"I don't remember Hazel Gillon," Sanderson said.

"Adela Rogers St. Johns talked to her. She told me what she said."

"Oh." Sanderson chuckled. "Adela Rogers St. Johns. Her I remember."

"So now that you knew all this, why didn't Buron Fitts go after Shelby? Did she get to him? Was Margaret's testimony not enough? Did they still need some kind of hard evidence?"

"They had hard evidence," Sanderson said. "Along with the check stubs to Stockdale and finding out that Shelby's other alibi, Jim Smith, was one of Woolwine's own men—Margaret showed us shells from Shelby's gun. The very shells the chauffeur unloaded and hid in the basement after Minter's suicide attempt."

"Thirty-eight caliber?" Vidor asked.

"Same size and weight as the bullet that killed Taylor."

"What about the gun?"

Sanderson set his cigar in an ashtray. "Here's where it really gets interesting," he said. "In August of that same year, nineteen twenty-two, the grandmother, Julia Miles, took the gun with her back to Louisiana and threw it into a bayou near her house. Margaret gave us the name and address of neighbors, a doctor and his wife, who would know where she threw it."

"And you found it?" Vidor said, excited.

Sanderson very slowly shook his head. "It was right at the point that I was taken off the case."

"But you said there was hard evidence," Colleen said.

Vidor responded to her. "Fitts found it."

Sanderson's smile congratulated him.

"So Fitts had not only Margaret's testimony, and all the others, but the actual murder weapon."

"That's right," Sanderson said.

Colleen grabbed Vidor's hand. "You were right. Charlotte must have gotten to Fitts, too."

But Vidor could tell by Sanderson's expression that this wasn't the explanation. It took him only seconds to arrive at an alternative.

"If Shelby didn't get to Fitts, maybe Fitts used all the evidence he had to get to Shelby."

Sanderson leaned forward, elbows on his knees. "You see, Mr. Vidor—King—Fitts had worked for Woolwine back in nineteen twenty-two. He knew damn well Shelby killed Taylor, but he kept his mouth shut, probably protecting his job. He did the same thing through the Asa Keyes administration. Then when he became top man himself, he wanted a little action from Shelby's bank accounts like his predecessors had been getting. So he let Shelby know he could put her behind bars, and got himself a little extra income. In exchange, he took care of the evidence for her."

"That's why the police files are so incomplete," Vidor said. "That's what happened to the nightgown and everything. Fitts got rid of anything Woolwine and Keyes hadn't."

"Once and for all," said Sanderson. "That was his deal with Shelby."

Vidor sat back in his chair. Finally, the entire picture was clear to him. Every question had been answered, every mystery solved down to its smallest detail.

"Amazing," he said. "But why didn't you just tell me this when I talked with you the other day?"

"Because I just know the story. Thanks to Buron Fitts, I don't have any proof."

"But you said you thought I could find the proof," Vidor said. "How? What proof?"

"Think about it. The gun's gone. So are the shells, the nightgown, the hairs from Minter's head, the Stockdale check stubs, every piece of hard evidence that ever popped up in this case. All carefully disposed of. What's the only thing that could solve this case once and for all?"

"An eyewitness," Vidor said. "Mary Miles Minter."

"Exactly. She was there. She saw her mother pull the trigger."

"What makes you think she'd tell me about it now, all these years later?" Vidor asked.

"I don't know if she would or not. But she certainly won't tell the police. When Thad Brown found out you were looking into the case, we decided you might be the last chance at ever solving it. You knew Minter. You were part of her world. You knew Taylor, too. We thought maybe, just maybe, she would say something to you. And without her, well, you'd have one hell of a time trying to tell your story. Buron Fitts isn't about to sit still while you destroy his career."

Colleen saw the pained look on the face of her companion. "He's got a point, you know, King."

Vidor nodded grimly.

It was late afternoon when Vidor and Colleen left. Vidor honked the T-Bird's horn at the Sandersons and pulled away. He felt a heavy burden on his shoulders. He would have to confront Mary Miles Minter about what happened on the evening of February 1, 1922.

He drove south on the San Diego Freeway. On the seat beside him, Colleen Moore rode in silence. When they reached Los Angeles, Vidor drove past the Sunset Boulevard exit that led to Beverly Hills. He turned east on the Santa Monica Freeway, heading toward downtown. Still Colleen said nothing. Finally, Vidor exited from the freeway, drove along Wilshire Boulevard for a while, then turned up a steep dark street. He stopped before a vacant lot. He turned off the car.

Colleen looked at the lot, a smooth expanse of fresh asphalt.

"Taylor's bungalow," she said. A sign in one corner promised a supermarket coming soon. "Sure looks different than it did in nineteen twenty-two."

"It is different," Vidor said. "Everything is."

Colleen said nothing. This was the moment each had been waiting for since Colleen's plane had set down. Vidor looked at her.

"Why haven't you said anything about Betty?" he asked.

Colleen took a deep breath. "I didn't think it was necessary. You told me everything I wanted to know when we went straight to the Sandersons' without even stopping to talk. I figured if anything had changed with her, you would have told me right off."

"I didn't know what to say," Vidor said.

"Maybe you just said it all," she said. "It's not nineteen twenty-two any more."

She slid across the seat, closer to Vidor. He held her hand tightly and looked out at the vacant lot, thinking not of everything that happened there on that fateful night forty-five years earlier, but of everything that had happened since.

37

King Vidor slept late. When he awoke, he could hear Thelma Carr already at work in her office. He stood up, stepped around the boxes he had brought from the Hollywood Ranch Market the night before, and started his morning shower. He didn't mind Carr's hearing his personal ritual this morning; after his weeks of living full-time in the office he knew she wouldn't comment on it now.

From the top of the largest market box he took his favorite suit, light nut-brown wool. He topped it off with a John B. Stetson wide-brim hat the suntanned color of a bay pony. "My," Thelma Carr said from her file cabinet as

Vidor stepped into the outer office. "You look nice today."

"So do you," he said, with an admiring glance.

It had been some time since Carr had had to deal with the Vidor leer. It caught her a little off guard. She quickly sat behind her desk.

"What's the occasion?" she asked.

"I have an appointment."

Carr glanced at her appointment book.

"It's not in there," Vidor said. "I made it myself a couple of days ago."

"Oh." Carr didn't ask what the appointment was. She had learned that meetings Vidor arranged himself, such as his meetings the past few months with "producer" Colleen Moore, were meetings she would just as soon know nothing about.

Vidor stepped outside. Nippy looked up at him from his shaded resting spot on the porch. It was a sunny morning, hotter than normal for so early in the summer. As Vidor walked to the T-Bird, Nippy followed.

"No, you're going to have to stay here," Vidor told him. He commanded Nippy back to the porch. He felt his meeting this morning would be awkward enough without having his dog along for the ride. It had been nearly fifty years since he had laid eyes on Mary Miles Minter. Back then, he'd only played a bit role in one of her films. Now, he had to ask her if she'd been a party to the murder of the man she loved.

He drove out of Beverly Hills, west on Sunset. As he cruised through the affluent foothills of Westwood, Bel Air, Brentwood, he couldn't help but think of how they, like everything else, had changed so much in what seemed like such a short time. When he had arrived in Hollywood in 1915, Sunset was a dirt road winding through citrus groves and evergreen canyons, passing through neighboring towns that had since all spread out and melted together into one sprawling city that extended all the way to the sea. Once distinct, autonomous communities were now distinguished only by the road signs bearing their names.

In Santa Monica he turned onto Ocean Avenue, then climbed up Adelaide Drive. He could see the steep sandy cliffs and clean white beaches below him. It was necessary to his project for Vidor to see Mary Miles Minter, but that knowledge did nothing to cease the discomfort he felt as he parked in front of Minter's red-brick house.

He rang the bell. There were no sounds from inside, no sign of life at all. He rang again, then heard something above him. Stepping back from the door, he saw a window opening on the second floor. A face appeared, indistinct behind the window screen.

"Yes?" Mary Miles Minter's voice said. "Is that King Vidor? Is that you, King Vidor? Oh, good, I'll be right down."

Vidor watched the window close again, then stepped back to the door. He found this greeting odd. He had arrived at exactly the time agreed upon. Why had Minter taken so long responding to his ring?

After another full minute, Vidor was about to ring the bell again when he heard footsteps behind the door. A lock sounded. Then another. A chain rattled. Finally the door opened, revealing a woman Vidor did not recognize at all.

"King, my dear boy," she said, unlatching the screen door.

Vidor was stunned. Throughout the past months he had always pictured Minter as he had known her, the beautiful, white-skinned, blonde-haired little Mary. He had expected her to have aged in the past decades, but was not prepared for the obese figure who stood before him now, her thin hair curled into mouse-gray wisps.

"Come in, dear boy," Minter said, pushing open the screen door.

Vidor stepped inside, squinting his eyes to focus in the darkness of the room. The only light in the house filtered through the thick curtains that hid the windows. Walking in from the midday brightness of the oceanside neighborhood was like walking into a summertime movie matinee. Minter grabbed Vidor's hand with short thick fingers and led him into the living room. Antique furniture, mostly from the 1920s, filled the center of the room while the walls were lined with shelves, tables, and an elegant bureau, all stacked with leather-bound books, newspapers, and the knickknacks of a house long occupied. The air in the room, though, was still and stale, like the air of a house not occupied at all.

"The servants are gone today," Minter said. "It's just you and I."

She showed Vidor to a chair. "I'll let some light into the room," she said.

She pulled back the curtains from a window, revealing through long-unwashed glass the contrast between the gloomy interior of the house and the neighborhood outside. In the light Vidor could see the layer of dust that lay untouched atop everything in sight.

Minter lowered herself onto a love seat.

"King Vidor," she said, looking him over. "It's been a long time since I've seen you. Are you still making Westerns?"

"Not lately." Vidor was struck by Minter's voice. It was high, almost childlike, exactly as Vidor had remembered it, but with that strange English-sounding accent he had heard over the phone.

"That's too bad," she said. "I love Westerns. I was in

Westerns myself, when I left the stage and started making pictures. I was in lots of pictures, you know."

"Yes, I know." Vidor wondered why she was telling him this. It was as though she were speaking to someone she had never met, someone unaware of who she was and all she had done.

"A child actress, that's what I was. Myself and my sister, also. Margaret was her name. She's dead now." When Minter spoke, her eyes seemed focused not on him but on some spot in front of him.

Uncomfortable, Vidor decided to try to channel the conversation in another direction. "Do you remember the picture we made together, Mary?"

"Oh, I surely do," she said, though her curious expression suggested she was not so sure. Then, as though the question had never been asked, she abruptly sat up straight. "What kind of hostess must you think I am? I'll serve cake and cider."

"That's not necessary," Vidor said, but she raised herself to her feet and, telling Vidor to remain seated, walked into the kitchen.

Vidor stood up. He walked around the room, looking at the memorabilia it contained: playbills, lobby cards from Minter's films, faded movie magazines. He wondered what Minter's mental condition was. All she had talked about since he'd arrived was the past, the early days of her career. And everything in the living room, from the furniture to the books on the shelves, was also a relic from that time. It was normal for people who had not seen each other in a long while to reminisce about past times, but nothing about Minter struck Vidor as normal. He wondered what her reaction would be when he mentioned Taylor.

Minter returned with a tray containing cups of heated cider and two thick slices of chocolate cake.

"Black Forest layer cake," she said. She set the tray on a low table and replaced herself upon the love seat.

"This is very good," Vidor said.

"Yes, Emma makes it for me. She's not here now, though."

Vidor watched her eat the cake with motions that seemed almost mechanical; she seemed no more attentive to the activity than she had seemed toward Vidor when speaking to him.

"I'm making a new picture," Vidor said.

"That's nice," Minter said. "You should."

"About the old days."

She nodded above the cake.

"About Bill Taylor."

Suddenly Minter stopped eating. She looked around the room, left, then right, everywhere but at Vidor. Her eyes finally came to rest upon the plate in her hand. She set it down on the table.

"Would you like to hear my poetry?" she asked.

"I'd love to, Mary,"

She left the room again, returned with a stack of papers. She shuffled through them.

"Here's my favorite. It's called 'Twisted by Knaves.' "

As she read the poem, Vidor tried at first to follow it, but finally gave up and simply watched her read. The third of Adela Rogers St. Johns's three Ms seemed to hover over the room like a cloud. Misery. Minter was a miserable woman, a gross caricature of what she had once been. When she finished the poem, she looked at Vidor for approval.

"That's very nice."

"I write all the time. I just sit upstairs in my little room and make up poems about everything I think about."

"Do you ever make up poems about the old days?" Vidor asked.

Minter shuffled through the pages again, as if looking for just such a poem. Then she stopped and looked up from them.

"You mean about Mr. Taylor?" she asked.

"Yes," Vidor said.

She shook her head. "No. No poems. I used to write him letters. All the time. He was a great man. He loved me very much."

"I know."

"Did you know I was the very last one to see him?" Minter asked.

The question startled Vidor.

"You were?"

"The funeral man promised me. He let me in after everybody else was gone. I brought roses and gave them to him. He was lying on a stone slab and was cold when I kissed him." There were tears in Minter's eyes.

"Do you know who killed him, Mary?"

Minter started rustling her pages again, but absent-mindedly, the way she had eaten the cake.

"I was home that night," she said, reciting the story Vidor had read in countless newspaper articles and the L.A.P.D. files. "I was reading to the family by the fire."

"Are you sure you weren't with Taylor?" Vidor asked. "Are you sure you didn't go see him after your mother locked you in your room?"

Minter looked at Vidor with a quizzical expression, as though he were an actor reading lines that appeared no-where in the script.

"Are you sure your mother didn't come looking for you, and find you there?"

"No," she said. "I was reading to the family by the fire."

She used the exact same words she had used seconds earlier, as though repetition of them through the years had ingrained them in her mind.

"Your sister, Margaret, said that wasn't true," Vidor told her calmly. "She said you were gone, and so was your mother, and that when you came home you told her something very bad happened to Taylor."

"No," Minter said again. "No. No. You don't know. You don't know anything about it. Mr. Taylor was a great man. He helped me. He took care of me. He said I didn't have to do everything she told me to."

"Who? Your mother?" Vidor asked.

She ignored the question. She stood up, the tears returning to her eyes.

"I didn't have to go to my room. Mr. Taylor said so. I didn't have to do anything. I could stay with him if I wanted to. Mr. Taylor loved me very much."

She walked aimlessly around the room, sobbing, passing the stacked and crowded mementos of her former life like—the thought sent a shiver up Vidor's spine—a bloated, exaggerated, real-life Norma Desmond.

"What did your mother think of that?" Vidor asked.

"She said I was an actress," she replied. "But I didn't want to be an actress. I wanted to have a boyfriend."

"Was Taylor your boyfriend?" Vidor knew the answer, of course; he wanted to hear what Mary would say.

Again she sidestepped a direct question.

"Jimmy was my boyfriend," she said. "We were married in the woods."

With each mention of her mother, Minter sobbed

loudly. She walked around in a circle, her hands trembling at her sides. Vidor had no doubt that she was unstable. He wanted to leave. He knew more than enough to write his screenplay, and knew that even if Minter did give a full accounting of what happened that night in Taylor's bungalow, her mental state was such that she would never erase the shade of doubt, faint though it was, that would hang over her testimony. Vidor started to stand up, then noticed the pages of poetry sitting on the table. He reached for them. What he saw on the top page made him sit back down. The paper was lavender, with pale yellow butterflies printed around the edges. At the top in a very elegant script was written "Twisted by Knaves, by Charlotte Shelby."

He flipped quickly through the pages. All claimed Shelby as the author. Yet Minter had said she had written them herself, in her little room upstairs. Vidor thought of Minter's face peering down at him from upstairs when he rang her doorbell, then of the rumors Adela Rogers St. Johns and George Hopkins had said they'd heard, that Charlotte Shelby had never died, that she was still alive and still running Minter's life as she always had. Vidor wanted more than ever to leave now. Then suddenly Minter stepped toward him and grabbed the poems from his hand. She flipped through them as though making sure they were all still there. Then she stopped and sank once again on her love seat, looking through tear-filled eyes at "Twisted by Knaves."

"This is my favorite," she said, again. "This is the same stationery I wrote my letters to my boyfriends on."

"What boyfriends?" Vidor said, tense, wishing he were gone. When once again she failed to respond to his questions, he said, "Is this the paper you wrote to Mr. Taylor on?"

Minter nodded, almost imperceptibly at first, but stronger as her sobbing grew more intense.

"My mother killed everything I ever loved," she said, and looked across the dark room at Vidor, tears streaking her bulbous face.

Vidor didn't know what to say. He couldn't look at her. He looked out the dirty window, then into the hallway where the foot of the stairs brought back the possibility that Charlotte Shelby was still alive, sitting above them at this very moment. Is that what Minter had been doing when he rang her bell, tending to her mother?

Vidor stood up and, without saying anything or even looking back into the room, let himself out.

He drove to the Santa Monica beach, walked to the pier. Coeds from Pepperdine peered in through windows at a decaying merry-go-round. A refurbished wood-paneled 1930s station wagon rattled by. But Vidor barely noticed. His mind was elsewhere.

The mystery was solved. He had no doubt about that. And its solution was more sensational than he ever could have imagined it would be, involving scandals and blackmail, sex and conspiracies, elements that would promise a sensational screenplay.

And yet he knew he hadn't gotten from Minter what Sanderson and Brown were hoping for. A vague, ambiguous statement from a crazy woman would not retire this case from active police files. Nor would affidavits from Vidor's friends and associates be any match for an ex-D.A. with a reputation to defend, and a penchant for taking matters to court.

Now, breathing deeply the ocean air as though sucking life back into his lungs after his visit to Mary Miles Minter's living tomb, Vidor wondered if all he had learned was worth the trouble. Hadn't there been enough misery?

Vidor was reminded of the question Antonio Moreno had posed, days before he had died: why did Vidor want to tell this story that would inevitably taint the remaining years, however few, of those involved? First he thought of Buron Fitts, polishing off his third martini over lunch at the Bel Air Country Club, looking nervously beyond Vidor as Vidor spelled out his suspicions, methodically chipping away the foundations of Fitts's career. And he thought of George Hopkins and the forty-five-year-old portrait of Taylor that Hopkins kept atop his brightly polished piano. Had Hopkins and Taylor just been close friends, or was it more? Then Vidor thought of Mary Miles Minter, once the sweetheart of the entire world, sitting in her dungeon of a house, surrounded by reminders of a world and time that no longer existed, a world and time she had once been a vivacious, vital part of, crying about a mother who "killed everything I ever loved."

Did Vidor want to tell this story now, and inevitably taint the lives of these people? Just to make his fifty-fifth film? Or should he wait, perhaps only a few years hence, for a better time?

He drove home. Nippy greeted him cheerily.

"Hi there, boy," he said.

He walked into the guest house, Nippy at his side.

"Sam Goldwyn called," Thelma Carr said, handing him the message.

"Thanks."

Vidor put the message on his desk. He changed out of his suit into a pair of jeans. He cleared anything related to the Taylor case from his desk and carried it down into the basement. He turned on the light.

Beneath his worktable he opened the metal strongbox in which he'd been keeping the notes and clippings from his investigation. Then he put everything he had accumulated—magazines, newspapers, police-file transcripts, interview notes, script pages—into the strongbox. He took his notebook from his pocket and started to remove the used pages, but decided instead to drop the notebook into the box intact.

He stood up, looked around the workroom for anything he might have missed, then closed the strongbox lid.

He clamped the padlock shut and shoved the strongbox well under the table, out of sight. He didn't even want to see it for a while. Maybe one day, he told himself, he would open it and tell the story it contained, but for now he would just let it rest. He had spent the last six months, both professionally and personally, chasing down the past, and he had had enough. Six months wasn't long—film directors often spent longer pursuing projects that never came about—but he felt it was time for something new. The past was a fascinating place to journey, but as he had seen in the sad eyes of Mary Miles Minter, it was a dangerous place to settle down.

He walked upstairs.

"Do you want me to call Goldwyn back?" Thelma Carr asked.

"Later," Vidor said, rubbing the brown spots around his temples. "I've got a few things to do first."

He picked up one of the boxes from the Ranch Market, filled with clothes and personal belongings, and carried it outside. Then, with Nippy barking at his feet, he headed up the driveway to talk to Betty.

AFTERWORD

BURON FITTS, former California lieutenant-governor and Los Angeles district attorney, raised a .38-caliber pistol to his temple on March 29, 1973, and took his own life. He was seventy-eight years old. Police reports indicate that the pistol used in his suicide was a vintage Smith and Wesson blue breaktop revolver, similar to the one used in the Taylor murder fifty-one years before.

CHARLOTTE SHELBY, mother and manager of Mary Miles Minter, officially died on March 13, 1957, at her daughter's home in Santa Monica. Acquaintances still living have provided eyewitness accounts of seeing her as late as June 1960. In an unpublished autobiography, made available to this author, she refers to William Desmond Taylor as the "kindest," "warmest," "most gentle," and "loving" director she had known, and posed the question: "Why would anyone wish to shoot such a man?"

MARY MILES MINTER, silent-film actress, died in obscurity on August 5, 1984, at her home on Adelaide Drive in Santa Monica. Shortly after King Vidor's visit, she unsuccessfully sued CBS and producer Rod Serling for his portrayal of her as one of three prime suspects in the killing of William Desmond Taylor. Until her death, she continued various forms of legal action and was known to have been robbed on at least three different occasions. After one such robbery, in 1981, she was gagged, beaten, and left for dead on the floor of her kitchen. A subsequent investigation revealed that one of her ex-servants had participated in this brutal act. An illegitimate child has recently come forward to claim her estate.

MARGARET SHELBY FILLMORE, elder daughter of Charlotte Shelby and sister of Mary Miles Minter, was reported by the Shelby family to have died on December 21, 1939, at her home on Valentine Street in Los Angeles, after a long, undisclosed illness.

EMMETT J. FLYNN, film director, former husband of Margaret Shelby and Nita Flynn, died suddenly in Los Angeles on June 4, 1937, at the age of forty-four. Rumors that circulated about his death were the result of an autopsy performed on June 5, 1937, but never made public. The final diagnosis revealed that he had died from a brain hemorrhage due to chronic alcoholism, and not from a blow to the head.

HENRY PEAVY, valet to William Desmond Taylor, moved to a ghetto in Sacramento, California, shortly after his employer's death. The last known statements he made to the press were in January 1930 when he stated that an actress had killed Taylor and that he had been silenced by the authorities and told to "get out of town."

GEORGE HOPKINS, Academy Award–winning art director and set designer, died in his Hollywood home on February 11, 1985, days before his eighty-eighth birthday. He had just completed his memoirs, a striking tale chronicling his life among such luminaries as William Desmond Taylor and James Dean.

ALLAN DWAN, film director, died on December 21, 1981, at the age of ninety-six at the Motion Picture Country Home in Woodland Hills, California. He was long considered the last great Hollywood pioneer, credited with over three hundred feature-length films and five hundred shorts.

HERB DALMAS, author, teacher, filmmaker, and financial analyst, lives with his wife, Elizabeth, who is also his editor and collaborator, in Santa Barbara, California. He is currently at work on his fifth book, a novel with an historical setting.

ADELA ROGERS ST. JOHNS, journalist, novelist, and film historian, is alive and well and living with her daughter in northern California. She is in her late nineties. For many years, her autobiography, *The Honeycomb*, contained the only no-holds-barred account of the Taylor slaying.

MINTA DURFEE, silent-film comedienne and ex-wife of Fatty Arbuckle, died on September 10, 1975, at the age of eighty-five at the Motion Picture Country Home in Woodland Hills. She remained active in her later years, playing small roles in such films as *The Singing Nun*, *The Odd Couple*, and *Willard*.

CLAIRE WINDSOR, silent-film star and artist, died at Good Samaritan Hospital in Los Angeles on October 24, 1972. She was seventy-four years old. After King Vidor's visit with her, she continued painting; her work was displayed in galleries and homes throughout Los Angeles. Because of her great civic contributions, the Alexandria Hotel in Los Angeles has named a suite of rooms in her honor.

GLORIA SWANSON, one of Hollywood's most important film actresses, died in New York on April 4, 1983. No one knew for sure how old she was. Some said eighty-four, others ninety. Regardless, her movie classic, *Sunset Boulevard*, lives on in the memories of millions.

BILL CAHILL, former chief of police of Arcadia, California, and twenty-two-year veteran of the L.A.P.D., celebrated his ninety-ninth birthday in 1985 at a Catholic nursing home in El Monte, California. During his distinguished career he was awarded over seventeen commendations for bravery in the line of duty, and medals for marksmanship.

RAYMOND CATO, former chief and active creator of the California Highway Patrol, a position he held for twenty-three years after leaving the L.A.P.D., died at the age of ninety-five on June 6, 1984, in Sacramento, California. He was remembered for his civic contributions to such organizations as the Shrine Temple, Royal Order of Jesters, and as chairman of the International Association of Chiefs of Police.

THAD BROWN, former chief of police of the City of Los Angeles, and seventeen-year chief of detectives, died on October 10, 1970, in Glendale, California. He was sixty-seven years old. Upon his death, Mayor Sam Yorty hailed him "as one of the great police officers of the world," and ordered that all of the flags on city buildings be lowered to half-staff.

LEROY SANDERSON, former detective lieutenant of the Los Angeles Police Department and retired chief of security for Republic Studios in Hollywood, died of heart failure on

July 25, 1981, at the age of eighty-six. He was remembered by many as L.A.P.D.'s "top gun," and the man police departments all over the country turned to when they needed help on particularly difficult cases.

THELMA CARR, former secretary to King Vidor, became a championship golf professional, and now resides in a lovely motor home overlooking the countryside on the outskirts of Hemet, California.

DICK MARCHMAN, former insurance executive and King Vidor's associate, continued to remain close to Mr. Vidor and his family throughout the sixties and seventies. He died on September 6, 1984, at his home in Park LaBrea, in Los Angeles, one week after his regular game of poker.

BETTY VIDOR, King Vidor's third wife, died of heart failure, brought on by anorexia nervosa, on August 21, 1978. She was seventy-seven years old. Except on rare occasions, she never permitted her husband back into the family home, and in her will left strict orders that this policy be continued. The house and all its furnishings were left to her German shepherd, Toby, who outlived Mr. Vidor by two years.

KING VIDOR, film director, writer, and private eye, died of heart failure at Willow Creek Ranch on November 1, 1982, at the age of eighty-seven. After putting aside his research on the life and death of William Desmond Taylor, he completely abandoned large-scale feature filmmaking and returned to the kind of smaller-scale documentary filmmaking he had known and practiced as a youth. He completed two successful feature documentaries: *Metaphor,* which he made with friend and admirer Andrew Wyeth; and *Truth and Illusion,* a film about metaphysics, art, science, magic, and life. He not only directed, produced, and acted in these films, but he did a fair portion of the camera work and editing. In 1979 he was presented with an Honorary Academy Award for Life Achievement.

COLLEEN MOORE, silent-film star, author, and former partner in Merrill Lynch, is alive and well and living at her ranch in Templeton, California, just down the road from King Vidor's Willow Creek Ranch in Paso Robles. In December 1983 she married Paul Maginot, a highly respected California contractor, and went on a whirlwind honeymoon in Switzerland. Other adventures have included trips to Japan, China, Europe, Russia, Africa, and the North Pole. Those close to her cannot help but feel that she is as young, vibrant, ambitious, and loving at age eighty-four as she was when she took Hollywood by storm at the age of seventeen.

NOTES AND ACKNOWLEDGMENTS

The most important body of research materials at this author's disposal was the King Vidor papers, graciously made available through the auspices of Suzanne Vidor, Mr. Vidor's daughter by his first marriage, and David Adams, Mr. Vidor's grandson and the executor of his estate. They made this material available without restriction, and it was only through their generosity, encouragement, trust, and insight that this book was possible.

Mr. Vidor's Taylor papers, principally found in the locked strongbox described in the introduction, provided the blueprint from which all further research was conducted. Approximately sixty percent of those papers consist of incomplete manuscripts that Mr. Vidor wrote for eventual incorporation into a book or screenplay, looseleaf pages upon which Mr. Vidor jotted his own thoughts and the thoughts of those he interviewed, and index cards on which Mr. Vidor and his secretary listed all the important clues under the headings Who, When, What, Where, and Why. The remaining material consisted of transcripts of actual police and court documents, business correspondence relating to Mr. Vidor's inquiries to both active and retired officers of the L.A.P.D. and others he interviewed and worked with, and, finally, William Desmond Taylor's diary and an assortment of his letters, notes, and photographs that Mr. Vidor either purchased or collected between 1966 and 1968.

Mr. Vidor's incomplete manuscripts—1,500 various pages bearing such titles as "Death of a Director," "A Bag of Peanuts," and "The Making of a Murder"—were principally written in the form of scenes that Mr. Vidor planned to use in a dramatic rendition of the Taylor story. With the help of Mary Anita Loos and Charles Higham, authors Mr. Vidor leaned heavily upon while writing them, I was able to gain the best overall view of the conclusions Mr. Vidor reached, his emotional responses to various aspects of the story, and, most significant, firsthand documentation in Mr. Vidor's own words of his motivations and personal connection to the story. Important incidents, phrases, and pieces of dialogue, as well as the epigram at the front of this book, were drawn directly from this source.

Mr. Vidor's original notes, transcripts of interviews, index cards, and appointment calendar were used to establish the exact sequence of events that have been portrayed, and much of the substance of each chapter. These documents, consisting of over 650 pages, ranged from mere fragments of conversations Mr. Vidor jotted down on loose pages of his notebook or on the backs of envelopes, to concise, typed transcripts or summaries of interviews. Instrumental to my interpretation of these documents was the advice and help of Dick Marchman, Mr. Vidor's brother-in-law and the man who worked most closely with him during his investigation; Colleen Moore, film producer, friend, and confidante of Mr. Vidor; and Thelma Carr, his secretary.

While all important events in these notes were documented by these witnesses and others, it was not always possible to delineate clearly Mr. Vidor's step-by-step progression. Given the nature of the story, accounts of the same episode would sometimes vary in detail, and in such circumstances, I have chosen the version that seemed the most likely, given an understanding of Mr. Vidor's personality and the manner in which he conducted his affairs and kept his records. I have chosen to delete from his story instances in which I was not able to corroborate events documented in Mr. Vidor's notes.

Certain liberties have been taken reporting the information. Dialogue, as described in the introduction, has been reconstructed in cases in which I have had only rudimentary notes from Mr. Vidor. In such instances, most specifically during conversations Mr. Vidor had with Laurence Stallings, Antonio Moreno, Colleen Moore, Herb Dalmas, and Betty Vidor, I have based my reconstruction upon interviews conducted with either the participants or, in the case that these persons have passed away, interviews with relatives or persons likely to have an intimate knowledge of the subject. I do not claim that the dialogue represents the exact words used by characters at the time of the events described, but feel, however, that the dialogue represents the essence and spirit of the conversations represented, as well as the personalities, styles, and characteristics of these persons.

I have also taken the liberty, in a few instances, of consolidating into one meeting interviews and meetings Mr. Vidor had over a period of time in different locations. This was done in the cases of Mr. Vidor's meetings with Allan Dwan, Herb Dalmas, and Laurence Stallings, all of whom were close friends of Mr. Vidor, and all of whom met with him many times. Such a liberty was taken purely for the sake of brevity, and done so, I feel, in situations that do not compromise the spirit or essential thrust of the investigation.

The police and court records represented in Mr. Vidor's files and described in this book have been quoted from and synthesized as professionally and accurately as I believe possible. All such transcripts have been verified by police or professional sources, and further supporting evidence has been gathered to corroborate all statements made. What remains of the original police records can now be found housed in the County Archives of the City of Los Angeles filed under case package #1947, Box No. 38, CRC #57456. What remains of the original court records are housed in the County Archives of the Superior Court, principally filed in cases #422468 and #426350. In situations in which only summaries existed in the County Archives of cases quoted from in this book, I have obtained and examined all important original documents provided to the defendants. Helpful to my endeavor to verify all findings have been Hynda Rudd, county archivist of the City of Los Angeles; Commander William Booth, Captain Arthur Sjoquist, Captain Bill Davis, Officers Jim Amormino and Wayne Mackley, and retired Lieutenant Jack Halstead, all of the L.A.P.D.; and Nicholas R. Burczyk and Associates, handwriting analysts.

Other certified police documents have been used to support Mr. Vidor's findings. Of greatest importance has been the June 13, 1941, "Summary and Résumé of Facts Developed During the Investigation of the William Desmond Taylor Murder, Submitted to C. B. Horrall, Director of Investigation, Room 26, City Hall of Los Angeles." This document, in conjunction with the James Kirkwood and Mary Miles Minter Memorandum, filed by the Homicide Detail, L.A.P.D., also submitted to C. B. Horrall, indisputably supports all of Mr. Vidor's findings in connection with his examination of L.A.P.D. files.

The King Vidor papers not part of his Taylor files were indispensable to my understanding of Mr. Vidor's personal and professional life. These papers, collected after his death from his ranch in Paso Robles, his home and office in Beverly Hills, and storage rooms throughout Los Angeles, represent over 75,000 pages of letters, scripts, diaries, journals, notes, and assorted documents. It was from this source that I drew pertinent details of Mr. Vidor's childhood in Galveston, his early filmmaking endeavors in Texas and Hollywood, the relationships he had with his wives, friends, and business associates, and, most significant, the daily records of his activities and habits in 1967. Photographs and motion-picture footage housed in his estate were used to chronicle his dressing habits. IRS tax returns, American Express charge receipts, canceled checks, and an assortment of bills and receipts from such sources as his auto mechanic, barber, grocer, and country club were used to detail all the important scenes portrayed.

The interviews used in conjunction with this book represented as significant a contribution as the King Vidor papers. At last count, nearly two hundred hours of interviews were logged with over forty-five different individuals interviewed in locales that included New York, Los Angeles, El Monte, Arcadia, Hemet, Ventura, Santa Barbara, Paso Robles, Templeton, and San Francisco. With the help of the Vidor family and the L.A.P.D., I spoke to all major living sources mentioned in the context of this book, and in cases where the individual had passed away, friends, relatives, or associates were contacted who, in my opinion, were best suited to provide pertinent information or corroborating evidence.

Individuals interviewed by this author whose names appear in this book were Dick Marchman, Colleen Moore, Thelma Carr, Robert Giroux, Allan Dwan, Herb Dalmas, Adela Rogers St. Johns, Bill Cahill, George Hopkins, and Rosalie Sanderson. Without their participation, most notably by Marchman, Moore, Hopkins, and Sanderson, I could not possibly have drawn such detailed accounts as reflected in these pages.

Of the many individuals interviewed or contacted whose names do not appear but whose contributions provided significant documentation of events chronicled, I would like gratefully to acknowledge the following: retired Lieutenant Jack Halstead, L.A.P.D., friend and partner of Ray Cato and Thad Brown; Willis Lane, friend of Claire Windsor; Margaret Tante Burk, historian of the Ambassador Hotel and friend of Adela Rogers St. Johns; Don Schneider, film historian and friend of Minta Durfee; William Stephenson, friend and bridge partner of Betty Vidor; Betty Fussell, biographer of Mabel Normand; Len and Leah Corneto, friends and companions of Mary Miles Minter; Ken Du Main, Minter historian; Cleve Dupey, friend of Mary Miles Minter; George Noonan, friend and associate of Brandon O'Hildebrandt; Mary Oldham, nurse of Buron Fitts; Sergeant Gary Blyleven, investigating officer of the Buron Fitts suicide; Mrs. Eliot Todhunter Dewey, friend of William Desmond Taylor; Eleanor d'Arrast, silent-film star and second wife of King Vidor; Charles Higham, friend and trusted confidant of King Vidor; Mary Anita Loos, friend and companion of King Vidor; David Bradley, film historian and friend of King Vidor; George McQuilkin, former student of King Vidor; Nancy Dowd, former student and associate of King Vidor; Rouben Mamoulian, neighbor and associate of King Vidor; Doug Whitehead, foreman of Willow Creek Ranch; and finally, Hollywood historians Kevin Brownlow, Kemp Niver, Michael Yakaitis, Marc Wanamaker, De Witt Bodeen, and Anthony Slide. Bruce Long, an avid fan of the Taylor murder, has been helpful in correcting errors in my manuscript.

There are others who need to be acknowledged with the recognition that they contributed far more than they realized: John Vidor, Cyndi Voltz, Mike Hawks, Robert Gitt, Peter Bateman, John Paoli, Jim Wait, I. V. Edmunds, Andrew Friedman, Jeffery Luna, Brian Borden, Jetta Goudal, Mary McLaren, Blanche Sweet, Betsy McLane, Bertha Hoagland, David Fritz, John Rapore, Katherine Berge, Henry King, Lee Shively, Mitchell Block, Vicki Hamlett, Belinda Vidor, Tony Vidor, Vickie Foreman, Sam Gill, Paul Killiam, Stephen Paul Cohen, Mindy Warren Pickard, J. Sandom, Michael Welsh, Harriet Baba, Jackie Cooper, Richard Partlow, Heinz Stossier, Marc Cohen, Carole DeSanti, and Judson Scruton.

Collections of research materials held in public libraries and private hands were consulted to clarify matters of historical record. Most significant, I would like to acknowledge the support and assistance of the following: Len and Leah Corneto for use of their private collections of papers on Mabel Normand and Mary Miles Minter; David Shepard for use of the Directors Guild of America oral history on King Vidor; Miles Kreuger, of the Institute of the American

Musical, for his collection of papers and research materials on William Desmond Taylor; and Tom McDonald, of the office of Los Angeles District Attorney Ira Reiner, for his historical papers concerning Los Angeles district attorneys. Other significant sources include the Mamaroneck Public Library in Westchester County, New York; the Cork County Library, Ireland; Shreveport Public Library, Louisiana; the Los Angeles Public Library; the National Archives and Investigative Case Files of the Federal Bureau of Investigation, Washington, D.C.; the Margaret Herrick Library of the Academy of Motion Picture Arts and Sciences; the Performing Arts Library of the New York Public Library at Lincoln Center; the Film Study Center, Library and Stills Archive of the Museum of Modern Art; the Motion Picture Section of the Library of Congress; the Library and National Film Archives of the British Film Institute; the Special Collections of the General Research Library of the University of California at Los Angeles; and the American Film Institute.

For use of their photographs or drawings, I would like to thank Brian Borden, Len and Leah Corneto, Michael Yakaitis, Marc Wanamaker, and Kevin Brownlow.

Finally, I would like to thank those who worked to bring this book into print: David Shepard, Special Projects Officer of the Directors Guild of America and close personal friend of King Vidor, who was instrumental in laying the groundwork that made my research possible; Michael Yakaitis, for his ingenious ability to track down and unearth major sources of original research materials and photographs; New York literary agent Tim Seldes and Hollywood film agent Evarts Ziegler, for their encouragement and counsel; Bill Whitehead, my first editor at E. P. Dutton, for his patience, confidence, and insights; Jennifer Josephy, my new editor at E. P. Dutton, for shepherding my manuscript into print; and author A. Scott Berg, my mentor and guide, whose example I can only hope to emulate. Finally. greatest thanks must go to Richard Woods, Hollywood screenwriter and my best friend, who never lost faith in this project, and who selflessly poured his valuable time and special talents into seeing that this story was told as King Vidor would have wanted it told.